C000061695

FORTHCOMING
VENGEANCE

MICHAEL PATTERSON

Cover design and layout by
JAG Designs

ISBN: 9781691633210

www.detectivestevemurray.co.uk

As DCI Steven Murray continually builds his readership (with a little help from myself). It is interesting to note how it comprises a wide and varied fanbase throughout the world.

- Firstly, there are those many individuals who can relate to his daily struggles with everyday life. That mix of emotions that involve family, friends and relationships.

- Then there are those of you that enjoy solving the crime or mystery… the whodunnit fans. Those that are looking for justice in the thrill of the chase. Where more often than not - the bad guy gets his comeuppance!

- Other avid readers, share his obsession with music. Of how song lyrics can influence our lives. They tap into that vibe of how words can inspire, lift us up and take us on exciting and exhilarating journeys.

"As a willing writer (a work in progress), still diligently striving to learn and improve each day. I thank you for your continued support. I believe I am a very different person from the one I was ten years ago. Looking a decade further into the future, I hope I am still evolving, still writing and most importantly, still smiling!"

Michael Patterson

Thank you to Scottish singer/songwriter
Mark Deans

for:

*"Been abducted by aliens,
drank whisky with Popeye the sailor man."*

I have loved those lyrics for years!

FORTHCOMING VENGEANCE

Prologue:

'Memory is the only true friend that grief can call its own.'

- Ronnie Drew (The Dubliners)

12th February 2016

The sun shone brilliantly. The virescent colour of the spring day under its glare was both offensively bright and cheerful. It was as if the elements had all cruelly conspired to show the sombre funeral goers, just how the world would continue to evolve without their cherished loved one.

Neat lines of pristine grey and black marble headstones, stood fully erect in reverent silence. Silhouetted both to the left and to the right, in front and behind. Row upon row they sprung up from the shimmering and lovingly manicured grass. The lingering smell of maturing old granite filled the dry air. Gravel paths weaved their way through the vast maze of graves. Allowing passers-by to pay their respects to those already lined up in the earth's tender embrace.

How the multi-faceted David Murray would have hated this place. The quirky David, who loved everything eccentric and unique, from top quality classical music to old, nineteen-seventies comedians. The enthusiastic Davie, who loved to go on outdoor adventures, sleeping in bothies and who could never sit still for a single moment. Finally the loving and compassionate Dave, a man who could be so rash and impulsive one minute, then instantly astounded by the serene beauty and simplicity of the world around him the next.

One

'Sail away, bright young man - love will anchor you. Leave behind what you have done - grace will see you through.'

- John Tibbs

Funeral etiquette demanded that Thomas and Hannah, the older brother and younger sister would be in attendance and they never disappointed. Both travelled home specially from separate parts of the United States. Neither sibling had seen or been in contact with their father since leaving home after their brother's prison sentence had been handed down to him five years previous. Many bridges needed to be repaired and mended. Deep wounds required to be healed.

The immaculate, dark rosewood veneer coffin, ironically sparkled into life in the daylight. It was pulled from the hearse by six strong figures. The two dressed in identical suits, were instantly recognisable as funeral director staff and they in turn were accompanied by invited mourners - 'Ally' Coulter, 'Doc' Patterson and David's brother, Thomas. The remaining pall-bearer, unsurprisingly, was Detective Inspector Steven Murray, the distraught father of the deceased.

'Inspector,' was sadly the last word his son referred to him by. Not lovingly, as it should have been, as 'Dad.' But a tired, distant and subdued offering of... 'Inspector.'

Vocally, the array of sounds at the busy cemetery were muted. From the gentle birdsong and grieving whimpered cries at the graveside. To the soft, authentic purring of the funeral cars. Visually however - that was a totally different matter entirely.

There was to be no nostalgic return of the prodigal son and the magnitude of despair and genuine heartache in Steven Murray's eyes was enormous. As the solid casket was gracefully released into the freshly dug grave, the grief etched upon the father's face was overwhelming. With each further foot it descended, tears streamed constantly from the 'Doc' and 'Ally' Coulter. Both men had known Davie nearly all his life. Over the years, he had affectionately referred to them as 'his guardian Uncles!' His well travelled brother Tom, dressed in a finely tailored all black suit, was not normally known for shedding a tear or two. But even he could not disguise the fine moist layer on his pale cheek, as he strived for composure. To accompany his suit, he wore a highly fashionable, charcoal grey polo-neck. The jersey constantly pulsed at his throat, as a build up of intense sorrow and regret, fought for freedom and release.

Steven Murray on the other hand, was never one to hide his emotions or disguise his body language. Sometimes, much to his later regret. Because, generally content for people to openly gauge his mood, he simply wore his large, generous heart on his sleeve. Whether it was filled with compassion, anger, understanding or rage - you generally knew where you stood with the man. Today on the front page - There was turmoil!

His very soul had been ripped out of him. Sure he was absolutely resolute and hellbent on catching his son's killer, but that was for another day. Here currently, his forearms shook uncontrollably, as he let the purple velvet cord slip uneasily through his tense, white-knuckled hands. As the coffin continued to be progressively lowered into the ground, emotional, audible gasps for breath were heard from his direction.

The thinning features of 'Ally' Coulter, held him by the shoulder and walked closely alongside. His long term friend steadied him, with each step, all the way back toward the funeral cortège. Coulter was not alone, in his support. In fact, Murray's whole team were in attendance to offer their condolences and ably assist in any way that they could.

Richard and Sandra Kerr were both there. For once without either of their twin girls in tow. Hayes and Curry, 'the two most notorious Constables now settled in the East,' were also present and accounted for. His old pal Constable George Smith stood and wept alongside their latest boss, Detective Chief Inspector Barbra Furlong. Detectives Allan Boyd and Joseph Hanlon made up the remainder of those work colleagues gathered around the graveside. A younger element, consisting of several of David's friends were also in the mix. Although, many of those weaker alliances had been severed, when he was sentenced to time in prison for the attempted murder of his father - Steven Murray!

Earlier at the church service, several hundred mourners had been in attendance to pay their personal respects toward the family and in particular to a diligent, hard working pillar of their community. To their favourite Detective Inspector. In many ways, you could have been forgiven for thinking that it was the man himself, that had passed away. Such was the praise, homage and deference being paid. In fairness, it was extremely poignant that so many people, from so many walks of life had the desire to express their love and respect to Steven Murray. Because, simply and sadly these days - he just didn't love or respect himself any more.

In his state of mind, Murray never had the chance to witness all of those that had attended. Often his concentration would wander constantly to other thoughts. He never fully recognised for instance, that each row of the three hundred seat church, was filled to capacity. So much so, extra seating had to be set out in the overflow area. Friends from his own West of Scotland school days were there. For although generally not a big fan of social media, it had been invaluable for keeping in touch with many of those from his past. Next up were neighbours from his local street that had made the effort to rearrange their busy schedules. Neighbours that every Christmas Eve would observe from their windows a lone figure dressed up as Santa Claus. This particular Father Christmas would leave gifts and presents on each of their doorsteps, before going into a familiar looking Volvo and heading off filled with the true spirit of Christmas to do a regular stint, serving up soup and food at a local homeless drop-in centre.

Also in the crowded congregation were other work colleagues. Many of whom would have their own inspiring story to tell of how a certain Steven Murray had influenced each of their respective lives for the better. There was even a smattering of grateful ex-cons in attendance. A small handful of men and women, whose lives he had in some way helped transform and turnaround. There were of course others, some surprisingly from the criminal fraternity were even present. Many of whom are just as slippery and shady as ever! However, those unchanged characters were old school and still wanted to offer up their genuine condolences. It was family after all and no one would wish what had happened, on anyone. But then, sadly, someone did… and it was front page news.

Perhaps though and possibly the most telling of all, was the numerous number of grateful survivors involved in previous cases throughout the years, that had come along. Individuals whose lives had been deeply blessed by the exceptional support, determined focus and the thorough investigative skills of DI Murray and his team. A close knit group of officers that had been taught their roles well and that had always tried their best to bring the victims and their families closure and justice. So now seemed like the ideal time, in some small way, for them to be there for the Inspector and his colleagues. They may never be able to repay him fully, but by being there in attendance today, they could at least recognise and offer an honest acknowledgement and a collective expression of gratitude.

Amongst that thankful number, were cafe owner Maurice Hynd and his daughter Iona. Iona had been the budding footballing starlet that had been rescued from a human sex trafficking ring in recent times. She had flown back specially from America, where she was currently fulfilling a soccer scholarship. Her ability to finance that University placement was all thanks to a certain anonymous donor! Alongside that father and daughter, sat an auctioneer. A man originally from Crieff in Perthshire. John Bennett had also assisted the Inspector on that particular case involving the Hynd family. The young, wealthy professional, always described Steven Murray as, "An interesting character!" Others included in cameo appearances that morning included Brian Pollok from Police Scotland in Dundee. Pathologist, Andrew Gordon offered a wave, complete with missing finger and then of course there was the mercurial Daniel George. Sir Daniel George, horologist to the stars to be precise. Murray, thought that he had witnessed a classic Aston Martin in the church car park, so was rather less surprised to spot the owner of the said vehicle inside. Up until his savage murder a year ago, DC Machur Rasul had briefly enjoyed, being part of Murray's high quality team. A killing that his Inspector knew could and should have been prevented. A death that to this day, he felt responsible for. So to witness Machur's father in attendance, humbled the Inspector greatly and instantly brought Steven Murray to tears. In the other extreme, however, whilst drying his eyes, a bright grin of optimism appeared on his countenance, as he waved at a young Caitlin Bell. On the far side of that young lady, was an elegant female in a red hat. But it was the woman on the near side, Caitlin's cheerful mum, that had brought most fleeting happiness into the Inspector's heart. The dress code of her mother was a clearly open, yet private message being shared between herself and DI Murray. She wore a beautiful, yellow, knee length, floral dress. It was accompanied with a rose coloured cardigan, and boy did those bright colours make him smile.

Joseph Hanlon had fortunately witnessed the exchange. He had at that moment remembered with clarity from a year or so ago, the profound question that Murray had felt comfortable enough at the time to ask of a woman. Empathising who was facing up to his or her own difficulties in life. He simply enquired of her that day...

"What is the merit of choosing the drab Ms Bell? When beauty hangs in your wardrobe." Today, both Murray and Hanlon fully recognised that Linda Bell on this occasion, had chosen exceptionally wisely from her wardrobe.

Steven Murray had indeed been touched by the outpouring of love and support. He had never for a minute doubted that there would be a good turnout for what would be a solemn day. He had only questioned - What he had ever done to deserve such support?

The day had consisted of a brief church service, the graveside burial and then a small reception back at

Murray's own home. An intimate gathering which was now just about coming to an end. Most of the visitors and acquaintances had gone, just like the earlier sunshine.

Kind remarks, smiles, loving anecdotes and uplifting stories from David's childhood had all been shared and reflected upon. Poignant memories and tears had been shed. The last of the friends had made their excuses and many of the Inspector's police colleagues were required back on duty. The general tidy up was finished and only three bodies presently remained. Steven Murray had always hoped that one day all his children would be reconciled back at home with him. However, this was far from the family portrait opportunity that he would have wished for. One dead son and his other two children, back through duty and obligation.

In the extreme silence that now prevailed, the Inspector sat slouched with his head dropped forward on a wooden dining room chair. The blue, finely upholstered, high backed piece of furniture had been brought through to the sitting room to provide extra seating, along with two others from the matching set. Thomas stood watching his father and quietly pondered proceedings in the adjoining doorway to the kitchen. Hannah sat opposite her dad on the aged green leather settee. Whilst her father and brother remained in their formal clothing, their sibling had decided to dispense with her morbid black outfit and had changed into some comfortable shoes, with jeans and a loose blouse. Her hair brushed to one side, swayed cheerfully over her left shoulder.

"It was never David's fault dad. You know that right?"

Murray heard those chilling words from his estranged daughter. But had no idea what she was referring to.

"She's talking about David's conviction," the quiet male voice from the hallway echoed.

"Where are you even living these days, Tom?" his father, shaking his head responded.

"Dad! I am trying to speak to you," Hannah interrupted. "He told you what happened, didn't he?"

She seemed to speak with a slight Stateside twang these days. Her father looked at his daughter's perturbed face. He witnessed anxiety and concern. This was close-up, personal and unexpected.

"Hannah, what is going on? I have no idea what you are talking about, and anyway, why bring something like that up from the past, today of all days? The very day we have just laid your brother to rest."

"It's just…" she trailed off.

"It's just what?" Her father's voice rose with each sentence spoken. "I visited David every week for five years. And every week for five years, he steadfastly refused to see me. How do you both think that made me feel? So no, he did not tell me anything! Except…"

"Except?" Hannah persisted.

Steven Murray then added quietly. "Except, that maybe through his actions, his unspoken words. He related to me clearly, his contempt, deep-rooted anger and hatred!"

An uneasy glance was quickly exchanged between brother and sister.

"He didn't hate you dad," Tom Murray felt the need to confirm. "Perhaps, he had lost a lot of respect for you that he had gleaned growing up. But he most certainly didn't hate you. None of us did."

Murray's facial expression seemed to hear the words, but was unable to manifest belief in them. The phrase - What was going on here? - seemed to nicely accompany, the quizzical look now being served up.

"Well, he was certainly found guilty of attempted murder on me. So I think hatred may have sneaked in there somewhere, Thomas. Don't you?"

14

"I can see how you would think that dad…" His eldest son spoke hesitantly. Desirous to possibly say more, but uncertain or unsure if he should.

"Well of course, I would think that. Why shouldn't I?"

A strong female voice felt compelled to speak. The tone was quiet and apologetic.

"That would be, because it was me that attacked you from behind on that day!"

Steven Murray's face washed blank with confusion and instantly drained of all colour. The internal cogs in his brain could not turn fast enough to register what he'd just heard. That key moment was the catalyst for his fragile, healing heart, to be broken… all over again.

"David never hit you once in his life, dad. It was me that lashed out at you on that day," Hannah continued to reveal. "Don't you remember? I was preparing dinner. We then got into a fierce argument. Over what? Who knows! The knife was in my hand and a ceramic pot was nearby. You had your back to me when I struck out at you. I continued to stab at you in a frenzied attack, as you lay motionless on the floor. Both Davie and Tom quickly grabbed hold of me. But it was too late, the damage had been done. Years of pent up frustration and teenage angst had been hastily and angrily unleashed. Both police and ambulance were called and whilst the paramedics rushed you to the hospital, David stepped forward to the police and admitted to everything. They had no reason to question things. Thomas and I reluctantly backed up his story and by the time you were in any fit state to talk, he had already been long charged."

Another voice then entered the fray.

"Davie was adamant, dad. There was no way he was having his baby sister, do any time for it," Thomas offered.

"With hindsight, I know I was wrong. But at the time I blamed you for everything," his daughter lamented. "Your obsessive gambling - mums death - family life at home - absolutely everything," she confessed. "I'd had enough, dad. And that day something finally snapped."

Her hands were now clasped tightly in her lap. Thomas wiped at her cheek. Tears of regret flowed freely at that point as she continued to unburden herself.

"That day I ruined and divided our family and I have had to live with it ever since. I am so, so, sorry, dad for all the hurt and pain that I have caused you with my stupid selfish actions - Can you ever truly forgive me?"

Hannah, simply slid down in front of her dumbstruck father and grasped and squeezed nervously to both his quivering hands on his lap. Their father was truly silenced. Five years of mixed up emotions, guilt and regret were all trying to find a place not only in his mind, but somewhere in the complex cauldron of his heart.

"It was you, Hannah? All these years your brother never spoke to me. He kept away because…"

"Because he was protecting his sister, dad. He knew that he could not keep quiet. That you would have continually kept on at him - Why? Why? Why? And he would have eventually told you," Tom Murray confirmed. "Then in turn, you would have done the right thing and told the authorities about a miscarriage of justice. Finally your precious daughter would have swapped places with her brother in prison and none of us wanted that."

Their father shook his head. Still unable to fully comprehend the magnitude of the situation and what was going on.

"Davie was willing to take full responsibility, dad. He then, unsuccessfully gambled on getting a lighter sentence. Sadly that wasn't to be and we're at where we're at today!"

Thomas Murray was always the pragmatic, philosophical one of the trio.

"I am also sorry, dad. Living with those actions just made it easier for us both to stay away."

Hannah tried to lighten the mood somewhat.

"There is someone that I would love you to meet though." She once again tightened her grip on his hands. "I am a married woman now."

But seeing no noticeable reaction upon her father's face, she added.

"We never left because we hated you, dad. It was the exact opposite," she said tearfully. "We just couldn't live with the guilt and knowing how much we had hurt you and let you down."

On hearing those gut wrenching words, Steven Murray decided instantly, there and then. That he did not want to dwell upon matters further. He released his grip from Hannah, stood up and took a tentative step toward them both. He then held his arms high out into the air. Taken by complete surprise at this unexpected gesture, both Hannah and Thomas Murray smiled and their eyes glistened as they embraced their father for the first time in nearly five years. His fraught emotions overtook him, his knees buckled and he fell to the floor. This time as their dad fell, their grip was unwavering. This time all three figures knelt, hugged and wept openly.

That night they each agreed to travel back after Easter and have a proper reconciliation.

Next day homeward bound to New York - Thomas returned. Next day homeward bound to Oregon - Hannah returned. Next day, still at home, Steven Murray's Bipolar returned. His black dog was on the attack...

Two

'We got too many gangsters doin' dirty deeds. Too much corruption and crime in the streets. It's time the long arm of the law, put a few more in the ground. Send them all to their maker and he'll settle them down.'

- Toby Keith

Six weeks later: *Good Friday morning: 25th March 2016*

Carpet and Tiling Specialists - At least that was the bold advertising claim across the side of the Mercedes van that pulled into the quiet, residential cul-de-sac. When parked up, only one of the rear doors required to be opened. The tousled haired driver dragged out a rather tastefully patterned Indian rug. A further assortment of floor coverings, including carpet tiles and expensive linoleum were all stockpiled in the back. Each due for distribution elsewhere later that day.

The residential address currently accepting delivery was modern. The actual estate itself, no more than three years old. It sat on the outskirts of Balerno, a respectable leafy suburb of Edinburgh. It's name was derived from the Scottish Gaelic - *Baile Airneach,* and this so-called, 'town of the hawthorns,' found itself situated, approximately eight miles south-west of the capitals bustling city centre.

This particular bespoke development had experienced serious delays in the building work, mainly due to important issues with planning permission. Initially the outlined plans were on the boundary of some crucial land required for access and that unfortunately, major conservation work was taking place on. Eventually, after various legal arguments, which included going to court, it was all amicably settled. After a whirlwind six months, the luxury homes and road infrastructure were in place and happy owners and families had moved in. It was now time for them to enjoy their new social status within their specially designed estate. Although, when one says estate - It's not like your local district council estate, complete with graffiti, litter strewn pavements and gangs of feral youth roaming the darkened streets. Here, only twelve houses were actually ever built on the land and no two homes were alike. Lawns seemed to be manicured to perfection. Customised wrought iron gates and fencing provided a high quality finish. Whilst well designed and professionally built garden walls, added enhanced security and privacy. Starting prices began at a very modest, by Edinburgh standards at least - Two point five million pounds... and that was for the humblest home. One could only wonder - Which poor paupers were going to be the black sheep of the community and end up there? The front door to the property was already fully opened, as the company employee walked up the path.

"I saw you park," the well groomed man in his designer jeans and snug fitted polo-shirt offered. He spoke in a manner typically associated with those wishing they had been born into a higher social class.

"Wrong address, I suspect though. I haven't ordered anything from yourselves. Could it be for my neighbour across the way?"

He then in a rather animated fashion went on to explain...

"This is Number 4 - The Birches. Number 2 is back there. With 6 directly opposite."

During all of which, his arms were gesticulating to every uttered syllable.

"I would hazard a guess, that last one is probably the one that you want. They almost always buy online."

With all his limbs now perfectly stilled and aligned. The last four words were delivered in such a sneering, supercilious, derogatory manner, that they seemed to question the very validity of how those particular neighbour's even managed to acquire a home in such a prestigious development. The black sheep had obviously been identified.

"Ross, Mister Ross Stevenson?" The delivery driver asked.

The homeowner was taken aback and genuinely surprised. His eyes raised up. He took a step away and his bare arms ventured wide either side of himself, fully prepared for - Animation, part two!

"But, I definitely never ordered anything," he maintained. "And I most certainly would not buy carpet or flooring via a website."

More of the self righteous superiority, the driver thought. Not an easy man to like.

"Because, that would be beneath you, sir?"

"What!" He initially responded with jagged condescension.

The cheeky driver winked and smiled.

"Oh, yes, quite. I see what you did there," Stevenson acknowledged, rather embarrassed and facially flustered. "Carpet, floor covering, beneath me. Yes, very good. Nice one."

He then paused briefly to regain his composure, to get back in control and take the upper hand. He always liked to have the upper hand, did Ross Stevenson. As a highly successful defence lawyer for over a decade now, he had a very definite sombre style and a well practiced routine. One that he was exceptionally comfortable with. Humour and lightheartedness threw him off balance. They played no part in his normally serious, aggressively animated manner and he needed a brief time-out to get back in step.

"I still never ordered anything."

The words were spoken in true lawyer fashion, firmly and forcefully. He stood absolute, like a stern-faced sentry guard. His arms securely folded. This time it was his rotating head that continually travelled from east to west on a regular basis.

"That's no problem," the driver said. "I'll take it back to the store and give Mr Reid a call. Just to let him know that you refused it. Thanks anyway."

"That's fine, you do that," the lawyer said, closing the door.

Still to fully process the information that had actually been passed on to him. Because then - Slowly, inch by inch, the beautifully panelled, white front door belonging to Number 4 - The Birches, began to gradually, delicately and smoothly reopen.

"Just a second. Wait a minute."

This time, it was a seemingly nervous, uncertain voice that called out.

"Did you say that a Mister Reid sent it?"

"I did, sir."

"Do you happen to have a first name by any chance?"

"I spoke with him myself earlier today," the driver answered. "His first name, I don't instantly recall, but he had a deep husky voice. Guttural I would describe it as, sir."

Ross Stevenson immediately swallowed hard and lost all colour in his face.

"Bring it back," he yelled.

"Honestly, I can take it away, it's not a problem."

As if in full courtroom persona, Stevenson focused assertively on each specific word…

"Bring - It - Back - Now!"

"Billy? Barney? No, Benny?" Were all questioned out loud. "Yes, that was it," the carpet specialist confirmed. "I'm pretty certain it was Benny Reid!"

"Uuuggghhh," Stevenson sighed. Frown lines contorted across his face.

"Whatever! Just leave it there in the hallway. That'll do nicely."

The rug must have been some length. It was short, maybe about four foot in width. Nothing unusual about that. But it was stocky, stout and appeared extra big in circumference. At that size it would roll out to about twenty five feet and that was somewhat unusual. Once inside, the driver carefully searched amongst several sheets of paperwork.

"Sorry, sir. It would appear I've left my pen in the vehicle. Would you have one handy to sign my receipt."

Another exasperated sigh, belched from the obnoxious, high flying legal expert, as he wandered off in search of a ballpoint. When he returned, he found his front door closed over and the newly acquired rug laid flat along his welcoming hallway. In total, it was only about six foot in length, rather cheap looking and nondescript. Meanwhile at the back of the door, sat a massive roll of industrial cling film. The mighty behemoth of cellophane wrap was obviously what had bulked out the rug in the first place and what gave it the appearance of being so impressively long.

The homeowners face screwed up into a courtroom scenario of - *'I don't understand M'Lord. What is going on here?'*

"Why would your obviously incompetent company provide so much extra packaging with such a small, ugly, insignificant rug?"

The afternoon air fell silent momentarily, before…

"And don't you dare tell the so-called, 'Benny' that I said that. Right!"

Obviously no cheap, retractable ballpoint had been available, as the hot-shot solicitor waved his recently retrieved, three hundred pound Montblanc pen at the driver in a scolding dismissive fashion. In fairness, the delivery driver quickly pointed back. But no individual delicate finger was involved in their particular hand gesture. Ross Stevenson, defence lawyer to half the crooks, misfits and aspiring gangsters in Edinburgh, instantly understood his predicament. He knew that he was presently staring down the short barrel of a Glock 19. The compact 9mm pistol was one of the most popular illegal handguns in the United Kingdom. But it was still a major surprise for him, to see it in the hands of a carpet fitter. By now though, he had also confidently figured out, that this individual was NO expert in laying anything - Except maybe wreaths!

"Yes, your beloved, 'Benny,' or should I more accurately say, 'Bunny,' would not have appreciated your uneducated appraisal of his gift. You know that right?"

Stevenson, once again swallowed. The driver had known full well that it was 'Bunny' Reid right from the start. Now a genuine look of impending fear ventured over the man's sudden pallid countenance.

"What have I done? What's wrong? What does he need? I'll drop everything. Of course, I will."

"You don't have to drop everything, sir. Just turn around slowly and drop to your knees to begin with." The voice was light, but carried authority.

"What!" He exclaimed. Again with the arrogant attitude.

On hearing a distinct click from the handgun, he instantly turned and fell heavily to the floor in one swift movement. The worrying sound from the revolver seemed to carry infinitely even more authority than the spoken word. The barrel of which was suddenly pushed crudely toward the nape of the cowering man's neck. The lawyer froze and remained perfectly still. The cold metal was drawn firmly down to the base of his spine, along his buttocks and outward bound across his muscled calves. On reaching his ankles, a plastic restraint was firmly attached and both feet were bound tightly together. As he began to relax, with the threat of imminent danger to his life diminishing, similar restraints were then placed around his wrists, as they were offered police style, behind his back.

Three

'It's supposed to hurt, it's a broken heart, but moving on is the hardest part. It comes in waves, the letting go, but the memory fades, everybody knows - Everybody knows.'

- Lady Antebellum

At police headquarters in Leith, DC Joe Hanlon had arrived early. He had undoubtedly missed his grumpy, music loving boss these past few weeks. The Queen Charlotte Street premises seemed to be lacking somewhat. However, he also knew all about grief. Having lost his young wife to pancreatic cancer only the year before. He had dealt with it differently though. The young widower had flung himself wholeheartedly into his work. At a time where he had been recently assigned to Murray's team, he felt he had a lot to prove to himself and to others. So daily, fresh challenges and new experiences were keeping him busy, active and alert. He was also fully aware that he'd never had the demon 'dog walking' experiences that his senior officer experienced on a regular basis and was continually thankful for that.

In recent days, 'Sherlock,' as he was known to his colleagues, had been given what seemed like a random, straightforward case. It was a suspected suicide and all Joe Hanlon had to do was literally, dot the i's and cross the t's. But with his thoroughness, generally like a rapid, starving dog with a bone. He had potentially, unearthed a rather sinister link to at least two other suicides in recent weeks. The possible connection made the overall series of events even more tragic and heartbreaking. DI

Steven Murray was himself delicately woven into the unfolding story and oh, how his young protégé could do with his help right now. In each case the name of a certain Mr Christian Blear had cropped up and that was enough to arouse the suspicions of a certain, intrepid Detective Constable.

At that precise moment, further west on the outskirts of town and beyond the city bypass itself. A solitary, self-imposed exile had allowed two unlocked suitcases to gather dust as they lay twisted and abandoned in the corner of the stale, airless bedroom. The tartan embossed luggage had never seen the inside of a plane, train or automobile for several years. Remnants of travels past adorned their canvas exterior. Stickers, stamps and various pieces of frayed ribbon from adventures throughout the world, could still be readily identified. Each one has its own special memory and story.

Outside, distant echoes of a howling wind thrashed wildly. In contrast, shuddering, sudden jolts, vibrated indoors from beneath the heavy cotton duvet. The supercharged body beneath it was in the midst of a mini physical tsunami. An aching heart shivered violently and those grieving, jittering pangs, caused an immediate ripple effect. Arms leapt up high, then anxiously crossed over shoulder to shoulder. Their grip trembled continually as they desperately tried to soothe and caress a pounding, explosive chest.

We all grieve in different ways. But every troubled road travelled, seemed to end up at the same prominent, densely populated, yet unfortunate destination, Murray had concluded. A much celebrated, well known recovery resort, that went by the name of: *'Hurting!'*

Without any extraordinary big budget advertising, it fairly brought in the crowds. It simply allows 'life' to unfold and awaits its daily influx! Normally, it's only once you have experienced the special pain and suffering that, 'Hurting' has to offer, that you really truly understand and appreciate what many others have gone through, as they traversed that difficult road previously.

Now, how long people choose to stay in that particular spot varies. It often depends on what the individual brings with them when they come to visit. Coping mechanisms - like family, friends and loved ones are often left unpacked. So too are jobs, daily routines, the practicalities of life and the uncomplicated, yet essential desire to continue on!

One, also has to remember, that 'Hurting' was not generally a place that people chose to go willingly. There was no fancy, illustrated brochure to be browsed through at your leisure. It usually sprung up unexpectedly, like a long abandoned truck stop. At other times, it was thrust upon individuals as they went about their daily business. A regular, mundane, twenty-four hour experience that would allow them to potentially, travel for long distances further and further away from the bright, satisfying light of happiness, contentment and satisfaction. A fairly recent, 'Hurting' resident had now been in situ for approximately two months. Again, let us revisit him, to see just how exactly he has coped with his extended, self-imposed stay…

Pills, medicines, liquids and a mass of scrunched up written notes, sat by the bedside cabinet. A pile of dirty, unwashed dishes with a host of mosaic gravy patterns, created a ceramic tower. The balanced, yet highly unstable structure, reached impressively up from ground level to the edge of the soiled, stained mattress. A united effort, consisting of dirt, sickness, urine and sweat all combined to give the man's room, it's very own specific and distinctive fragrance. His laundry basket was a whole corner of the room. In certain instances that would no doubt resemble a mini Everest.

However, for this individual a change of clothing was more likely weekly than daily. So his well worn and foul smelling apparel, was even shorter than his china plate collection. On the opposite bedside cabinet, sat a mobile phone and a well thumbed bible. In the background, an ancient digital clock radio played constantly on low. The familiar, flashing red display had been deliberately covered over and blocked out by several grubby, well-used paracetamol packets. In tandem with this man's life, the room itself remained in total darkness. His whole being, had become void of illumination these past two months. How or when would that ever change? The introduction of a bible may have at least offered a semblance, if not a tunnel of light. However on his current trajectory, there would appear to be no imminent sign of a transformation, or a personal desire to leave that little hick country town of 'HURTING.'

His youngest son was dead. An assassination would almost always seems to be associated with world leaders, politicians or the criminal hierarchy. But in this specific instance, nothing described it better. His middle child had been cruelly assassinated. Slaughtered suddenly and premeditatedly on the steps of Barlinnie Prison in Glasgow. A son that it has since transpired, had actually committed no crime in the first place. Except for bravely taking responsibility for the actions of another. That special individual, being his beloved sister. Although ultimately and ironically, it was on the day of his actual release, that he had arguably been given - a life sentence. A sentence that his broken father would now have to live with for the rest of his natural. Which, given his own recent track record and current state of mind, might not necessarily be too long.

The fleeting tremors from his weary limbs began to ease off. His body stilled. Each day for the past two weeks, he had experienced violent, hourly shaking. The fact that except for toilet breaks and front door grocery deliveries, he seldom dressed, showered, shaved or left his darkened solitary space, obviously never helped. The room had a severe stench. Not only from the rotting food products and his personal hygiene, but from the all too familiar malodor of his deeply entrenched melancholy. Wow, melancholia! Who would have guessed it? Steven Murray could have written a best-selling book on each of the various descriptions listed: Bleakness; Dejection; Desperation and Cheerlessness. And that is before the Inspector even got started with: Discouragement; Misery and Sadness.

His imaginary black dog, whimpered, sighed and desperately ran for cover as this heavy-hearted, tearful individual, binned another series of emails from Joe Hanlon seeking his help and assistance.

Detective Constable Joseph Ian Hanlon was an only child and had been introduced to DI Steven Murray about fifteen months ago. In that brief period of time, 'Sherlock,' as Murray had nicknamed him for his dogged detective skills, had not only become a widower and valued member of his team, but also a close and trusted friend. He offered Murray a younger person's investigative perspective. He was clever, shrewd and thorough. All top qualities that Steven Murray admired greatly in an individual. Hanlon had also come to fully appreciate his Inspector's honest, west coast humour and cheekiness. He remembered with fondness the first time they walked together past a well known, family run bakery in the city centre. The freshly baked aroma lingered in the air and the less experienced detective, was licking his lips and beginning to salivate as they sauntered past. Shrewdly, Murray had spotted this and in an unmistakably, generous tone offered up…

"We all deserve a nice treat every now and again, don't you think, DC Hanlon?"

Joe smiled in mutual agreement. "I absolutely do, sir," he murmured in anticipation.

"Right then, let's turn around," the Inspector decided firmly.

Hanlon grinned like a Cheshire Cat, as Murray (tongue firmly in cheek) announced…

"Okay and remember Constable, this is my treat…… Let's WALK BY once again!!!!"

There had been a definite father and son vibe between them. One that often went unspoken. However, close colleagues could not help but recognise it. So over the past several weeks, DC Hanlon had probably been more disappointed than most, that Murray had chosen not to respond to his various calls and emails. More so, especially in the last 24 hours to texts relating to a case, or possible cases, that he felt sure his mentor could or would, want to assist with.

One of those specific cases, had involved the suicide of a local politician that had apparently hung himself. The sensationalist, yet sad reasoning behind it, was that the poor man had allegedly embezzled huge sums of money from his Parliamentary funds. That he had used racist language on several occasions over the years and whilst still at University, the accusations were that he had met weekly with underage rent boys. All of which, every last word, was proved beyond doubt to be clearly untrue. On two of the alleged dates, he was actually out of the country doing intern work in Sweden. It had simply been lies, lies and more lies. Headline grabbing FAKE NEWS!

'Sherlock' was totally intrigued. He had remembered that only a month before, another MP, this time a female. Had driven her car at high speed off cliffs, in nearby East Lothian. The online photograph that the blogger had used in their horrific article, was of the MP and her husband, alongside a friend at an Edinburgh Chamber of Commerce dinner. Two days later, after hate mail, death threats and thousands of disgustingly personal tweets and comments, the highly emotional and troubled woman, oblivious to the normality of life at this point, had tried inconceivably and thankfully unsuccessfully, to take her 13 year-old daughter with her. Strapped securely into the backseat, the teenager, Mhairi, had desperately thrown herself out of the door at the last minute and was still in hospital recovering from back injuries. Her deceased mother's body was later recovered from the car's wreckage on the rocks below. Her funeral had taken place two weeks previous.

Yet again, the simple premise and candid reason behind her personal desperation and anguish was the online story that ran alongside the picture. The main headline in bold print stated unequivocally, that she had been an underage prostitute during her teenage years and had several convictions for soliciting. Not only that, but during that period of time, she had, on more than one occasion aborted a child. No wonder there was outrage, profanity and personal insults directed toward her one would think. But think again…

Joe Hanlon read on with total disgust and astonishment. It contained line after line of fabrication. Dates didn't match up, timelines were skewed and the article was riddled with inaccuracies. It was all the figment of someone's vivid imagination. Again it was all proved to be untrue, untrue, untrue. Pure fiction. A fantasy that was sadly confirmed after the fact, as genuine FAKE NEWS.

That poor, innocent women's world had been turned upside down by some faceless, invisible individual behind a keyboard. Her good character and personal integrity was torn to shreds and lay in tatters. However, her depression was instant. Her turmoil guaranteed. Her precious life is gone, and with it also, so nearly that of a beloved and cherished daughter. She and her husband Stuart, had been pictured at that Gala evening next to someone who was very rarely caught attending any of those large corporate, sponsored events - The man in question being the notoriously enigmatic - Detective Inspector Steven Murray.

Elsewhere in the city, returning south-westward, it took a steady nine mile drive from the busy, rejuvenated Port of Leith streets to reach the beautiful, picturesque Balerno countryside. There the panic-stricken Ross Stevenson was being gloriously mummified from head to toe. Or more accurately put: Foot to Face. The Glock 19 had been laid to rest on the hallway table. Alongside it, sat a carpet fitter's constant companion. An ever reliable and razor sharp Stanley knife.

 Cling film - The thin transparent sheeting, with its low permeability to air, oils, bacteria and water, made it exceptionally useful for packaging. That's why in every home in the country, it would be used regularly for food products. But on this scale, these enormous rolls were mainly busy sealing large screen televisions, washing machines and electrical appliances. It would keep them safe from damage and the outside elements, during transit. Currently trussed up and cocooned to the top of his slender shoulders, Defence Advocate, Ross Stevenson was crazily and hysterically pleading his own case and his fully fledged innocence. His calm, smug, imperious legal persona had disappeared faster than a Scotsman's wallet at New Year.

 "What does 'Bunny' think I've done? Because I haven't! I've always been there for him - No question. I constantly looked out for him and did what was required."

"And therein lies the problem." A slow deliberate nod of the head accompanied those words.

"I don't understand."

"You - have - always - done - what - was - required. Legal or otherwise."

He hesitated. "Well. Yes. Mmm. Sometimes we all have to…"

"James Baxter Reid never sent me here you fool!"

"What?" Stevenson's voice radically shifted up an octave or two.

You would have thought that those words would have reassured the wealthy lawyer. But in fact they seemed to have the exact opposite effect. He became even more concerned than ever. Sure, whatever Reid's grievance with him was and whatever humiliation and pain he wanted to put him through, Stevenson was at least confident that he would have still been alive at the end of it all. Now however, that arrogant assumption had been almightily kicked into touch.

Who was this person that dared to visit him in the middle of the afternoon in his own home? What did they want? They were certainly prepared to live dangerously, going up against Reid. But who had actually sent them and why? And would he even survive the ordeal to find out the answer to any of those burning questions?

"Who then?" He then quickly vocalised. No longer prepared to silence his thoughts.

"What is this all actually about, then? If it's money you want, my safe is upstairs."

He smiled ironically and spluttered…

"You do realise, if 'Bunny' never sent you. He will track you down and finish you for this."

There was a sinister, satisfactory tone to the encased man's comments.

"You mean like - deliberate payback, retribution and retaliation? That I will be privy to and experience some form of forthcoming vengeance?"

This time - A huge, gratifying grin, chillingly surfaced on the deranged face of the captor.

"Then bring it on. Because maybe, just maybe - THAT is exactly what this is all about."

As another length of cling film dutifully made its way around Stevenson's throbbing throat, he made to speak. That though, only enabled his host to grasp, pull firmer and narrow his windpipe even more.

"I'm sure that by mixing with your regular, established clientele, you will be very familiar with the Urban Dictionary," the voice stated in a rather matter of fact way. "The site where people look for slang or dirty, filthy definitions of everything."

The male cocoon at this point, could only offer the slightest of head gestures, as the cling film had reached his chin and lower lip.

"Well the word, 'Sonder' has made its way into that popular, iconic, online tome. For the vast majority of people though, Mr Stevenson, they will have never heard and more than likely, will never hear of that word."

Just before covering his nostrils and sealing his airways permanently. The thin faced assassin paused and stared at the now terrified legal counsel.

"Sonder - Is the realisation that each random passerby is living a life as vivid and as complex as your own."

At that moment, Ross Stevenson seriously doubted that anyone was currently living a life as complex, as his presently was.

"You would have done well to have remembered that in your Law Courts, sir."

His victim's fear was palpable.

"It means: A life that is populated with their own ambitions, friends, routines, worries and inherited craziness. That they all have an epic story that continues invisibly around you. Like an anthill sprawling deep underground, with elaborate passageways to thousands of other lives that you'll never even know existed. One in which you might only appear once, as an extra sipping coffee in the background."

The Advocate's nostrils flared repeatedly. Cloudy, marshmallow tears streamed from his reddened, ripe and repentant eyes.

"You denied so many good people justice. Your deceitful, devious, greed-filled actions allowed murderers, rapists and drug barons to walk free, time after time and on countless, numerous occasions. You simply knew no shame and fully merit your punishment."

Stevenson's frenzied eyeballs danced from side to side as his friendly, neighbourhood professional continued to rant.

"You should have been a Spider-man fan Mr Stevenson. Maybe then you would have given more heed to the following: *With great power, there must also come–great responsibility!*"

What was this deranged lunatic on? This was serious, deadly serious. The lawyer could hear it in their carefully chosen language, in their deliberate intonation and inflection. This individual's specific speech pattern clearly indicated to Ross Stevenson that the end was near. The words he heard were menacing, frightening and caused genuine need for alarm. Finally, yet another stretch of cling film screeched effortlessly from the roll. It was instantly thrust defiantly around and around the man's well groomed, although petrified features. His nostrils were gone and the bridge of his haughty nose was soon covered over. Impending suffocation was most definitely on the cards. The wrap was taken precisely to under his bulging, bloodshot eyes and immediately snapped off. Job done!

Right away, almost instantly in fact. Small patches of dampened mist filled the miniature air pockets surrounding his earlier trembling lips. You could feel his heaving lungs ache, as his docile eyes continued to dilate and pulse. Internally, he screamed in agonising silence, gasping desperately for the faintest breath. His weakened heart, once beating rapidly, had now slowed moderately in tempo. His head fell forward, his courtroom fight had diminished and his grasp on life was soon to be no more. Flight was no longer an option and all of his legal arguments had come to a close. In the final summation, the experienced carpet fitter had obviously seen enough. A hand was hurriedly extended to reach out and grab the waiting Stanley knife. Instantly it flicked into action. The triangular blade violently slashed downward from head to waist. Blood gushed at will from the severe wound and Stevenson's nose parted like the Red Sea. As the cling film fell from his face and chest, loud audible gasps for air were frequent and continuous. Wheezing, coughing and spluttering were all par for the course, as a seriously deep, three inch gash was revealed at his naval. His eye sockets began returning to normal. He'd had a lucky let-off, of that there was no doubt. As a mighty relieved, yet badly injured soul, he was again about to articulate his defense and offer up a further tedious appeal.

However, the Stanley knife was still located tightly in his assailants hand. Ross Stevenson never even saw it coming second time around. It was swift and clean. One vigorous strike, straight across the gullet.

"Guilty!" the voice stated bluntly. Before carefully closing the front door of Number 4 - The Birches.

Four

'Mixing pop and politics, he asks me what the use is. I offer him embarrassment and my usual excuses. While looking down the corridor out to where the van is waiting, I'm looking for the great leap forwards. One leap forward, two leaps back, will politics get me the sack? Waiting - for the Great Leap Forward.'

- Billy Bragg

Unaware of the bloodshed in Balerno, Chris Blear took a tentative sip of his morning coffee. The aroma competed with the elegant floral display on a nearby cabinet. With mug in hand, he carefully monitored one of the five screens directly in front of him. The early bird had been awake for several hours and he was sitting comfortably in his home office. Located all of thirty-five minutes outside Edinburgh city centre. The sparsely furnished, minimalist styled, three bedroomed retreat was nestled in a quiet, sleepy, East Lothian village. Longniddry was a traditional close-knit community. One where the main focus of the villagers attention throughout 2016, was taken up by recognising and honouring the Scottish Women's Rural Institute in a variety of scheduled events.

  Exactly one hundred years previous, the first meeting of the SWRI took place in the local village hall and 37 members were enlisted. Today, old Etonian Christian Blear had over 37 million people following his escapades. Now that may only be a humble third of the ardent loyal fan base that Kim Kardashian has, but in fairness to the glamorous US celebrity, she does not

37

directly influence the death by suicide rate in Scotland or the UK.

Stroking his thick, dark beard, the overweight man looked anxiously at his bookmarks bar. Then before his decaffeinated coffee went cold, he took another sip, inhaled long and hard and proceeded to log into the back end of one of his many websites.

Firstly, he began by choosing a subject. Which 'lucky' politician would be on the receiving end of his attention today? Would it be Theresa May, Vince Cable or maybe even Nicola Sturgeon herself? Was it to be the turn of an MP, SMP or once again an unfortunate local Councillor? In fairness, maybe the subject of the 'Trapper John' lookalike, won't be a person at all, but possibly a Government policy? Migrant workers? Police brutality? Scottish Independence? Each of those headers had all worked very successfully in the past. Because anything that would raise blood pressures, ensure outrage and quite literally get people pushing buttons was all that this particular individual required. Next the details.

It could well be, he'll invent a highly controversial incident, a crime, a new law or an Act of Parliament. Creating a new law was particularly fun, he had found. Having already devised sixteen highly original ones in recent months. At this point, Blear sat back on his chair and once again focused intently on the main screen. He briefly nodded, tipped himself forward and placed both hands at the ready. There was to be no doubting his nimble agility on the keyboard and he soon began typing the same way he did every time. Bold. Cap lock. BREAKING. Colon…

BREAKING: *Ex-First Ministers holiday home in the Highlands sealed off, as drugs, guns and black bags of money are seized.*

The words flowed effortlessly from his vivid imagination. Each gathered from the random array of thoughts desperately playing tig-tag in his unsettled head. They were however, unconnected to any actual reality. They required no thorough research, no official reports to confirm or deny and no writing pad for notes. Like performing a piano concerto, his adept fingers struck rhythmically upon the waiting keys. Each letter formed a word. Each word evolved into a proper sentence and they in turn morphed into a killer blog of about 200 words. In the modern, high tech world in which we live, each post was in actual fact an incredibly dangerous incendiary device. A highly destructive blog, constructed and edited by a man with no moral compass whatsoever. He was totally oblivious to the mayhem, chaos and grief that he would doubtless leave behind.

Or was he?

Each completed masterpiece, did not take long to compose or write and for that matter, hey presto… **Publish.**

As their four year old son, Luke, accompanied Jane Blear on the daily school run for his seven year old sister, Sariah. Christian Blear would casually sit back, much like a sinister James Bond villain and stroke the fur of his delicate, precious pussycat. However with no four-legged, white feline predator present, he would have to arrogantly content himself by steepling his fingers, tapping each opposite one together and watching the numerous *likes* and *shares* roll in.

Joe Hanlon continued to scour diligently through the report Radical Lizzie had prepared recently. 'Sherlock' was determined to ensure that he'd left no stone unturned in this FAKE NEWS enquiry. As he did so, in Leith - More than 300 miles away in a seaport market town in Norfolk, England, there was a similar office in another home. Upstairs in the large, open plan kitchen, three young children all still under the age of five, desperately indulged in a breakfast war with their father.

Martin Smith, whose name also appeared in Lizzie's findings, found himself battling with remnants of milky cereal being thrown behind his ear. With that, he beat a hasty retreat and navigated swiftly down the steep set of stairs to his basement office. There, sat an L-shaped desk in one corner, whilst a mini fridge, filled with an assortment of chilled drinks, occupied another. It rested peacefully on an old, beige formica worktop. His own daily working desk, greatly resembled that of Christian Blear's. On it were positioned several ultra modern computer monitors, with machine hard drives all tucked away neatly underneath. On his centre screen he suddenly noticed a lot of frenzied activity. Around the country people were waking up. UK commuters were heading off on their travels and catching up with the latest street savvy influencers as they did so. Many more, working from home and back in their businesses, would want to see who or what was trending online. Impressive numbers spiking on one page in particular, caught Smith's swift attention. He cautiously watched as that one specific news story gathered momentum. It was quickly being shared on Facebook and other social media networks. Martin logged into his own website and started to type.

His job, as far as he was concerned, was to tell the world that what they were seeing online - the story of a previous Scottish First Minister's holiday home, allegedly hosting drugs, guns and numerous sack loads of money - was in fact, a complete fabrication. It was fake news. Simply untrue on so many levels. Actually on every level. It was entirely a complete work of fiction.

DC Joseph Hanlon and DI Murray had met with a lady known as Sarah C nearly three months ago. She was a friend of the Inspector. Sarah was an ethical hacker and had assisted Steven Murray with a few cases in more recent years as I.T. and tricky web issues had become more prevalent. Sarah C had then in turn, introduced the officers to another colleague within her close sisterhood ranks. Social media, networking and fake news was the area of expertise for Radical Lizzie. This was her world, her domain and her specialist subject.

Earlier in the year, whilst DI Murray was busy figuring out his '3rd Degree Burns' case in Edinburgh. Reporters across the Atlantic on the trail of the US presidential election, began noticing a rash of viral made-up stories on Facebook. Bizarrely, many of the pages appeared to be posted by people from the Balkans. After Buzzfeed reported on an unusual cluster of pages, a 'scoop' of journalists, as Murray liked to refer to them, flocked to Albania. The city of Kukes, surrounded by sweeping mountains and high terrain, was the humble 'David.' Situated and engulfed by its, 'Giant' landscape.

The Americans loved the stories, Hanlon recalled Lizzie telling them. She had said...

"Fakers made lots of money. Their attitude - Who cares if the stories are true or not?"

Joe remembered, Murray's sudden yelp of surprise at that.

"What!" he had stated. Followed by an incredulous facial feature.

Lizzie continued. "The stories were in the main pitched to Donald Trump supporters."

Both officers had shaken their heads at that claim.

Radical Lizzie went on. "They included rumours about Hillary Clinton's health problems and illegal dealings.

Stories about such luminaries like Pope Francis, being lined up in support behind the Republican candidate and other false news sure to either please or rile Trump's campaigners."

With those particular memories of his first meeting with Lizzie so strong in his mind. It seemed to help 'Sherlock' remember that even earlier last year, Hillary Clinton gave a speech in which she slammed…

"The epidemic of malicious fake news and false propaganda that has flooded social media over the previous twelve months. It is now clear that so-called fake news can have real-world consequences." Clinton went on to state.

Initially, on hearing it, Joe Hanlon felt it wasn't immediately clear if she was referring to the election. At the time some journalists interpreted her remarks, as a reference to "pizzagate." A conspiracy theory that grew to tremendous proportions online and which prompted one man to storm into a Washington DC restaurant and fire an assault rifle.

Today though, Detective Constable Joseph Hanlon was fully aware of the devastating consequences that FAKE NEWS could lead to. One Scottish Nationalist MP drove her vehicle off a clifftop. Whilst another politician, unable to deal with the malicious, vile gossip being spread about him, felt the only way out was to hang himself. Both deaths were wholly unmerited. They'd simply been unable to handle the vitriolic lies and deceit being distributed about them. Both were innocent parties that had been targeted for no other reason, than sensationalism, greed and ego.

However, regardless of Mrs Clinton's meaning, the term was taken up by her opponent and used in a completely different way, several weeks later. At an awkward, disorderly press conference, Donald Trump refused to take a question from CNN reporter, Jim Acosta.

"I am not going to give you a question," he said. The Trumpster then declared, "You are fake news."

Since then, *'fake news'* has been a topic of mainstream obsession and debate. Although what is meant by the term varies hugely. Some insist on the original definition - 'fake stories' of the type pumped out by those *'Balkan Banditos.'* Others lump in 'politically motivated conspiracy theories' - perhaps, exactly what Hillary Clinton was getting at. With that said, people have also used, *'fake news'* to describe honest mistakes, opinion, spin, propaganda or like Donald Trump - news outlets or reporting, that they simply didn't like! Not only that, but often stuck under the banner of, *'fake news'* is satire or parody. Which, although on the surface appears harmless, could still fool a high percentage of people - with potentially negative consequences.

Joe Hanlon persevered reading through all the various materials, right into the early hours of the evening. By studying, pondering and questioning, things were becoming much clearer in his mind. Unusual links, strange coincidences and a multitude of dots, soon looked like they may possibly be about to join up. A serious, satisfactory unravelling had begun.

Christian Blear had grown up in the south east of England. Located directly across from Aldershot army barracks, he had been raised in a small town called, North Camp. It was an unimpressive suburb of Farnborough in Hampshire. For although, he had often referred to himself as an 'Old Etonian,' that in itself may well have been - FAKE NEWS! It had also come to light recently that his aged stepfather was a committed Conservative. A man who once ran unsuccessfully for office as an MP for Aldershot.

Although academically astute, Blear spent more than two decades in the construction industry. A trade that over the intervening years took its toll on his ravaged body. Nearly ten years ago, the 'Great Recession' of modern times hit and his industry slumped. It was then that he had started in earnest, to look for another viable source of income. That was when his first political blogging began. He soon discovered that he loved to write. Found that he had a natural flair and ability for making words come alive. So he began a blog, the first of many. He found it liberating. Being able to say what he wanted. Arguing in favour of a range of positions on the left-wing side of initially, English politics. However, although it was fun and a few people had started reading it. After four years, he acknowledged blogging simply didn't pay. However, that was when he decided on using another tact. The Hampshire man began to write fabricated tales that looked like real news headlines. When he saw the results online, the hundreds and thousands of likes and shares his posts were getting, he felt validated. Far more people were interested in fake news, than in Christian Blear's own tepid opinions or lack-lustre true stories. Although not everyone was fully convinced.

"You're wasting your time," his Scottish wife told him. "It'll never amount to anything."

But once his fictional 'fake news' started to get clicks, he was soon able to use Google's advertising platform to convert those healthy views into money. Shortly after that, he was able to quit his day job.

"Once writing became lucrative enough to not destroy my body in construction any more," he reportedly said with a laugh to a journalist. "That was when it became time to stay at home and do this full-time."

He then generated multiple online identities, using pseudonyms and aliases such as Cracka Troll and Aware Enuff. He took on a whole series of personas - Of Anti-Scots, Feminists, the Scottish Parliament and many more. He delighted in people who took the lies for the truth and shared stories, as if they had come from real news websites. The overwhelming success of the fakes, led Blear to construct a Facebook page called Scotland's Untold Story. It was dedicated to fake news stories aimed at staunch Scottish Nationalists and supporters of First Minister Nicola Sturgeon. The standard headlines were sensationalist and mainly offensive. They had one sole aim - to provoke a reaction, to conjure up an emotional response, one that would get people to share and discuss.

* BREAKING: A tawdry basement in Treasury Minister's home, once described as a torture chamber.

* BREAKING: American tourists snubbed, by SNP supporting tour guide.

* BREAKING: Local SNP Councillor groomed his own children.

That last one was the one that interested Detective Constable Joseph Hanlon the most. Christian Blear himself described many of the headlines he wrote as "racist and bigoted." But they went viral - and those shares turned into clicks. Which then turned into hard, fast cash.

Back in Norfolk, computer programmer, Martin Smith had cleverly created software that could detect which stories were currently trending on Facebook. He called it the Popularizer. He would then write about them on his blog, but he also struggled to find an audience. He was up against some of the world's biggest media organisations. By the time he noticed a post was trending and wrote about it, big news sites had already covered it. However, like Blear, Smith soon discovered a niche when it came to fake news. For all the people who liked and shared fictional stories, believing them to be real. There were a host of others who appreciated someone who could readily identify those that were fake. So when Smith discovered false stories and blogged about them, his site traffic went up. Not by an astonishing amount. He wasn't making as much money as Christian Blear. But he did well enough for him to concentrate on debunking fake news. His blog *Lead Stories,* became focused on the fakes, with the tagline: "Just because it's trending, doesn't mean it's true."

Martin also noticed patterns and repeated online behaviour. For example on a weekly basis he saw fake stories about the death of David Cameron. Every Saturday, he would read that the Prime Minister had died - either in a dramatic car crash, an explosive boating accident or from a sudden heart attack.

As he debunked the fake stories, Smith began to collect information about fake news sites and the people behind them. His database allowed him to track the fakers across the Internet, even as their websites and Facebook pages were taken down. He noticed broad themes. In addition to David Cameron and Hillary Clinton, voter fraud was a popular subject for fake news, as were immigration and Islam. And given the wild west nature of the fake news world, he increasingly found that more and more sites - including some of those from those Balkan states - were stealing content and simply copying and pasting from other fake news sites. In fact, many were stealing content from just one source. That source was of course, the inimitable Christian Blear!

Five

'Breakin' rocks in the hot sun - I fought the law and the law won. I needed money 'cause I had none - I fought the law and the law won. I fought the law and the law won.'

- The Clash

Friday evening - 25th March 2016

In low, strained tones of muted anger, the emotional voice whispered…

"The judiciary of Scotland are the office holders who sit in the country's courts and make decisions in both civil and criminal cases. Your role was to make sure that justice was carried out. That those cases and verdicts were kept within the parameters set by Scots law."

Now openly filled with disgust and disdain, the voice rallied.

"People trusted you and you let them down badly. The everyday man and woman in the street depended on your integrity and honesty to serve them. They relied on you to hand down appropriate judgements and sentences. You basically betrayed them and now through myself, they seek redress M'Lord."

Mockery and ridicule were now joint bedfellows in derision toward the cowering figure.

The sinister voice echoed. "We are not going to get a Good Friday agreement here tonight are we?"

"No, no, no, I beg of you," the bespectacled, white haired man, pleaded passionately.

With his complexion drained of all colour, he sat Dickensian. Comparable to Ebenezer Scrooge getting his first festive visitation. Desperately, the newly retired judiciary statesman tried to lift his small, wiry hands from the vintage, antique desk top. They were stuck fast, superglued firmly in place to the gleaming, shiny mahogany surface. Only his thumbs were left with any available movement. Over each knuckle the wrinkled lines and sun spots on his skin, indicated, like a tree trunk - a rough estimate of the man's timeline here on earth. The matching chair having been wedged underneath the beautifully varnished bureau, made any further exertions near impossible. However, no doubt the one inch wide nail about to be hammered agonisingly through the back of his left hand would also curtail his desire to struggle further.

"Aaaagggghhhh."

The excruciatingly, tortuous scream would ricochet dramatically from wall to wall. Disappearing, almost unheeded, through the vast patio doors and down toward the sixty yard driveway. It would finally be lost out into the almighty ether of the rolling green Lanarkshire hills nearby. His captor had fully appreciated balance in all aspects of life. So undaunted, another rigid piece of greying metal was positioned centrally, this time onto the back of the distressed man's right hand. As the sharp point pierced the skin, the enlarged flattened end…

"Aaaagggghhhh."

With slender sinews crushed and bone fragments shattered, the intercom to the man's front gate rang out loud and clear. The distinguished hands of the large, imposing carriage clock approached 10pm. The deed was done and the impending 'Scales of Justice' were nearly, but not quite balanced. They still remained slightly out of kilter, not yet fully in synch. As the front gate remained closed, a raw mixture of burning tears and pain related sweat ran forcibly down the face of the honourable Judge Gordon B. Menzies. With no further distraction from any outside intruder anticipated, his countenance presently indicated, acute anguish and horror. However, the individual that had just delivered the two terrifying blows was not yet witnessing appropriate remorse or regret from their pitiful captive. A pair of red rimmed cufflinks that had been located in his upstairs bedside drawer, was further proof, if any was required, that this individual had indeed been part of TIME. The 'tears in my eyes' teenage human trafficking ring. The sickening all male group of corrupt, depraved, deviant souls that had been unearthed the year before. Many of whom in recent months had even been found, 'Not Guilty' and several more, 'Not Proven' by this very man.

'Not Proven' - now wasn't that a very interesting Scottish option. There have been constant calls to scrap that verdict since the middle of the 20th century. So was it a strange coincidence that on the very day of Judge Menzies' personal dilemma, a private members' bill to scrap the verdict had once again been debated in the Scottish Parliament?

As his tormentor was about to leave the magnificent, two million pound, plush luxury bachelor pad, the Judge's resolve had weakened. Barely able to stay conscious, he had desperately tried to listen as a soothing voice made to reassure him. An iPhone had been carefully positioned between Menzies' thumb and forefinger on his right hand. Several fine wires seemed to run out from the base of the mobile. Each one a different colour, they travelled vertically downward between his 'right honourable' arms and dropped off the edge of the desk like a mini zip-slide. At the end of which they were delicately connected to a small, sealed, oval package. One that was now firmly ensconced between the quivering legs of the corrupt, aged lawmaker.

"Listen carefully," the voice, quietly instructed. "This can save your life. In the next couple of minutes, someone will call this number. Do you hear me? All you simply have to do is before the fourth ring, hit the answer button. No connection will be made and you'll survive until your fat, elderly cleaning lady, calls again in the morning."

The voice spoke menacingly, but with a rather bouncy, upbeat rhythm to it. It was coupled with a definite air of satisfaction and finality.

"Got it?"

The frenzied head of white hair nodded forward. Both his thumbs trembled incessantly.

"Before the fourth ring," he repeated. "I hit answer. Sure. Okay, I've got it," a pained and deeply desperate rasp offered.

Thirty seconds later his cold caller had gone. Disappearing back into the night, as quickly and as unexpectedly as they had arrived.

Menzies' head shook uncontrollably from side to side. He had to remain extra calm his inner voice told him. *Rat-at-at-at*, his thumbs beat like a snare drum. *Rat-at-at-at*, as his eyes focused on the tiny screen. Outside at the bottom of the lengthy tradesmen's entrance, the lurking figure in the shadows proceeded to dial. *Rat-at-at-at*, the sound historically heard before the body dropped at a gallows. *Rat-at-at-at*, and suddenly the darkened screen turned white. The ring tone sounded once and his over-anxious thumb immediately burst into action, reaching out and tapping instinctively.

"Noooo-oooo," his terrified voice rang out.

The phone was upside down. His heart was beating faster than his drumming thumbs. A second ring broke the momentary silence. How would he reach that button? In a millisecond he attempted to flick and swivel it with his thumb. Too fast, too hard. It had travelled a full 360 degrees and was now caught up in the wires. The third ring was about to begin as he managed to launch his thumb once again back into action and at that, the mobile seemed to magically turn into a mini, ultra slow version of 'Wheel of Fortune.' It felt never ending, before eventually stopping within reach of his short, thick, inner digit. This time his thumb instantly and accurately hit the green answer button. No fourth ring was heard. The Judge's head fell solidly between his chest, knocking the phone well out of future reach. A large, expressive sigh of relief was offered as two exhausted thumbs remained perfectly still. It would appear that on this occasion the verdict favoured Lord Gordon Menzies. He was physically safe and sound. His bloodied, bruised and battered hands would eventually heal, although mentally, he may well be scarred for life!

As a certain so-called vigilante headed off at speed. The serene calm and relative quiet of the awe-inspiring Clyde Valley countryside was about to be broken. A faint, weakened tremor was initially felt, before a full realisation of what was actually occurring dawned. The Judge opened a weary eye. The vibration was the iPhone receiving another incoming call. Colour sprang to life once again on the screen, Menzies' eyes grew wide into a crescendo of disbelief and fear. His mobile then delivered another ring. His sharp legal mind realised immediately that this would be its fourth. The prosecution would argue that - *No one said they had to ring consecutively.*

Creating a perfect silhouette for the lone motorcyclist travelling unhindered in the opposite direction. The massive, almighty, sandstone explosion erupted and lit up the Lanarkshire skyline. Earlier that day Scottish politicians had been required at the parliament building. Plans to scrap the 'Not Proven,' verdict had been overwhelmingly rejected once again: 80 votes to 28!

Entering into the early hours of a chilly Saturday morning. The hands on the customer's knocked-off Rolex approached 2am when the slim frame of the so-called, hospitality manager, went to escort him vigorously off the premises and finally lock up. The dingy gathering place was a rather dated and well-worn drinking den of iniquity. A degrading hostelry situated in one of the less salubrious parts of the historic town. Yet it still continued to thrive and be a favourite regular haunt, for half of Edinburgh's gangland community. One wondered why? Although the word, 'Connections,' sprung instantly to mind as an answer to that particular question.

They'd had by all accounts, a very successful and busy night. Takings were up and numerous scores of shady wheelers and dealers had been in selling their various wares over the busy holiday weekend. Out of which, only two disruptive, unruly strangers required to be unceremoniously ejected. 'Papped out' in other words and told in no uncertain terms to make themselves scarce. It must have been bad, to find yourself getting slung out of that particular establishment.

Earlier in the evening, a serious heavyweight crew from Newcastle, had been busy touting their upmarket goods and arranging test drives the next day for serious bidders. Their uncommon product was high quality and not for the faint hearted. Nor for that matter, any cash strapped shyster. Their special merchandise consisted of a luxurious mint green Porsche and a rather more traditionally coloured, blood red Ferrari. Both vehicles came unsurprisingly with 'free delivery and road tax.'

As the tawdry manager, eventually exited out into the car park at the rear of the grubby watering hole, he began to pull down the rumbling roller shutters. Only a solitary motorbike and a run down, battered Mini Cooper remained to be partnered up with their respective owners. The slight man had been totally oblivious and unaware of the single figure astride the bike and although muffled slightly by their bikers helmet, a soft voice asked politely...

"Mr Johnson?"

Without turning around and fully crouched down at this point, the arrogant publican finished padlocking his metal shutter before offering up a high, shrill voice. One that matched his tall, wafer-thin, wine glass figure.

"Who's asking?"

The full beam of the bike's headlight, was then dramatically switched on and it's engine revved fiercely. A rampant bright sphere shone directly toward him, blinding him completely. However, two quick crab steps to the side, soon edged him out of the direct spotlight. With his eyes still seeing clusters of shooting stars, he could only just make out the leather clad upper body of the individual as they approached. Their helmet had now clearly been removed.

"Actually, that would be me," the quiet voice stated. "And I am in fact - a Sir!"

The lofty publican stared dismissively at the dark figure now stood right in front of him. And a slow, less than impressed question left his lips.

"You? You would have me believe that you are a, Sir? Are you having a laugh? Although, hang on a minute, don't I know you?" Came the over confident, *'gallus'* announcement.

The sneering question was volunteered up in a tough, derogatory, street-wise manner. On hearing it, the shadowed stranger's voice changed abruptly. In a swift heartbeat, patient and calm had been instantly replaced with fast, furious and frenzied. It was well seeing that Dr Jekyll and Mr Hyde was indeed written by a fiery Scotsman.

"Oh, I am a very distinguished, Sir," the words lightly cackled. "Sir Ringe!"

At that precise moment, not one, but two piston powered metal syringes made directly for Johnny Johnson's fear-filled, bulging eye sockets. Plucking one instantly from its chamber with such force, that it detached itself fully from the optic nerve and muscles. The resulting high velocity scream would have woken the dead from every cemetery in town.

Six

'2-4-6-8 ain't never too late. Me and my radio truckin' on through the night. 3-5-7-9 on a double white line. Motorway sun coming up with the morning light.'

- Tom Robinson Band

Saturday morning - 26th March

It was the Easter Holiday weekend, with extensive sales at well known furniture outlets and sofa superstores. Which meant endless congested traffic jams on major motorways. It may well have been a time for much needed family get-togethers and celebrations, but today, all hands on deck were required at the Queen Charlotte Street police station. Chaotic school children on ski slopes or in fully enclosed holiday parks, were no match for the twenty-four hours of murder, mystery and manic mayhem that had just kicked off.

First a prominent criminal defence lawyer was killed in his own home, on Good Friday afternoon. Then an explosive Easter extravaganza was experienced in the evening, with the named fatality being a distinguished Scottish High Court Judge. Any link between the two remained to be seen. But surely not a coincidence, was the thinking of those in charge at Police Headquarters.

In quick response, a security notification had been sent out to leading members of Edinburgh's legal fraternity. It included all lawyers, sheriffs and judges. Even the Crown Office and Procurators Fiscal staff were put on high alert.

If those two significant acts had not been enough for the boys and girls in blue (although now it's officially black). Then just for good measure, a dodgy publican had been found in the early hours at the back of his shady premises. What a gruesome discovery that had been for a poor 'jakey' on the prowl. The homeless man had been hoping to sniff out remnants of a possible liquid breakfast to begin his day with. Instead, he found himself spewing up last night's 'Buckfast' dessert. The dead man's eyes had been viciously removed from their sockets. They sat disgustingly at his side in a congealed pool of maroon.   Each with a seven inch syringe embedded. If that had not been enough barbarity. One of his ears had been cruelly sliced clean off and placed alongside his severed nose, on the dank, moist concrete. The forensics team were going to have a field day with this one. Definitely a little bit of, *'see no evil, hear no evil.'*

At present, travelling in haste from her new home in the old mining village of Lochgelly, Fife, to her workplace in the congested, busy streets in the north of the capital, Sergeant Sandra Kerr had hoped desperately that today was not going to find her, as she so eloquently put it…'chasin' her tail!'

What a fascinating statement those three words were. Implying that one was busy doing a lot of things, but actually achieving very little. With recent developments, 'Sandy' could not afford for that to happen. At around 7am, her husband Richard had headed off. He drove at speed up toward Angus with their twin daughters in tow. They had ALL been scheduled to visit Richard Kerr's aging parents that holiday weekend and enjoy Easter together. Alas, ten minutes before the 'family' were scheduled to leave, DCI Furlong phoned her in despair. She begged Sandra Kerr to come into the workplace.

"Ma'am, do you happen to know what goes with potty training?"

Barbra Furlong literally pulled the phone from her ear and stared at it. Am I talking a different language she wondered.

"Eh, 'Sandy,' did you hear…"

"Oh, I heard you alright, Ma'am," Kerr interrupted.

There was frustration and angst in her tone.

"Now let me enlighten you… and tell you exactly what goes with potty training."

After what seemed like eternity, but was actually a three second pause, ADI Sandra Kerr offered up in a mightily relieved voice…

"A great big, ice cold… double vodka and Coke - that's what!"

Gentle laughter echoed down the phone line from her female superior. She had just been subtly reminded that 'Sandy' was the mother of twin toddlers.

The team was currently still a man down and had experienced three suspected murders since yesterday afternoon. What could she say? 'Sandy,' as she was affectionately known to her colleagues for her flaming red, vibrant hair was still adjusting to the position of Acting DI. So there really was no way she could refuse, or actually wanted to refuse.

Several friends in the force had already made her aware of the deaths of Ross Stevenson and Judge Menzies, literally within minutes of them being confirmed. If truth be told, she would have happily volunteered her services and turned up in the middle of last night. But she had been unwilling to do that to Richard and the girls. However, being called up and requested in specially, well that gave her own pride a welcome boost and obviously created a perfect excuse.

How did HE, do it she thought? All these years and HE, has made it look so effortless. HE took it in his stride, or so it appeared. But she, more than most, was well aware of his Bipolar. Although, HE himself had never really, fully openly acknowledged or confirmed the fact, even to himself at times! HE always seemed to be in control and fully aware of what was going on, often without even trying. Maybe that was her problem. She was trying too hard. For many years now, the so-called, exemplary, 'HE' in question. Had been her role model, friend and mentor.

Within fifteen minutes and 'Ba-boom... Ba-boom... Ba-boom...' her tyres sounded at regular twenty yard intervals, crossing the old world famous road bridge. Its appearance was tired and jaded these days. Having served Scotland for well over half a century, it was now nearing time for partial retirement for this stalwart, faithful and vital Fife commuter link. Soon, it would be replaced for the majority of journeys by the gigantic, super sized Lego structure, rising up majestically at her side. This latest behemoth on the landscape had popped up gradually and surprisingly quickly in recent months. The new, unoriginally titled, Queensferry Crossing, would be ready for use in 2017.

Sweeping back the tousled mane of glorious hair from her brow, Murray's current deputy heard herself ask internally. Would the familiar 'Ba-boom... Ba-boom... Ba-boom,' be gone forever? Would it have a suitably, reliable and up to speed replacement? And at the present time in her own busy workplace - Was she equally suitable, reliable and up to speed?

Driving over to the east from Glasgow, Allan Boyd was another member of the team, scheduled to be late. The M8 motorway, the main thoroughfare connecting

Scotland's two major cities was at a virtual standstill in both directions. The radio reports and traffic news seemed to indicate that an incident involving an articulated lorry and an overhead gantry were the alleged culprits. Coupled that particular morning, with holiday makers of all descriptions heading off to various Easter destinations, meant that an immediate heavy build up of congested traffic had ensued.

This disillusioned officer was going to take at least another two hours to arrive at the station. Ex-armed forces, DC Boyd was a '5ft 5in,' thirty-eight year old male. A team player that had enjoyed his six year stint thus far building a career with the aptly named Police Service of Scotland. Sandra Kerr, his initial partner had described him as, 'a mini, red-haired Murray.' Having worked with each of the men, she was probably the one best placed to offer an honest opinion. 'Both had generous hearts and were rather wacky and off base in their respective manner and styles,' she'd said. By using humour to hide behind, the pair also seemed reluctant to talk about their respective demons from the past. Currently, whilst 'Sandy' was Acting DI, Detective Constable Allan Boyd was teamed up with Sergeant Mitch Linn.

'Mitch' was short for Mitchell. Although his official nickname was 'Baldy!' Which was genuinely ironic and maybe, why they teasingly called him it. Because his regularly tanned complexion hosted a healthy crop of bleached blonde hair up on top. Detective Sergeant Mitchell Linn had operated out of Edinburgh for three years, but had never been a part of Murray's, so-called elite team before. Either under the command of the late, deceased DCI Keith Brown or its most recent incumbent… Detective Chief Inspector Barbra Furlong.

Seven

'Food, glorious food! What is there more handsome? Gulped, swallowed or chewed - still worth a king's ransom.'

- The Musical: Oliver

The generally mild mannered Barbra Furlong was still trying desperately to give up her two decade long habit, of continually cursing and using profanities. Today she had been given a heads up on a Scottish Television piece that was airing live, on the local news, that very morning. Whilst various members of her team were delayed getting into their Queen Charlotte Street premises that day, the DCI had arrived super early and made herself comfortable in her office. She had then changed the appropriate channels and was all tuned in, settled and ready to go.

The global reach of the Scottish Crime Campus (SCC), had targeted more than 440 organised criminals. With three new countries – Nepal, Germany and Slovenia having been added to their international crime map, since it became operational two years previous. Multi-agency investigations led from the Lanarkshire hub had spanned the world since February 2014. That was when its doors first opened, marking a significant boost to the fight against crime. The £73 million site has also added a state of the art forensics capacity, through an additional £6 million development. The brand new laboratory housed DNA 24, the most advanced profiling facility in Europe. Doctor Tom Patterson, aka 'The T'inker,' now worked out of that busy lab at

Gartcosh. Having made the transition just over a month ago, his travel time has greatly increased from his little 'bolt hole' of a cottage in Athelstaneford, East Lothian. But the Doc figured that he may not be too far behind 'Ally' Coulter in the retirement stakes, so could stick it out in the interim.

Organisations based in the new Lanarkshire location have tackled fugitives, dismantled international commodity networks and countered the threat posed to communities by co-operating and sharing information. Which in turn has helped underpin operations and investigations in all four corners of the world. Police Scotland has a right to be rather pleased with themselves.

Officers working with agencies based at the Campus had also caught up with more than 300 international, 'most wanted' criminals. Villains who were either in Scotland and wanted abroad or who had simply fled justice here. Those included certain individuals being returned from Jamaica, Spain, Portugal and Thailand. Either for firearms offences, stalking, sexual abuse and even murder.

Today, Police Scotland's Chief Constable and the current Justice Secretary joined with SCC partners, to hail the facility which they had said truly placed Scotland at the forefront of modern crime-fighting methods. Presently on camera, live, a rather self-assured white haired man, the Chief Constable himself was about to begin.

"The impact which the Scottish Crime Campus has had in just two short years is truly breathtaking," he stated. "It has led to a sea-change in how organisations, including law enforcement, share information and develop opportunities to detect and disrupt criminality."

He looked good Barbra Furlong thought. He came across well on camera. His face and words spoke volumes. They said: decent, honest and down to earth. Someone that the public could put their trust in. He was very articulate and open in his remarks, the DCI noticed. 'Continue,' she heard herself say aloud. Hoping for more inspiration.

"Through working more effectively and smarter. Through sharing information and intelligence and by linking our resources, then if there is a real threat posed by criminality connected to any part of the world, we will go and we will seek to nullify it for the benefit of our communities here."

Whilst DCI Furlong considered his further comments, more carefully in the morning privacy of her neatly kept room. She was conscious that her team was still cautiously getting over and coming to terms with the death of a colleague's son. A death that they were all hurting from. A loss that has affected each of them. One which they will always feel should have been avoided, that should have never happened. A death that no one felt more guilty about, than the deceased's very own father. For a full eight week period since the emotive funeral, Detective Inspector Steven Murray has locked himself away from the reality of the world.

Food and an assortment of supplies had been dropped off every few days by members of his team. 'Danny Boy' continued to play mournfully on his doorbell. *The pipes… the pipes are calling,'* but no one ever answered that call. However, at random times throughout the day or night, the door would eventually get unlocked, open briefly and the most recent delivery dragged swiftly inside. Then the familiar slamming of the door followed. That deeply distressing and upsetting routine was currently - on week nine.

"Morning Ma'am."

The slim figure that stood at her doorway belonged to a dishevelled and tired looking Detective Constable. A man that had been DI Murray's partner for this past year. At present, 'Sherlock' had been temporarily reassigned to desk duties and his most recent investigation, had led him to staying in the station all night.

"Elementary, my dear Hanlon," his Chief Inspector smiled. "Come in Constable. How are you doing?" she asked. Noting immediately his wrinkled and ruffled clothing. "Was there something specific you wanted to see me about?"

Catching the early morning TV news article that she was watching, 'Sherlock' felt the need to contribute.

"The Doc is permanently over there now. You know that right? Well of course you know that, Ma'am," he said feeling rather foolish.

His face blushed like a bright beacon, as he continued.

"I was just speaking with him two nights ago. He says it's a superb facility and that we should continue to see a noticeable turnaround in result times."

Barbra Furlong raised her head slightly.

"Was that a work related enquiry with Patterson? One, that I should know about?" she asked curiously. Although with a bright mischievous glint in her eye.

"Or was it a non-work related item, that you were in discussions with him over? One, that I would be better off, not knowing anything at all about?"

Both her head and her eyebrows dropped whilst delivering that last remark.

Joe Hanlon's cheeks were ablaze once again. That was, answer enough.

"PUSSYCAT FLAMING DOLLS!" she exclaimed. Replacing a swear word or two.

"You lot are all up to something. I should have known," she said. Her pitch raised, she ended with - "Unbelievable!"

"Moving into Gartcosh wasn't just about doing the same as we were all doing before, but in a new building, was it, Ma'am?" Joe Hanlon questioned quickly, by way of distraction.

"Surely, the aim was to build a new network for tackling crime and to establish new ways of doing that? It has been about putting collaboration at the heart of what we do to make communities safer, isn't that correct?" 'Sherlock' then added quietly…

"Because, trust me, that is exactly what we are doing as a team, Ma'am."

He then opened out the palm of his hands, in an unspoken gesture of honesty, that said - Would I lie to you? As Murray's partner-in-crime went to exit, his CI began to respond…

"The last two years have seen important changes in the way we work with our partners to tackle serious and organised crime Joe," she said boldly. "And all through the collaboration, we have shared resources, tactics and information with great success from the outset. Undoubtedly, this has helped us by bringing extra strength to bear on the people who were profiting from criminality and has helped us immensely in our efforts to systematically dismantle organised crime groups from all angles."

Hanlon was baffled by that rather lengthy and politically correct response. What was she saying?

"So, remember please," she continued. "When and if you feel the time is right to collaborate and share your findings, I would encourage you to do so."

Hanlon offered a nod of understanding. He got it now. The message was simple and clear. Furlong appreciated that she was still new and had not been fully accepted into their private members' club just yet. After a brief moment of quiet reflection, Hanlon once again diverted the route of the conversation.

"You attended the crime scene at Stevenson's yesterday afternoon, Ma'am, I was told. How did you get on?"

"Our Acting DI, had not long finished her shift and so with your buddy still absent, I thought I would take it on and run with it."

"Any joy with the vehicle then?" Hanlon persisted.

"It belonged to an independent, self-employed carpet fitter. He had it stolen from outside his flat in Gorgie between seven and eight that morning. We'd had a report. It had been circulated and we were on the lookout for it from about eight-fifteen onwards.

"That seemed rather risky, wouldn't you say?" Hanlon opined. "Stealing some transport and then within the next couple of hours or so, using it as cover to murder someone."

"Possibly the exact opposite I would suggest, Constable," Furlong answered. "By the time we get it reported to us and we update our system, including messaging patrol cars and officers on the streets, he'll be well gone, suitably parked up in some secure, isolated spot. Probably, nearby to his target no doubt. Then later, within ten minutes of arriving at the lawyers door, the deed was done!"

The uncertain shrug that Hanlon offered, would have been sign language for 'I guess so.'

"Also Joe, I would add, rather than risky, this person was… Well, where should I start? Confident, self-assured, assertive. They were certainly organised. Possibly even watching our flooring expert for weeks, to ensure that their regular evening schedule or ritual was kept up. They were definitely level headed, poised and calm…"

"Any witnesses?" Hanlon interrupted.

"Not really. A long haired driver with a baseball cap and overalls. Pretty cliched actually, if truth be told. That bland description was from a neighbour across the way."

"A neighbour?" Hanlon repeated.

"Yes. Seemingly they had been waiting at their window, watching out for an Amazon delivery. The killer even had the audacity to wave over to them, as they pulled away. Literally it would appear he was no longer than ten to twelve minutes."

"Fastest carpet fitter I've ever come across," 'Sherlock' joked.

Knowing full well as soon as he had said it, that he had overstepped the mark.

Barbra Furlong shook her head in disappointment. Joe Hanlon recognised fully that although plenty of Steven Murray's seasoned character traits were impacting on him positively. Unfortunately, several others were less welcome and should be best avoided altogether.

"Sorry Ma'am. Apologies, that was in bad taste."

The DCI's gentle nod said - Accepted.

"DC Hanlon," she then announced in a stern voice. "Boyd is going to be held up for an hour or two… and you are wasted here. So I want you to team up with ADI Kerr. She should be in shortly. Get yourselves over to Judge Menzies' home, or at least what remains of it and see what you can uncover or literally unearth."

Strangely, the DCI did not get the excited, positive response that she had expected.

"Is there a problem, Constable Hanlon? Joe?"

As he bit down nervously on his lip, his thumb and forefinger on both hands danced a nervous jig. His tongue began doing backward somersaults in his mouth. 'Sherlock' was in a quandary. At first he was delighted to be asked to assist Kerr. For he knew all the top brass would be all over this story, as well as the newspapers and TV. However, never one to sit on his laurels and take things easy while his boss was recovering, Detective Constable Hanlon had stumbled across something recently that piqued his interest.

"Ma'am, it's just that there is something extremely odd about some recent suicides that have come across my desk. I was hoping to check them out and discuss them with you. I was hoping that the DI would have been back. Because I think he may have some personal insights to shed on at least one of them."

Warily and in an exhausted, tired manner, he also added. "Plus, I believe there have been another four more possible tit for tat, gangland attacks last night also."

"Some of Reid and Scott's foot soldiers?" she surmised.

"It would appear so. Officers are at various scenes now."

"Agghhh - FRIGGIN' GIGANTIC GOLLIWOGS!" The Chief shrieked.

Hanlon coughed. It was a discreet, yet chastising, politically correcting cough. Whatever one of those sounded like!

"I would suspect fully fledged swearing would get you into a lot less trouble than that particular word," he reminded his Chief Inspector.

"What word? GIANT?" she questioned. Then in a more intense voice, she remonstrated further with, "BOLLOCK-SEY BLUES."

"That would be Biloxi, Ma'am," he smirked. "It's the name of a place, not someone's..."

"Get out!"

"But Ma'am..."

"Go! Disappear! Depart! Leave! Join 'Sandy' and get to the scene of that dreadful explosion and forget gangland squabbles and your supposed suicide theories for now."

"But... Ma'am."

"Go!" She bellowed.

Hanlon turned swiftly on his heels. Disappointment was etched all across his face. At that precise moment he saw a rather harried Sandra Kerr arrive in, through the bottom doorway. The tiniest of smiles surfaced from her lips and an early morning wave was exchanged as Joe walked down the lengthy open working space toward her. Out of the side of his eye, the detective turned just in time to glimpse a body take up the spot he himself, had previously occupied with DCI Furlong. 'Sherlock' gave a somewhat concerned look. With his billowing eyebrows ceiling bound and his mouth crooked and pulled back. 'That is not a good sign,' he thought to himself.

By now Acting Detective Inspector Kerr was astutely staring over her approaching colleague's left shoulder. Joe Hanlon had recognised that she too had spotted the elephant in the room.

He went to ask...

"It is," 'Sandy' said.

With his curiosity now fully aroused, he then went to...

"I've no idea what it's about." Again she anticipated the obvious question to be asked.

At that, a rather troubled nod of her head was offered. 'Sherlock' was uncertain which number Murray would have allocated to that particular movement.

"I'm not a fan, Joe. I don't hear good things on the grapevine from fellow female officers and I repeat... I have no idea why he is here."

DC Hanlon raised his head warily. "Sarge, sorry Inspector, you know that this fatal explosion we are on our way to in Lanark was carried out on a prominent Judge's house, right?"

They both quietly nodded to each other.

Kerr went to speak…

"Yes, you're right 'Sandy,' that could be the very reason he is here," Joe Hanlon said, before his ADI could utter a word!

A broad smile came over his features, as he walked smugly to the car park.

His, "Get you outside!" trailed off into the distance.

As the two officers headed over to join the busy forensics team, both individuals wondered - Why are we travelling all the way to Lanark?

The answer to that specific question was possibly about to be discussed and disguised in more depth, somewhere within the political, cat and mouse maneuvering that was currently taking place in Barbra Furlong's refrigerated room. The atmosphere between the two officers certainly appeared to be rather chilly to say the least!

Eight

'I practise nightly, I try to keep ahead. This art of surfacing is all but dead. Wind chill factor minus zero. Wind chill factor minus ten below.'

- The Boomtown Rats

The actual temperature in the Chief Inspector's room was more than a match for the bitter March weather outside. The chill factor was all to do with the physical and verbal interaction, or lack thereof. The recently divorced, Assistant Chief Constable Paul Martin's body language was an instant giveaway at his dislike, or certainly perceived disdain, toward the recently appointed Detective Chief Inspector. Several times over the years, Barbra Furlong had turned down his amorous advances. Back then, she was disgusted by his lewd comments and suggestive foreplay. All of which were supposedly disguised as fun banter. She knew full well what to expect today and so far he had not disappointed. It was not an impressive character trait and it was guaranteed to hinder this discussion right from the start.

"We are all under pressure here, Chief Inspector. We need to come up with some answers quickly." Martin's staccato voice was lofty. His words were full of self-importance and well polished rhetoric. The 'We,' he spoke of, Furlong clearly understood to mean - everyone, but himself.

"That is why the Chief Constable is desirous to have a team from here oversee the Menzies' case. A local squad from Hamilton would have done a pretty good job, I'm sure. But you guys, will have a much stronger, immediate connection with it. Given that they appear to be linked."

The Chief Constable my backside, Furlong shrugged. She had already spoken to the man himself, late last night after the incident had taken place and that idea was certainly never discussed. However, earlier that morning Scotland's highest ranking officer had called her personally, to say that ACC Martin had an interesting proposal. One that he'd wanted to come over and visit with her about. Ideally, so that he could discuss it more fully in person. DCI Furlong had gotten the gist of it from her Chief Constable and was ahead of the game, by sending out Kerr and Hanlon. But, 'The Chief Constable's idea?' Aye right, she thought. Paul 'don't believe a word I say' Martin, was a born liar, coward and cheat. Which had already been confirmed to her five years previously, when he himself was a humble Chief Inspector. She remembered it as if it were yesterday. Although to be fair, how could she forget? That was the very first occasion that he had asked her out. It was for an expensive evening meal at one of the city's exclusive eateries. At the time his beautiful fiancé of three months, was lying constrained in a hospital bed, having her inflamed appendix removed. Their doomed marriage was to last unsurprisingly, all of two full years!

"You do know that, Menzies was one of the men that Inspector Murray named as being at the under-age sex trafficking roulette game?" Paul Martin questioned arrogantly.

"And so was, Stevenson for that matter!" Barbra Furlong submitted. "And yet they both continued daily, to take up their respective seats in court?" She questioned.

"Yes, however and correct me if I'm wrong Chief Inspector, neither individual was ever charged you will recall. Innocent until proven guilty. Don't you remember that rule of thumb, DCI Furlong? Because that is how we operate in Police Scotland. Not…" he continued slowly, "On the dodgy word, of unreliable officers. Or maybe that should be the unreliable word of dodgy officers?"

Barbra Furlong contained her anger and contempt, by grasping tightly onto her desk chair and digging her recently manicured nails deep, down into the soft black Italian leather. This man was a tormentor and trouble maker. Not someone to be trusted. Never mind the fact that he was the current Assistant Chief Constable of Police Scotland. His heavy handedness and intimidating bully boy tactics had gone unhindered for years. In another world, it could easily have been 'Bunny' Reid looking to track down Martin. At least Reid could turn on the charm, was principled and had integrity of one sort or another. By all accounts… ACC Paul Martin - Not so much!

"Last night it was one of the country's top Judge's. Earlier in the afternoon Barbra, it was one of the city's most brilliant legal minds. Obviously with everything else that is going on, we initially thought Andrew Scott would be good for it."

"I can see why," DCI Furlong steepled her fingers and agreed.

"Far too public though, Chief Inspector. We've watched Scott grow his team and his wealth and influence in recent years. Unfortunately, this is definitely not his style. Although my guess would be, he'll be delighted at the toll it must be taking on the 'little fluffy rabbit' guy.

"Surely, several of Scotland's other crime lords, would be equally delighted to move in on Edinburgh's historic streets? I know many of them were angry and mightily unimpressed by Reid killing Andrew Scott's mother and holding his young niece prisoner," Furlong contributed.

"Maybe!" He replied. "But there are other individuals also, who may well be out for revenge."

Furlong's eyebrows narrowed, as she stared at her superior officer cautiously.

"Possibly that kind of individual, may already be regarded by many as a loose cannon. Someone that is in desperate need of revenge or vigilante justice. Someone that knows the game well and has accrued a wealth of insider knowledge." He then paused…

"Possibly even someone with nothing left to lose, but plenty to gain. Someone that is a little bit closer to home."

The Chief Inspector hoped he was not going where she thought he was going with his lazy, snide and disingenuous remarks. But sure enough, in his own uniquely tasteless assumption, he continued with…

"At this point you have to seriously question, where is Steven Murray in all of this? How long does an experienced officer like himself, stay absent? What mischief has he been up to or involved in whilst away? Plus I mean, have you actually even been watching him? Keeping close tabs on his daily whereabouts? Because, knowing the man. I would have."

Furlong stood in amazement at what she had just heard.

Her ACC continued with. "And from the look on your face, I would have to ask - If not? Why not?"

Bewildered. His female officer, ruthlessly stared daggers at him.

"I believe he's not been seen out and about for fully two months. Would that be correct? If so, he's having you on. He's playing with you woman."

Martin's voice had an added edge to it. It had become aggressive. His words seemed to have taken on a very personal malice.

"The same way, he plays with everyone. It's always about him, about our Steven isn't it?"

His female underling considered his outburst. She reflected on his words, his tone, his cadence and delivery. She took a second or two to ponder her next move in this particular game. The DCI made a decision and chose familiarity.

"You can't seriously be suggesting Paul, that DI Murray…"

"You must admit Babs…"

Babs! I'll friggin' Babs him, she thought silently. But then quickly acknowledged that she had opened the floodgates on that score.

"Right now, for him, it would certainly be the ideal time to get all those debts settled in one easy swoop," the ACC continued. "Hit Reid where it hurts and take out a few of his major players into the bargain. Starting with his defence lawyer and a continually helpful High Court Judge."

"You think?" Furlong wailed in a surprised yelp.

"I absolutely do," he maintained. "Especially one that, Murray already reckoned 'Bunny' had an unhealthy, long term connection with. Both men claimed that they were members of similar clubs - and that was Murray's very point. For example, the ABC Casino. The very location, he had supposedly witnessed them both, on the evening of the 'Live' roulette game." Martin paused slightly. "Plus, it's Assistant Chief Constable to you Inspector," he whispered surreptitiously.

Continuing to play the soft and cuddly, subservient card, Furlong remained silent whilst the pinball machine whirled violently inside her head and broke all new world records. As she glowered angrily at the sanctimonious, self-serving git, her fiery eyes were igniting every single inch of him. From matchsticks at the soles of his feet, to a plastic lighter flame burning slowly up each of his nostrils and across his eyebrows. Hurriedly, she tried regaining her composure, but only somewhat. Because those thoughts were soon followed by a further silent tirade of... **YOU OVERSIZED, FUDGE FLICKING, VANILLA VAGRANT!** A further satisfactory smile surfaced upon her determined face, as she breathed a heavy sigh of relief and relaxed.

"What are you so happy about? This is an extremely serious matter, Chief Inspector. In fact, were you even aware that the man with the body parts removed and eyes gouged out, was also a part of Reid's little inner sanctum? He certainly played a minor role, but pivotal nonetheless."

"Sergeant Linn and DC Boyd are covering that," Furlong responded. "I take it, you ARE referring to the body found in the car park at the rear of the pub?"

A smug, to be expected comment rebounded.

"Unless you are aware of another incident in the city overnight with a dead man's body parts being removed, Detective Chief Inspector?"

Furlong's face became more anxious. I wish it had been yours, she thought to herself.

"You had no idea that there was a connection did you? You haven't been here long enough."

"Do you actually have a point to make, sir? Or was the point just to make this junior, female subordinate, feel truly inferior to you yet again?"

"Careful DCI Furlong. Stay within our professional boundaries, woman."

Woman! Wow! That's two strikes! - Furlong was about to rip up the 'play nice' card, stick her taloned fingers down his weaselly throat and then slowly bring up his grotesque innards. Purely for entertainment value and nothing else. Oh my, he really was an ignorant, overbearing, pompous prat, she concluded.

"It was The Doctor's pub," he informed her.

"I was well aware of that. Thank you, sir."

"It's owned by our cuddly 'Bunny.' James Baxter Reid."

The DCI's face fell further on hearing that news. This time there was no disguising her surprise. Why had none of her team thought to inform her of the relevance of this fact. She then quickly realised that the officers she'd assigned, both Boyd and Sergeant Linn were relative newcomers to the team also.

"The dead man was the landlord. Well in fact, he was 'Bunny' Reid's loyal man on the ground there. It's where a certain young, promising DC had her throat slit, nearly 16 months back. So it would seem that our Inspector Murray, has struck it lucky yet again."

Furlong appeared puzzled. Her eyes questioning.

"I mean really? What are the chances? Do you really believe in that kind of good fortune, Barbra? I reckon old Stevie boy got his man! What do you think Babs?"

"That would be Detective Chief Inspector to you," she said robustly and confidently.

"Professional boundaries and all. You understand."

Her next line exuded passion from every pore. But before uttering it, she had deliberately and graciously pulled back her room door. Which in turn, ensured a capacity audience from the open setting. Many curious heads were already firmly focused in that direction anyway. But now ears were also pricked up. An office silence ensued and a variety of colleagues were on the lookout for an outright victor.

"We run a clean ship here now, ACC Martin," Furlong confirmed. And then with increased volume, just in case some people missed out. "Thank you for the visit, sir. But we have already kept you back, far too long."

Firmly and with a genuinely insincere smile, she added, "Good-bye."

Now all of the prying eyes and ears were concentrated on the ACC.

Paul Martin's cheeks reddened as he lifted his official cap, placed it strategically under his arm and with a nod of his head was gone as quickly as he arrived. Although, all DCI Barbra Furlong saw departing was a pair of dark coloured trousers with a tail tucked firmly between them.

The glass door then swung shut. You can't help, but see a 'pink elephant,' even when you are told not to think about one. So as much as she tried, Barbra Furlong could not get her grieving Inspector, Steven Murray out of her busy, turbulent mind. So was he still grieving? She now questioned that option. Or was he set solely on revenge? Who could even say with certainty, exactly where he was at mentally? He was perfectly entitled to be angry, to be hurt and to be seeking justice. A son that had been imprisoned for five full years, had just been shot dead on his release. An emotionally charged and sensitive father had been finally looking to make amends with him. To rebuild any semblance of a fractured relationship that had once existed between them.

Had it been the bold James Baxter Reid that had been responsible? You would put nothing past him and everything would initially seem to suggest his involvement. He owned the Riddrie flat where the gunman had stayed. Where the lone sniper's rifle had been fired from and discovered. The weapon itself had been abandoned deliberately. Thus making it easier for the marksman to walk or run away and blend in with the panic and public mayhem that had soon gathered outside. He may even have been within the first few people that had crowded around the early morning scene that day. Possibly to check out and ensure that his macabre handiwork had been successful.

'Bunny' Reid though, ultimately owned hundreds of rental properties throughout Glasgow and Edinburgh. Nothing had been proved. They had no way to directly tie him to the shooter. The gunman, an expert marksman and possibly ex-forces, had never been captured. Yet DI Murray always felt that Reid was NOT the man. For plenty of other crimes, yes absolutely. Including the innocent slaughter of Detective Constable Tasmin Taylor. But not on this occasion. The evidence he was reliant upon… was his gut.

With the judge, the lawyer and one of Reid's trusted cronies all taken out. Was it the ideal time for retribution? Would Murray go that far? Cross those lines? The day was only just beginning. Crossing swords with ACC Martin had been an exhausting experience for the Chief Inspector. As her drained and wearied body collapsed effortlessly into her chair, she knew that she had some careful decisions to weigh up and make. Including several, puzzling 'pink elephant' questions. Delicate ones that wouldn't just go away, but would require fast, solid and dependable answers. Barbra Furlong reached for her landline, made a quick call and soon afterwards departed the station.

Nine

'And now they are trying to take my life away, forever young I cannot stay. On every corner I can see them there. They don't know my name, they don't know my kind. They're after you with their promises, they're after you to sign your life away. Sixty-eight guns will never die.'

- The Alarm

Earlier that morning there had been an equally chilly bedroom in the western outskirts of the city. All it's curtains remained closed and the crispy, crusted eyelids of its occupant were firmly clamped shut. Which made a disgruntled and dishevelled Steven Murray instantly cross-examine - Why do we close our eyes when we pray? When we cry? Or even when we kiss for that matter? Also he began to question - When we dream? He had no need to ponder any of those thoughts for too long. The overwhelming, burning and aching pangs from within his heaving chest responded immediately. His sweat stained duvet was pulled closer and tighter, as the answer came to him loud and clear and in the solitary isolation of his darkened bedroom. Each word felt and sounded like a hammer blow, causing immense physical pain. He realised and fully recognised at that precise moment, that it was because, often important events in our lives, key significant events, ones that really truly matter are most notably not visual. They are not seen, nor discernable. They are not necessarily witnessed or often observed. Special momentous occasions such as that are felt only by the heart.

Murray's own heart had been severely broken and beat infrequently over the past two months. Ever since the cruel, fateful day that his son David had been mercilessly gunned down outside Barlinnie Prison in Glasgow. From that moment, DI Murray had been placed on compassionate leave. After his two remaining children returned home, he had been posted missing.

No one had any idea that the full story of David's non involvement in his father's attack had come out. That revelation had remained a secret. There had been no contact with his team or with the top brass, including DCI Barbra Furlong. Not even with his long standing colleagues and friends, head pathologist Dr. Thomas Patterson and retired Sergeant, Robert Coulter. 'Ally' now operated freelance, as a Private Investigator and he especially knew to give his buddy's home a wide berth at present.

"When he is good and ready," Coulter was heard to state on more than one occasion to many of Murray's workmates and friends.

The DI was still a popular man. Well loved and respected by the majority of his fellow officers. The funeral itself was testament to that. But again, the Inspector often failed to recognise the fact. In fairness, those upstairs were another issue entirely. As well as locking up his previous Detective Chief Inspector, over the years, the passionate DI had kept the 'top brass' on their toes with his 'out on a limb' theories, his 'gut instinct' arrests and his 'clearly outspoken' opinions. He would always hold them to account, often publicly and that was not a popular move. So in turn, they would often investigate him more than most it appeared.

Only two months ago, the so-called troublemaker, had been cleared yet again at an internal enquiry. The two investigating officers were DCI David Cleland and DI James Mare. At the conclusion of their investigation that very same day, Inspector James 'Jimmy' Mare was found dead in his car with a bullet wound to the forehead. It would appear that 'The Complaints' had been making enquiries into the wrong man with underworld connections after all. Mare had failed to complete his errand and was in the final analysis - dismissed. Again the hand of 'Bunny' Reid seemed to be suspiciously involved there. Yet with that said: No proof and no evidence equalled - No accused and no case to answer.

However, the relationship between 'Bunny' Reid and Murray was surely now at an all time low. The police themselves had favoured Reid for sanctioning the assassination of David Murray on the steps of the prison. Although the boy's own father always had other ideas. Inspector Murray had no actual inkling of who had ordered the hit, but experience had told him, that although 'Bunny' was probably well aware of it. That it was a high priority on someone's 'to do' list. He had then also recalled several jibes, quotes and various utterances that the Reidmeister had made in the days running up to his son's release. Comments that he had openly stated to Murray, as the Inspector lay in bed recovering from a brutal assault. An attempted murder it had actually been recorded as. Unsurprisingly, so far, that assault had gone unsolved. Mainly because both DC Hanlon and his DI knew the truth behind the random, yet vicious attack. During one of his darker episodes mentally, Steven Murray had enlisted the help of an underworld middleman, to alleviate the problem. The problem being...... himself. The wheels had been set in motion. Luckily however, that evening, Joe Hanlon saw an assailant carrying a blade running toward his boss. He immediately cried out to his Inspector and when Murray turned around swiftly, death was averted by mere inches. Initially promised that it would only be a one-off attempt, successful or otherwise. Murray, could not help but question - Had the hitman a reputation to protect? If he'd realised his target was a police officer, would he willingly take another crack at him, free gratis? So at the end of the day, was that high velocity bullet meant for him? Had DI Steven Murray been the real target? He now had no way of confirming or denying those suspicions, but just lived with the continual guilt of... 'If Only.'

Raymond Armour, the Irish go-between that Murray had used to set up the deal, was gone in the wind. He was now a fugitive on the run. Wanted in connection with the death of a young girl on a train at Waverley Station. She in turn, had been a deranged serial killer. One that the whole of Police Scotland were now desperately searching for. What a sad, tortured and complex world we live in - and at that, his eyes eventually opened.

Ten

'Lawrence of Arabia, British Beatlemania. Ole Miss, John Glenn, Liston he beats Patterson. Pope Paul, Malcolm X, British politician sex. JFK blown away, what else do I have to say? We didn't start the fire...... it was always burning!'

- Billy Joel

Joe Hanlon ensured he took his laptop with him as they travelled the thirty to forty minute drive out to Lanark. He was not disobeying his DCI, but just making good and productive use of his valuable time. It enabled him to make some delicate enquiries enroute.

There had been widespread talk about the rise of Facebook-enabled, fake viral news stories. But that did not mean that social media companies were doing anything about it, Hanlon thought. In fact, Facebook founder and Chief Executive Mark Zuckerberg had famously scoffed at the suggestion that fakes could actually sway voters.

"Personally, I think the idea that fake news on Facebook could influence elections in any way - I think is a pretty crazy notion," he was quoted as saying throughout the run up to the US elections. However the frenetic political climate in America, meant fake news writers like Blear were more successful than ever before. At one point, he in turn hired other writers to churn out the fakes and the money kept flowing in.

'Sherlock' read of how Blear stated, "It was every day, all day," he said. "We were getting results with what we were doing."

But the good times didn't last forever. The political winds had begun to turn against him. Christian Blear, a committed Socialist was being lumped in with a whole host of people accused of peddling lies about the Tories and the Scottish National Party. This had been done in a bid to inflate support for Labour leader, Jeremy Corbyn.

In East Anglia a certain Martin Smith was increasingly being drawn into an enterprising game of cat and mouse. One in which any weakness you might have, would be fully exploited. Fake news writers were finding better, more creative and devious ways to capture an unwitting audience. But at the same time, Smith was developing his systems. Getting wiser and better at identifying the fake news writers and crucially, getting his debunks in front of a wider audience.

"I just want to be a Google search away, when people think they're looking at a false story," he said. Smith estimated that there were about 200 or so dedicated fact-checking organisations worldwide. "Not nearly enough," he stated. "As long as there is potential for profit, people will keep trying," he ventured. "People will find new filters and then they (the fake news writers) will find ways to get around the filters."

In August the year before, a huge hurricane tore through parts of the American state of Georgia. Killing dozens and causing billions of pounds of damage to Atlanta and many of the surrounding areas. At that time back in the UK, Blear sensed an opportunity once again to use his creative writing skills. He wrote a story about a fictional Imam in a made-up mosque in Georgia. The Imam, he wrote, refused to provide shelter and safety to non-Muslims during the storm. It would clearly whip up Blear's fan base, and yet it was all untrue.

There was however, a problem. The photo that he had used to accompany the story was of a real Imam. He himself was the leader of a mosque in Seattle, Washington. Aahil Askrat had never even visited Georgia, but he was suddenly the target of fake news.

"He found out and he got really upset," Blear said. "He was all over Twitter about how we were racists, xenophobes. The whole nine yards. I immediately removed it and sent him a million apologies."

However, it wasn't the only time that Blear's falsehoods had snared real people. Another of his websites carried a story about a Royal Marine who was a deserter. The only problem was, he had used the name and picture of a real person who had nothing to do with the story. Smith noticed it going viral and when he checked it out, he realised that a real person had been unfairly inserted into a fake story. He then for the first time messaged Blear and got him to remove the story. The two men then continued to message online at regular intervals. And that is where Christian Blear revealed his secret. His real reason for writing fake news. Blear liked it that Smith had called him out. That was something that made him stand out from the other fact checkers. Simply by the fact that he had willingly communicated with him.

"Other fact-checking websites," he said, "write debunking blog posts, but never actually talk to me before they do."

Smith stood up to Blear, pointed out the mistake and got the fake story removed from the internet. And so Blear invited Smith into a secret Facebook group with fans of his work. It was there that Smith learnt the truth about Christian Blear and got an insight into what drove one fake news writer.

"He basically explained his whole schtick," said Smith. "How they (fake news writers) work."

There were heavy hints in the disclaimers that Blear had slapped all over his websites and Facebook pages. The Last Line of Defence has one that read: *"We are here to provide you with information you can use to continue being as informed as possible. Please don't use our page in conjunction with Google or the news, it will only serve to confuse you further."*

So SATIRE - Not news; not opinion and not propaganda - is how Blear describes his work. His clever aim however, is to trick individuals into sharing false news in the hope of showing what he calls, *"their stupidity."*

"We've gone out of our way to market it as satire. To make sure that everybody knows that this isn't real," he said. Pointing out that some of his pages have more prominent disclaimers than the world-famous satire site The Onion. Once his stories go viral, Facebook comments burst forth and that is when Christian Blear, the fake news writer - Becomes Christian Blear, the crusading left-wing troll.

"The mission with trolling first and foremost, is that we pull them into the comments section underneath each fake article."

It's then that he starts on the offensive. The faker becomes the exposer, weeding out and reporting the most extreme users among his fans.

"I can show you hundreds of profiles that we've had taken down," he said. He then claimed that he'd exposed many British National Party members and other hardcore racists.

"We've had people fired from their jobs," he stated. "We've exposed them to their families. Say what you want about me being a monster. But I'm pretty proud."

As public awareness about fake viral stories grew, so did pressure on social media companies and their bosses to do something about it. Mark Zuckerberg had said…

"His personal challenge for the year ahead was to 'fix' the social site. To combat hate and abuse, but also address fake news."

Their co-founder had been called in front of Congress to answer questions about a host of issues. The fakers on his platform, being one of them. As a result, Facebook announced algorithm changes designed to boost content from 'friends, family and groups.' The company, realising it had an image problem, launched an ad campaign to reassure users that they would be protected from spam, clickbait, fake news and data misuse. Many Facebook pages were deleted, while other publishers found that their posts were not travelling as far or as fast as they once had.

For Blear, the money began to dry up. Largely because of those Facebook changes. He said, "I now make a fraction, of what I did, at the height of the fake news boom." But he insisted money was never the motivator and instead, he claimed to be a 'leader of the resistance' against the First Minister and her SNP cronies.

"I'm not some monster," he said. "The goal was never all about money. There hasn't actually been any money in the last six months. But go look at my page, I'm still active, I'm still doing it. I'm still writing. I still believe and I always will."

Martin Smith meanwhile, declared quite openly and surprisingly that he had a quiet admiration for Blear.

"He's very good at what he does," he said. "His stories have always been quite easy to debunk because they mostly say, right at the end, that it's all fake - and also, it says the same in the header of his sites."

But Smith will still write about them constantly, if they go viral. The fact that something is presented as satire, doesn't stop him from debunking it.

"I see my job as a fact checker. My job is not to give an opinion about it," he stated.

"Whether you agree with it or not, what I do is an art form," Christian Blear boasted in recent weeks. "The stuff that I write a lot of the time - I read it and I laugh at it myself. It's ridiculous."

Smith pointed out that Blear's posts often lead him to other fake news writers, the ones who don't use disclaimers and who are much more straightforwardly spreading lies. Those Balkan teenagers aren't the only ones copying and pasting from Blear. Other fake news writers around the world do the same.

"Because of this," Smith says, "He's a great way of finding actual fake news sites."

DC Hanlon felt sick. The dossier Radical Lizzie had supplied him was intensive and thorough. In his mind though, Christian Blear had clearly continued to overstep the mark and only took down offensive or blatant lies when pulled up or caught out. Which was now too late for the families and bereaved of those cases, 'Sherlock' was currently working on. Nevertheless, the third and final case file that he had been given, would turn out to be the most tragic of them all.

Eleven

'Deep in the castle and back from the wars. Back with my lady and the fire burned tall. Hoorah, went the men down below and all outside was the rain and the snow. Yea - Over the hills with the swords of a thousand men.'

- Tenpole Tudor

Craignethan Castle was a ruined fortress in South Lanarkshire. It was located in an idyllic setting, high above the River Nethan. The historic building lay two miles west of the village of Crossford (pronounced locally as 'Crisfird') and 4.5 miles north-west of Lanark itself. Built in the first half of the 16th century, Craignethan was recognised as an excellent early example of a sophisticated artillery fortification. Albeit, back then its defences were never really fully tested. Unfortunately, the night before, the defence of the Right Honourable Judge Gordon Menzies' nearby dwelling had been! Sadly, they had failed that particular assessment, in rather spectacular fashion.

As Acting DI 'Sandy' Kerr and Joseph 'Sherlock' Hanlon parked close to the electronic gates, at what had once been the Judge's iconic home. They were instantly struck at the sheer devastation on show.

"It makes you think, doesn't it?" Hanlon declared from out of nowhere.

"About what?" Kerr asked.

Joe Hanlon pointed at the buzzer and camera system attached to the wall at the left of the entrance.

"What about it?" She persisted.

"So," he began with an impish, mischievous grin on his face.

"Go on." Sandra Kerr, encouraged. Although knowing full well, she'd regret it.

"So, Amazon's almighty Alexa can monitor everything I say at home. The all powerful CIA can hack into my TV and listen to every opinion I have…"

Joe, paused for effect. Deliberately milking the moment.

"Yet for some unfathomable reason, McDonald's can't hear me say, 'No Pickles.' Over their drive-thru speaker!"

Hanlon creased into fits of laughter, whilst ADI Kerr pulled rank, with a dismissive shake of her head and…

"Me thinks that you've spent far too much time with a certain Steven Murray, M'lord."

She delivered a brief wink. Before re-commencing with…

"Let's get serious, Constable."

Neither had experienced anything like it before. A glossy, movie production or a TV soap portraying a small airplane crashing into their local village or hillside, would have been the closest they'd previously encountered destruction on a scale of this magnitude. But this was way different. This was for real. Up close and personal. There was a deep grounded honesty on display. A dark, brutal overtone that seemed to manifest itself as - vulnerability. This was no production set, with special effects, props or extras on stand-by. Everybody present today was a professional in some capacity or other. Dependable individuals going about their business - trying to serve, protect and repair. Or in the case of officers Kerr and Hanlon, trying desperately to understand what had actually happened and who or what was ultimately responsible.

The male deceased, had many years ago been a first rate student. Law was his thing and he was always determined to succeed and get to the top of that field. During the course of 1986 and after nearly 19 years as a practising lawyer, advocate and sheriff. Gordon B. Menzies did just that and became a High Court judge at age 44. In Scotland's High Court of Justiciary, judges hear the most serious crimes such as murder and hear appeals from all of the other criminal courts. As the holder of a judicial office, the Honourable Judge Gordon B. Menzies would, in theory, make sure that each accused would get a fair trial. Knowing full well that his decisions would impact people's lives. It was his job to ensure that justice was done.

The modern frontage and east facing, side wall of his 1990's bespoke villa, was totally gone. It now lay fully open to the elements and was desperately being secured and covered over. To make it as wind and watertight, as best they could. Debris had been fired at random across the normally finely trimmed lawn. Plants and flower beds had been rained down on by a combination of domestic kitchen appliances. Remnants of the fridge, freezer and washing machine had created a brand new avant garde water feature, sponsored by Hotpoint. The powerful blast had fully dispatched everything from that specific side of the house. It's overwhelming force would have taken out anything in its path. An assortment of broken furniture, charred books and burnt bedding had taken refuge thirty yards from what had previously been the welcoming front door. Hopefully there had only been one casualty, but that was still to be fully ascertained.

Gordon Bryce Menzies was born in Hamilton, Lanarkshire. He worked three part-time jobs to survive University. His father Frank was a street corner newspaper vendor. That was back in the day when print was still king. There were even two editions on many of the more popular titles. Twelve hours a day, his dad would stand on his pitch in the High Street. Rain, hail or shine the locals knew that one, overweight, Frankie Menzies could be depended upon. He would be squeezed in tightly, under his worn out red and white striped rainproof awning. It gave him shade and shelter in equal measure. Although in South Lanarkshire, Scotland, shade was very seldom required.

Morag Moffat, who had always been a fairly industrious girl in her youth, left school on her sixteenth birthday. She had been a diligent Saturday worker for the previous two years. So it was no problem getting a full-time role as a humble shop assistant in her local Co-operative grocery store. It was at that point that she first met Francis Menzies. Frankie, as she called him, was seven years older than herself. But that was no deterrent for that young lady and by age seventeen, she was engaged. Two months after her eighteenth they were married and before her next birthday celebration came around, she had given birth to one Gordon Bryce Menzies. The infant was named after each of his grandfathers, Gordon Menzies and Bryce Moffat. No further children ever presented themselves and they seemed to be content, as a reasonably happy, working class family.

Frank Menzies' sweet tooth as a child, followed him into adulthood. Over the next two decades as a married man, he continued to pile on the pounds. He'd developed a real predilection for confectionery, crisps and cake. Not ideal when you stand on a street corner all day. Through his son's teenage years, Frank on numerous occasions would joke with him that...

"When I inevitably choke to death on gummi bears. I hope that people will just say that I was 'killed by bears!' He would then end it, with a rather half-hearted and embarrassed laugh. Indicating to his son, that he felt he was not necessarily joking.

As fate decreed, when Gordon Menzies was only in his second year at University, his father suddenly dropped dead from a massive heart attack. He was one week away from his 45th birthday and still standing on 'his patch,' selling newspapers. He weighed 32 stone! Two years later and before she could witness her only child graduate from University, Morag Menzies also passed away. She died peacefully in her sleep. At only 41 years of age and unusual as it may seem, it was suspected that she ultimately died of a broken heart. As fate would have it, and as Gordon Menzies life was to unravel in later years, maybe it was just as well that neither of his parents were alive to witness his excesses in life.

The blues skies were out early over Lanarkshire, but so too was a biting, chilling wind. Scenes of crime had four major tents erected by the time the two officers had arrived. Dozens of uniformed colleagues kitted out in traditional white SOCO suits scoured the gardens, paths and driveway for relevant clues and evidence. A mass of vehicles involved in the investigation thronged the narrow road approaching, what had previously been Gordon Menzies home. From journalists to medical support. Fire Brigade to public utilities. Even dog handlers and specialist illumination riggers. The latter had begun setting up temporary lighting at midnight, so as to allow investigation work to begin as soon as possible that morning.

Police, civil servants and Scottish Parliamentary figures one suspected, had certainly ensured that all the stops were pulled out for this case and it was somewhat noticeable. Whoever was in overall charge of the Police Scotland budget had, at the very least, been gently encouraged to loosen the purse strings. Anyone currently watching this spectacular scene from neighbouring properties or adjoining homesteads, especially those from within the farming community itself, would instantly think - disease, infection or widespread contamination. However, to those in the know, it would appear that in the last twenty-four hours, the only 'major outbreak' in these parts, was that of a seriously unbalanced bomber.

Overhead, a prying helicopter flew perilously close at times. No doubt chartered by a group of anxious reporters trying desperately to clarify matters for themselves. They could all feel a scoop or a front page exclusive coming on - shared or otherwise.

The 'T'inker,' Doctor Thomas Patterson met up with Acting Detective Inspector Kerr and young 'Sherlock' at the gates to the property. Where some further temporary protective measures had been taken to secure the area.

"Good day to you both," the Doc offered in his genial Irish brogue. "We've got a couple of interesting finds for you, for sure."

"Which would be?" Hanlon piped up firstly. Much to the chagrin of his senior colleague.

"Which would be, young DC Hanlon - Fingerprints and footprints."

"Footprints?" Kerr offered with surprise.

"Yes, sure it would appear 'Sandy' t'at someone rang at the gates intercom and foolishly placed t'eir left foot on the soft soil at t'e edge of t'e path."

"Seems a rather inexperienced, juvenile mistake to make." Hanlon said.

"Unless, they had nothing to hide. No expectation of having their presence here ever monitored or checked up on," Kerr added. "Simply an innocent visitor. Possibly someone from earlier in the day."

"Out here? In the middle of nowhere? On foot?" Hanlon scoffed dismissively, whilst continually shaking his head. He certainly wasn't buying into that theory.

Elsewhere at that moment, DS Linn had already been at the crime scene for over twenty minutes. Before the much delayed, Detective Constable Allan Boyd finally joined him on site. It was nearly 11.00am. Boyd had taken some 'scenic' detours, through the neighbouring districts of Springburn and Kirkintilloch with their heavy granite clouds and extensive mist. Eventually, he had managed to manoeuvre himself onto the M80 and in due course the M9, taking him all the way into the crisp, radiant blue, cloudless skies of sunny Edinburgh.

The cobbled parking area at the murder scene was still covered in a heavy frost. Any hint of a thaw was never going to filter through onto that stretch of ground until much later in the afternoon. Currently the neighbouring tenement buildings stood guard on sentry duty, as the bright springtime rays of sunshine slowly made their way to the rear of the property. It was there that Detective Sergeant Linn pulled back the sheet from the body, to reveal the extent of his injuries to the approaching Boyd.

"He bled out," Linn said. "A fatal knife wound to the heart."

Boyd though, pointed at the disfigured, bloodied face.

"Obviously, the killer blow was delivered after his nose and ears had been lopped off and his two bloodshot eyes syringed from their sockets." Linn added.

With his stomach churning and his shivering hand at his mouth. Boyd recognised that he had seen much worse during his military days, but it didn't make it any easier or less horrifying.

He began to mumble. "Symbolic. This was symbolic. You get that right?"

"I may be new to the team, Allan. But I do have plenty of experience on the job. Give me some credit at least."

"Sorry, Sarge I didn't mean to…"

"It's okay, I get it. And I get this scene also - Symbolic, like you said. He is…"

"Jojo," Boyd interrupted. "Johnny Johnson, one of Reid's men."

"Like you said, Constable - symbolic! Because, what I was going to say was - I guess the message sent was, that he is or strictly speaking was, Reid's eyes and ears on the street in this part of Edinburgh."

"And that he always had his nose to the ground," Boyd added with a hint of schoolboy humour. "For he certainly turned a blind eye to the events going on in his pub, on the night of Tasmin Taylor's death."

"What do you mean?" Linn asked.

"Well, let's put it this way. One retired Police Sergeant, named Coulter. Will be delighted to witness this skinny runt on a slab in the morgue."

"Ally? Our Ally?"

"The very same," Boyd confirmed. "I spoke with him a few months ago and he recounted the whole thing. Jojo here, was on duty the fateful night that Detective Constable Tasmin Taylor got her throat cut by Reid."

"So how come he's still out and about running his illegal empire?"

"Because he had one of his terminally ill minions, take the fall for it, by all accounts. But Ally could still remember to this day the self-satisfactory smirk, that

Jojo here gestured to him as he arrived at the premises that evening. With hindsight, the Sarge recognised fully that Johnson knew full well that something unsavoury was about to go down that day. Or at the very least that something had been planned as a nasty surprise for both detective's - himself and his DC. Did you know that they were both hung upside down? Whilst Taylor's throat was slashed, Coulter spun helplessly, around and around."

Sergeant Linn's mouth hung wide open, but no words came forth.

"Ally may well have survived physically," Allan Boyd continued. "But mentally, he was a goner."

Several months, after initially being talked out of quitting by his long term friend DI Murray. Coulter eventually took his pension package. Now as a registered Private Detective, he was exceptionally happy in his retirement. He enjoyed the flexibility to pick and choose his cases and take things at a slightly steadier pace. Nodding along to Boyd's recollection of previous events, Linn decided to speak. Suddenly he expressed aloud…

"But why, the need to use syringes?"

As both men looked up. The large hostelry sign loomed over them. There, in what had once no doubt, been bright, blood red paint, lay the answer. The bold scarlet lettering was now faded and weather beaten and had certainly seen better days. But the regular punters were all fully aware of where, 'The Doctors' was.

The two officers collectively nodded and once again, this time in unison said… "Symbolic!"

"I would agree wholeheartedly, gents. Symbolic."

The softly spoken accent belonged to Doc Patterson's trusted assistant pathologist, Danielle Poll. Known to her friends and colleagues as Danni. Dr Poll loved the outdoors, animals and travel. Every weekend when she was not on call, she could be found seeking a fresh adrenalin rush. One that probably involved climbing mountains, visiting new places or helping out at animal rescue shelters. Either of those exhilarating activities, would have the North American, smile in anticipation.

A white SOCO tent had been securely erected around the body of the man whose optic nerves and eyeballs had been so crudely severed and removed. Noticeable tyre marks, which appeared fresh, seemed on initial inspection to belong to a motorcycle. There was no CCTV surveillance footage at the rear of the pub, because who in their right mind would knowingly mess with premises owned by 'Bunny' Reid? Someone did. Someone stupid? Someone with something to prove? Someone oblivious to the consequences or that couldn't care less. Someone with nothing to lose? Or has already felt that they have lost everything? Maybe then, someone with a specific grudge to settle? And given the severe intensity of the assault on Jo-Jo, it certainly appeared exceptionally personal. So who was this elusive someone?

Danni Poll and her team went about their business in a professional and diligent manner. Meanwhile Sgt. Linn and DC Boyd sought the warmth and cover from the elements in their squad car. As they travelled back the short distance to Leith.

Twelve

'Give us this day all that you showed me. The power and the glory, 'til my kingdom comes. Give me all the storybook told me. The faith and the glory, 'til my kingdom comes.'

- Ultravox

"What is it?"

'Sandy' asked Hanlon. As the DC carefully placed his mobile phone back into his pocket.

"And people call me, 'Sherlock,'" he exclaimed. "It's just that DCI Furlong had asked me to call her with an update when we got here."

"And?" Was the first word Kerr actually said.

When she desperately wanted to know why her DCI, never asked her to report in?

"You know that she has a thing for origin trivia, right?"

"Origin, what?" 'Sandy' looked confused.

"You know. Like the back story of how things came to be. Where 'they' or 'it' originated from. For example, I just made the mistake of telling her that half this property had been blown to kingdom come."

Kerr smiled. She now knew where this was going.

"You can grin all you like, but it's totally fascinating and possibly, slightly addictive. Did you know it's origin, it's birthplace was in fact biblical?"

Sandra Kerr shrugged in meek surprise.

"Thought not," Hanlon said. "Neither did I. I just thought like most people, that it was an exaggerated way to express your feeling that it would last until the end of time, or into the next world."

"Biblical?" Kerr prompted.

"Ah, yes. It's because it is thought to come from the Lord's Prayer. From the line... *Thy kingdom come.*"

"You and her are two peas in a pod," his red haired colleague uttered, with a bewildered, amused look.

"Now let's get busy Joe, or we'll both be here until kingdom come!"

At that, one of the engineering experts on site, gave them the okay to walk about the rear of the property. It had been found to be structurally sound inside and the forensics team were keen to get started.

ADI Kerr ventured into the remains of the modern bespoke bathroom. It's normally crisp, arctic white ceramic floor tiling, was covered in a fresh layer of blackened fallout from the explosion. Both herself and 'Sherlock' were fully kitted out in the standard disposable crime suits. The look included hood, mask, gloves and although not colour coordinated, blue crime scene overshoes. The plastic all-in-one outfit was not figure hugging or fashionable. It actually gave Hanlon an enlarged bulk to his body and at least now, he looked more like the astronaut Neil Armstrong. As opposed to the long term children's favourite...... Stretch Armstrong!

The mirrored bathroom cabinet held no surprises. Standard mouthwash, toothpaste and cotton buds. Toothpicks, aftershave and one or two familiar creams, including a Vicks VapoRub. It soon became apparent that the retired Judge was actually in reasonably good health. Sandra Kerr had been in plenty of younger victims homes and experienced a vastly different scene. Numerous premises had been turned into fully fledged pharmacies. She recalled visiting the home of an overweight, thirty-five year old male, in Edinburgh's Stenhouse district one time. He had a private collection of anti-depressant tablets, pills to control his heart rate, blood pressure and cholesterol. She found capsules for angina, several empty oxygen tanks and an unused mobility scooter. At the time, as a relatively young and inexperienced Constable, Kerr felt inclined to put his name forward to the Guinness Book of Records for the owner of the most pharmaceutical products in an enclosed space! Surely at least, he was in with a shout for the man with the most outstanding illnesses and conditions ever!!!!

Over the intervening years, 'Sandy' had come to realise that with a certain section of society, that is their sad, private and very insular world. On a daily basis, their small-minded lives constantly and continually leapt from one mini crisis to another. That, coupled with a myriad of medication to battle against their ongoing ailments and to give them the much needed strength to garnish Facebook sympathy, from their wide array of followers. All fifteen of them! Kerr exited the bathroom and eventually came down off her moral 'High Horse.'

Joseph Hanlon meanwhile, was carefully 'walking on the moon' in a luxurious bedroom nearby. He soon realised that he was gradually turning into Murray, just like Sandra Kerr said. The clue was when he heard himself gently sing…

'Giant steps are what you take, walking on the moon. I hope my legs don't break, walking on the moon.'

After soot, dust and charred cinders, the first word that came to mind upon entering this room was - Dated! It was without doubt, furnished and decorated to a very high standard. However, those touches included deep pile carpet, quality cotton bedding and hand-made, fitted oak bedroom units. Much more in keeping with a 'Conservative' Lanarkshire Laird, than a 'Playboy' sugar daddy.

There was no fancy big screen, high definition TV. But the king size bed did have a remote control to activate a 12" television monitor. It appeared, as if by magic, from the foot of the leather upholstered bedstead. Yes definitely dated, the Detective Constable thought. As he slowly drew back the sliding doors, on the inbuilt wardrobe unit. Joe Hanlon was now undecided whether it was a surreal episode of Baywatch or Hugh Hefner's 1970's 'Bunny' infested mansion that he had entered into?

The man hung up his ironed underwear. It ranged from standard boxer shorts and cotton jockeys, to silky thigh length garments. He even had several pairs of black, open meshed briefs. Hanlon's mind was working overtime to keep up. As each pair hung separately on individual hangers, 'Sherlock' managed to conjure up a faint, distant sound. A sound that seemed to make the whole creepy scene more palatable, at least for him.

Growing in confidence, he once again exercised those finely tuned vocal chords…

'Feet they hardly touch the ground - Walking on the moon.'

Shelves in the room were nondescript. Two colourful, decorative figurines adorned them. Along with several framed photographs and occasional holiday snapshots from around a sunny pool. A pair of miniature plates on stands, represented that last sector perfectly. One with heavy green influences, shouted out, 'Dublin.' Whilst the other small piece of pottery, was rather more traditional. It consisted of a wide range of stylish brown inks depicting Buda Castle, Parliament Buildings and the River Danube. The word 'Budapest' was prominent around its rim. Again from his time with Murray, Joseph Hanlon knew that when impressed, one had to act. That 'gut feeling' was not to be ignored, Murray would constantly tell him. So as the *'astronaut'* came to the end of his moon exploration, he quietly encouraged one of the crime scene officers to ensure that they had plenty of images of everything in that bedroom. Just a feeling, he thought to himself. A niggling impression.

"Thank you," he said.

Thirteen

'We lost faith in the omens, we lost faith in the gods. We just ended up clutching at the empty rituals, like gamblers clutching long odds. But I don't want to spend all my life indoors, laying low and waiting for the next storm. I don't want to spend all my life inside, I wanna step out and face the sunshine.'

- Frank Turner

Beep... it was a follow up message to a strange cryptic text sent to him yesterday. That particular communication was the first one in a long while which seemed to, if not bring him to his senses, at least make him sit up and take notice. This one however, startled him back into reality.

His youngest son was gone. Buried over two months ago. Yet here he was, the solid, dependable, seemingly unflappable policeman - Detective Inspector Murray. 'Stoic,' they would describe him as. However, Steven Murray recognised that those individuals either never knew him, or what that particular word meant. Because those that could tell you that its definition was along the lines of: long suffering, patient, tolerant, uncomplaining and accepting - also knew full well that the West of Scotland man with the healthy Irish lineage, embraced none, absolutely none of those charming character traits.

So how did he find himself here? Had he finally been held to account? Was this the resulting consequence of his actions in recent years? Did his God hold him responsible? Did he even believe in a God any longer? It was the Easter season after all. Was this the intended time for Murray to rise again? To possibly be born again, change his ways and make amends? This certainly seemed to be a culmination of the man's very own variation on Lent. For the previous forty days and more, he had endured a prolonged period of deliberate fasting, prayer and penance!

Often over the past few weeks, on more than one occasion, he had deliberated with himself. Questioned many of his actions and his motives in recent times. Had he crossed the line once too often perhaps? Had he mixed with the criminal fraternity for so long, that his own version of right and wrong had become badly muddled and confused? Had wickedness, sinfulness and criminality merged into one and become acceptable to him? Were they no longer a violation of the law of the land or a problem in Steven Murray's judgemental eyes either? Over two prolonged months, he had even come to question if any actual line existed any more? Was it his own moral compass that was corrupt? Or was there a very specific time and place to apportion blame? To identify when things changed?

To that last question, the Inspector had decided overwhelmingly that there was. It was definitely all down to himself and his gambling. It probably seemed too easy and so straightforward to pinpoint. But there you have it, he thought - 'No More Bets' and his wife would still have been alive - None of his children would have felt the need to attack him and David would not have ended up in prison.

No gambling and they would still have been a family. Or was that just too simplistic? Who could know for sure? And who really cared? Not it would appear Steven Murray at this point and that was the real problem. He currently felt detached fully of emotion. In his mind he had nothing left to live for. Except, the uncomplicated fact that he had always helped and assisted others. It had been a natural part of his upbringing. In more recent years it even seemed to be a part of his basic DNA. He'd deliberately set out and try to seek opportunities to help, assist and better support people's lives. Now sitting up in bed, he once again re-read the recent texts he'd received, that had deeply alarmed him.

Firstly, yesterday's read: *Your friend needs your help. Tomorrow is D-Day!* At the time the DI had mistakenly thought, like lots of others in the past few weeks, that it was just a rouse. Some gentle encouragement to get him back to work and out of his so-called 'depression.' Although it had been sent from an unrecognised number and no sender details were attached. That fact intrigued him greatly.

Today's follow-up however, had him definitely more concerned. It jolted him upright in bed for the first time in nearly two months. He clawed at his eyes, scratched at the grubby foliage hibernating on his cheeks, chin and neck and then tried his darndest to focus on the worrying text and getting his pulsing heart rate back down. This latest message read: *Steven - Your team seems either hellbent on setting me up or trying to take me down. Either way it is my turn to pay a visit to one of your own. But which one? Get up and back in the saddle MY FRIEND. You have ten minutes before the off!* The last word was what triggered his nervous and deeply worried reaction. It was signed: *Best Wishes... BUNNY!*

Dirleton was a small parish in East Lothian. It lay nestled comfortably between the coastal dwellers of North Berwick to the east and those graceful golfers of Gullane to its west. It was most notable for Dirleton Castle. Which according to its current owners, Historic Scotland - *'Was a well preserved medieval fortress.'*

  Tonight a certain village resident had maybe wished that she had made her own delightful home, more of a fortress - 'a place of exceptional security and a mini stronghold.' With its laid back style, charming craftsmanship and comfortable neutral interiors, DCI Barbra Furlong's cosy cottage was a property to dream about. One to salivate over in a monthly, glossy, homestyle magazine. Given its picturesque setting and the bushy brown welcome mat on the outside, one could quite happily assume her door was always open... and one would be right.

  For all her years as a police officer dealing with petty crime, break-ins and burglaries, you would have thought - But no! She was not one for wondering if she had her house keys with her, transferring them from one jacket to another, checking which bag she had left them in, etc, etc. Her century old door would remain unlocked at all times. Except, ironically, when she herself was inside! Many of her friends and neighbours knew that she would walk three miles in both the morning and evening. It was a little guilty pleasure that the woman of the house liked to share with people. However, only her closest work colleagues had been privy to the insider dealer trading, and that was, that 'three miles' was actually in fact, the name of her dog! Often the Chief Inspector only ventured to the local green, let her pet do its business and duly returned home again. So three miles in ten minutes? Now that was impressive.

"Home, home is wherever I'm with you…"

The shower was on and his music playlist read: 'Favourites.' Steven Murray was cavorting around under the powerful jet of steaming hot water. That was of course, after a thorough and well deserved close cut shave had already taken place. He was determined to be ready with at least two minutes to spare before that next text came through.

'MY FRIEND?' he thought. Typical 'Bunny' Reid and his mind games. The very man that most people were convinced was behind his son's tragic killing, sending him a personal text. And a mildly threatening one at that. Regarding Reid, being responsible for David's murder. Murray himself, didn't think so. He was more inclined to believe, just like today, strangely, that James Baxter Reid had in actual fact tried to pre-warn him that a contract had been put out on someone close to him.

As his phone vibrated, all of those thoughts would need to go on the back burner for now. He was kitted out in a new suit that had lain untouched for a couple of years and for good reason. Because even with the unhealthy food that had been delivered, Murray had lost sixteen to seventeen pounds during his self-imposed sabbatical, and the outfit had now become a welcome option. His face was thinner, his features tight and sharp. A few unwanted chins had been sent packing. Whoever this was that had risen, they were certainly intent on embracing life again. As he opened the waiting text and closed the bedroom door, a disappointed 'black dog' was to be heard left whimpering inside! And there it would stay for the foreseeable future. Or at least the next 24 hours, Murray had hoped. The purposeful Inspector took up a seat in his kitchen and began to read.

The veiled threat stated: *There is no need to take you all out! Who is your current favourite? Or is there one that is Not Reliable? I am in this for the long haul Steven. I don't like having obstacles placed in my way. I'm a level headed kind of man, but I'm in a hurry to resolve our issues. You enjoy your gambling - Who is the lucky recipient to be? Will you get there before me? It's gonna be tight!*

On returning home and casually opening her front door, Barbra Furlong could instantly tell something was amiss. There was a noticeable unpleasant whiff, an unusual odour, a faintly offensive lingering smell. People know their properties. Just like they do their cars, their workplace and their partners. They have a scent, a familiar fragrance or distinct aroma to them.

They offer an essence of home and belonging. They reassure and comfort you. They confirm to you that you're in the right place. A 'this is what I'm used to' feeling. Unsurprisingly, this was not the emotion DCI Furlong currently felt. The tangy musk that trailed in the air, was out of step with the overall freshness of her home. She had quickly identified the culprit, but that wasn't the problem. The real issue was how did it find itself wafting its way throughout her house in the first place? It was a no-smoking zone!

As she cautiously entered her quaint, intimate sitting room, small circular rings of smoke were being expertly blown toward the low oak-beamed ceiling. Casually and slowly they rose - puff... puff... puff. At that precise moment the police officer's normally glowing expression was lost in the overt paleness of her skin. All of her colour evaporated and made a hasty retreat on recognising the unwelcome guest. Leaving the female detective to once again spar, verbally at least, against a familiar adversary.

Tonight, awaiting her arrival, the male visitor in her front room was in fact the individual that only two months ago, broke the news to her new workmates about the name of her dog. DI Murray had been recovering from stab wounds in the Royal Infirmary when the man at his hospital doorway spoke. In his highly recognisable, familiar, thick, hoarse tone, the voice simply stated - "You do know that *'three miles'* is the name of her dog, right?"

James Baxter Reid, aka 'Bunny' Reid, was aptly ensconced in Furlong's brown leather upholstered, so-called - 'smoking' chair. Although the property owner herself, normally only used it to snuggle up on, in the evening with a good read.

"Make yourself at home, Mr Reid. Why don't you!" Said a rather shocked, but resolute DCI.

"I already have Chief Inspector. Haven't you noticed?"

By way of a reminder, another gentle circle of smoke was sent on its way upward. As his heavy voice sounded, its pace as always was slow and laborious. As if dragging a hundredweight of metal chain behind every word. Whereas the Chief Inspector's nervous energy produced a rapid vocabulary.

"How did you get in here and what is it you want Mr Reid?"

Furlong had realised things were different as soon as she opened her door. But she had concentrated on the smell and forgot all about the sound or lack of.

"Where is three miles?" There was no barking. "What have you done? You know I'll kill…"

"Now, now, don't be rash to make promises, Chief Inspector. Especially ones that you cannot keep. Now may I call you Barbra?"

"No you may not," she yelled. In a clearly aggressive and angry tone.

"I like the name Barbra though. So I think I will." He began to gradually raise and lower his hands in tandem. "Calm down, calm down and relax woman," Reid said in an old fashioned, chauvinistic manner. Much like ACC Paul Martin.

"I only want to talk, a little cordial chat. If I'd meant you any harm, 'Barbra,' it would have been over and done with by now. I'm not known for wasting time."

Furlong was well aware of DC Tasmin Taylor's fate at the hands of this seemingly charming, yet brutal man.

"And as for that yapping dog of yours. It's quite safe in your kitchen. Although I have to say, it is one excessively noisy beast when you knock on your front door. You trained it well."

Furlong's mouth twisted and her lips gnarled, as she deposited a toxic glare in Reid's general direction.

"However, you really should lock that front door," he beamed. "Especially in a much neglected, run-down area such as this."

The edge of his smile nearly touched the ceiling.

"Talk? Talk about what? What do we have to talk about?"

She duly stepped up onto her imaginary soapbox.

"You and Mr Scott are currently trying to desperately wipe each other out. Measuring parts of your anatomy, to claim the full bragging rights. It would appear that at least one of each of your respective employees are being either taken out or maimed every twenty-four hours. I presently have a caseload of serious murders on my hands and thousands of normal, everyday tourists and punters are being scared off the streets of Edinburgh. So really… really… what do you and I have to talk about?"

Rant over. The stare offered by Reid was intense. The voice as always, guttural, gritty and grim.

"Take a seat, Barbra."

'Bunny,' ever the gentleman, stood up to offer his chair. "I would rather…"

"It wasn't actually an invitation, Chief Inspector."

This time, as he gestured a firm hand toward the sturdy, elegant piece of furniture. She sat and braced herself upright.

"Let's talk about me," he began…

Back in the recently rejuvenated, yet extremely tormented mind of Steven Murray, a list of names had been busily formatted. Part of Reid's text had mentioned:

Is there one that is Not Reliable? - Who is it to be? Who is your current favourite?

This was not the Inspector's strong point. At that moment, he'd wished 'Sherlock' had been at his side. He studied the text again. Repeated it aloud. Hyphens, capital letters, the actual wording.

He's in it for the long haul, hurdles, gambling, level headed.

It suddenly clicked. He'd figured it out! But surely not. It seemed far too easy he thought. He then studied remarks in his earlier text like…

'back in the saddle,' 'ten minutes before the off.'

Was this some sort of trap? He tapped a few more buttons on his phone.

"Inspector Kerr," a confident voice answered, without having looked at her screen.

"That suits you, 'Sandy.' Murray offered up in a kind, polite manner."

She was flabbergasted.

"Sir, sir," she said excitedly. Having not heard from him in weeks. "It's great to hear from you. Just to hear your…"

"Let me stop you there, Inspector. This is not…"

"Don't call me that. You're the Inspector, I, or rather we, we are just waiting on your return."

"So keep quiet then, Sandra." Murray offered hastily. "And put DCI Furlong on the phone immediately. I couldn't reach her on her own mobile and her direct office line just rang out. Please, please tell me she is still in the station and hopefully with you?"

He had asked that with such genuine concern that it was beginning to worry ADI Sandra Kerr. There was only silence.

"Sandy?"

"I am actually out and about, sir at the minute. But the DCI called me about three quarters of an hour ago, to tell me that she could be reached at home in the next twenty minutes. She should have been there by now, sir. What is wrong? Why are you suddenly contacting us to track down the DCI?"

Trying to be more practical, Sandra Kerr then added.

"I suspect her mobile was in her bag, sir. Plus you know that the reception can be quite patchy and temperamental in and around that area that she lives."

"It's nothing to do with dodgy cell phone reception. It's all to do with a dodgy 'Bunny' Reid."

"What? No! Not again. I don't understand."

"You don't have to. Just listen. I believe he is on his way to the Chief Inspector's home right now. Possibly he's already there. Let's hope not. Send a couple of local teams, 'Sandy.' Get those sirens heard and the sooner the better. I am not losing another officer on my watch. I'll meet you there."

"You will?" She questioned. Half in utter surprise, half sheer delight.

"I will," he confirmed. "Now get moving!"

Fourteen

'Sometimes we get it wrong, stick the kettle on. And if you're low, you're not alone, I hope you know. Sometimes we get it wrong and we come undone. Sometimes we get it wrong... stick the kettle on.'

- Lucy Spraggan

The conversation in the Dirleton cottage continued...

"This supposed, 'an eye for an eye' business, between me and Scott." Reid paused. "Well it's not happening."

"What do you mean, not happening?" Barbra Furlong scowled. "You took his young niece captive and blew up his mother's house. Killing the poor woman in the process. He's now out for revenge and it's basically, 'anything you can do, I can do better.' It's tit for tat carnage on a daily basis. Oh, and don't forget the murder of his brother. Thug or not."

"Chief Inspector," the rugged voice stated. "Enough of the female hysteria and drama. Plus we all know that taking his brother off the streets, makes this country a safer place to live," Reid quipped.

Furlong was livid. Her face contorted with fury. "There is no place safe with you around Mr Reid. Or have I just massively misjudged you?" she asked.

Her reddening face continued to distort and show disgust, distaste and dismay in equal measure. His sluggish delivery continued…

"The problem is Barbra - You're not listening and I don't take kindly to people when they choose not to listen to me, or take me seriously. Why do you think I have taken the risk of visiting a high profile Police Scotland officer in the privacy of her own home?"

"Uninvited!" I hasten to add.

Reid said nothing. A raised hand and a mild smirk were as much as he could muster. He needed this Detective to calm down and start to focus. He then sat on the matching two seater settee opposite. He remained silent. His relatively new image of suited and booted, certainly appeared to give him more gravitas in these situations. With her breathing slowing and her level of anger decreasing, the homeowner delivered a deep sigh. It was followed up with a rather reserved…

"Go on. I'm listening."

"And it's about time Chief Inspector," he rasped. "Firstly, you need to get our good friend DI Murray on this case ASAP."

"OUR good friend?" She questioned. Before adding, "Inspector Murray is still on leave Mr Reid. Compassionate grounds - I would have thought that you, more than anyone would have been well aware of that?"

"Oh, I am very well aware of his CURRENT position," he smiled as he spoke those words.

What is he up to? Furlong watched him carefully. Inwardly, she conceded that the latest events must have been a major concern to Herr Reidmeister. Otherwise, like he said, why would he be doing house visits? That in itself was a potentially reckless decision. A move that Reid had admitted was quite possibly, very foolish and that could backfire badly.

His words soon came up for air. They were tinged with years of blood, death and misery.

"You will be well aware I guess, Detective Chief Inspector, that Messrs Stevenson, Menzies and Johnson were all good friends of mine?"

"More good friends?" Furlong questioned.

The guttural tone continued. "Okay, so maybe not friends exactly, but that I enjoyed an exceptionally close and beneficial working relationship with each of these men."

"We certainly thought someone had it in for you. That they were intent on ruining your operation, or at the very least, creating some major disruption for your core business."

"And automatically, you thought it was Andrew Scott's crew? You have been treating it as part of an extension of all the retaliatory attacks that you guessed were being carried out."

Furlong said nothing.

"Well, here's the thing Barbra…"

The female Chief Inspector squirmed everytime he called her that.

"I have pretty reliable sources."

"I bet you do," Furlong agreed. "Mainly, bent police officers!"

His slow rasping tones, continued to reverberate throughout the intimacy of their surroundings.

"And these sources of knowledge, tell me in no uncertain terms. That Andrew Scott has not been involved in any single one of these attacks. Neither the major killings, nor the attacks on some of my…"

"How do you know they are totally reliable sources?" Furlong interrupted.

"Because they are still able to walk DCI Furlong - That's how!"

The vulnerable woman swallowed hard at that statement. Momentarily dismissing the fact that she was a high ranking police officer. Fear for her own life, had fleetingly entered her thoughts.

"Just have Murray, our music loving, friendly policeman, speak with him. I'm fully confident, he'll figure Scott out. He'll soon know whether he is telling the truth or not."

"That is all good and well, Mr Reid. But like I said, he is not on the team right now."

"He's a clever man our Mr Murray, Barbra. Don't underestimate him. You do him a disservice. I've already sent him 'Best Wishes.' Along with a little kindly encouragement. A modest re-introductory offer, inviting him to the party!"

"What the…"

"Mind that language of yours DCI Furlong. We expect so much more from those in authority these days. And I hear that you've been doing ever so well with your continued rehabilitation."

A condescending laugh accompanied that last remark.

"What have you done this time, Bunny?"

"No need to fret or concern yourself, Chief Inspector. It was just a friendly little incentive, to get him back to work. I am led to believe that his remaining family members wouldn't even recognise him right now. Either physically or mentally."

Barbra Furlong could not genuinely argue with that assessment. Reid was fully up to speed. Just as she had imagined that he would be. Then, as if sounding the bell during a boxing match, Furlong's phone began to ring. It had been in her bag previously and she had never gotten around to syncing it with her new car, so it would have gone undetected on the short drive home.

"Don't let me stop you," the hoarse voice echoed within the naked timber of the cottage.

The Chief Inspector hurriedly tracked down her mobile. Quickly flicked it open and froze. She turned the screen toward Reid. There, clearly in bold font flashed up the caller's name. STEVEN MURRAY it proclaimed. His ears must have been burning.

"Again, don't let me stop you," offered the undaunted bully.

DCI Furlong herself was uncertain. She also, had never heard a thing from her DI in recent times. Was this actually him? Was Reid or Scott for that matter, playing mind games with her? Was it going to be bad news? Had someone found her Inspectors body and located his mobile? A multitude of logical and very illogical scenarios played out in her mind, all over the course of five short seconds.

"He doesn't do patience very well," 'Bunny' growled. "I would answer that, sooner rather than later."

That last statement was delivered assertively as an instruction. One that she should obey without delay.

"Hello, hello, Steven is that you?" Her voice was curt and polite. Slightly wavering, but confident.

"It is indeed, Chief Inspector." He paused nervously. "But how are you? Is everything alright?"

She knew, from those few brief words. That he knew, that she was in danger.

"It's just I got a cryptic message from 'Bunny' Reid and I…"

Furlong, interrupted abruptly. So that he would not give anything away about his whereabouts or his theory regarding Reid's clue.

"I'm fine, Inspector."

Her uninvited houseguest smiled. It was an insincere grin that said - Be careful young lady, be very careful.

"I'm just making myself a nice cup of coffee after returning home. It's so good to hear from you. Are you coming back to work soon? I really could be doing with your help."

Her nerves seemed to be getting the better of her. She was just talking ten to the dozen, as the phone trembled nonstop in her hands. Obviously she was more nervous than she'd fully realised. There seemed to be just the slightest of delays from Murray. Before he responded slowly, yet assuredly with…

"Sure, I'll be back in your company in no time, Ma'am."

"Great to hear that, Inspector," she said.

A great surge of relief seemed to come over her. She knew that he was on his way. But how did he know Reid was even there? She now questioned - What had that introductory offer been? Whatever it was, it had obviously been successful and had enticed Steven Murray back to work.

"I'll call you back," she added. "That's the kettle boiled. We'll speak soon enough. Bye for now."

Murray had already hung up. His spirited boss, then gazed curiously across at James Reid with real fascination and interest. What made this man tick? As if on cue, the aging gangster offered some delicate words of wisdom for her to reflect upon and ponder over.

"You know DCI Furlong, wallowing in your own self-pity makes you weak, not strong - and my great adversary, Steven Murray knows that. So I reckoned he just needed a little personal motivation."

Then, as if endeavouring to read her mind, Reid stared directly back at Barbra Furlong. He focused only on the area around her eyes, her temple, the bridge of her nose. It seemed like a definite attempt to get inside her mind. To probe, to unsettle or maybe just to play with her emotions more than he'd already done so. Eventually he spoke again...

"I guess you've been wondering what the introductory package consisted of?"

Now that was well deduced Furlong reckoned. She hadn't moved and no noticeable outward sign would have indicated that, that was exactly what she was thinking. So to give him his due - Impressive! Reid hastily looked down at his mobile and smiled broadly.

"My information seems to tell me that our beloved DI is on his way here currently. So maybe it is best if I don't hang around much longer. Please remember, Barbra, that I could have hurt you. But I didn't. For that was never my intention. Because obviously, YOU, were my introductory offer!"

Furlong appeared startled, but offered a gentle sigh of relief under her breath.

"Me?" she then exclaimed, unwittingly.

"Of course, Barbra. The very thought of you coming to harm was the incentive required. So, like I said, make sure you put him to work, Detective Chief Inspector. He figured out that it was you that I was going to pay a visit to. I had every confidence that he would. So he must have his old Mojo back. That's what I had hoped for."

The lifelong criminal began to walk away, but paused briefly.

"Just one more thing by the way," he rasped. "That was a nice try with the coffee. But if I know you don't drink it... Really? Now remember, Barbra, the most important message here is.... He would have been too late. Not just a fraction late, but far too late. You would have been dead, if that is what I had really wanted!"

With those chilling words still ringing in her ears, a solitary, reluctant tear ran down DCI Barbra Furlong's cheek. She was then left all alone to gather her thoughts. Although the faint barking of a dog could be heard in the distance... a lot closer than *'three miles'* away.

Fifteen

'Don't waste your pucker on some all-day sucker and don't try a toffee or cream. If you seek perfection in sugar confection, well here's something new on the scene. A mouthful of cheer, a sweet without peer - a musical morsel supreme. Toot Sweets, Toot Sweets - the candies you whistle, the whistles you eat!'

- Chitty Chitty Bang Bang

Going back out into civilisation for the first time in weeks, Murray began talking to himself incessantly.

"I have severe depression and many people think that means each day I cry and that I'm sad," he vocalised loudly as he started the car's engine.

He then pummeled his fists aggressively into the dashboard before replying to himself, whilst shaking his head intensely.

"But that's just not true. What it actually means is that... every day, I try not to kill myself! And relax..." he said calmly.

He then adjusted the rear view mirror, crunched into first gear and drove off.

Seventeen minutes later, driving at high speed throughout the narrow, twisting country roads of East Lothian, the troubled Inspector ran through it all again in his chaotic mind. Trying to first rationalise and then tie up the loose threads of his simplistic theory. He could visualise the list, the usual suspects - Hanlon, Kerr, Hayes, Curry and Boyd. Then he continued with The Doc, Ally Coulter, the DCI and Sergeant Mitchell Linn. That was nine in total. Well strictly speaking, Ally was no longer with us. So down to eight, he thought. Why mention my gambling though? Reid was always deliberate with his choice of words, so it must be relevant. He had reached out to me specifically. So rather than excluding me, he still recognised me as head of the team. That took us back up to nine. Absolutely, Murray nodded to himself. But with that thinking and logic, then he must remove his DCI. If he's in charge, no one is above him. Back to eight then. And that was how he was sure.

 If he was only going to take out one of them - the lone target must be his Chief Inspector. Reid had typed 'Not Reliable' with capital letters. Again, within the racing fraternity NR was significant. It stood for Non-Runner! Reid would have been well aware of his gambling and horse racing addiction of old. Bunny's text spoke about being level headed - so that would refer to the Flat courses, not National Hunt courses which involve jumps, hurdles and fences. He was in a hurry - so it would be a sprint. Reid also knew the name of her dog was 'three miles,' but again he reminded himself, it was *only the one* that would be targeted - So possibly just one mile, which was still regarded as a sprint. Then using more racing terminology to narrow the field even further. Murray concluded his thought process with a fact that all regular racegoers already knew, and that was… What every eighth of a mile was referred to in the sport of kings?

An answer that his Detective Chief Inspector, with her great wealth of trivia knowledge, would no doubt be fully familiar with its actual origin. Of how dating back to Anglo-Saxon times, it was once a common way to measure farmland. In fact, as well as being one eighth of a mile, the length of a furrow in a ten acre field was also referred to as…… A Furlong!

As the Inspector screeched abruptly to a halt outside the well maintained garden of the cottage. A dark coloured SUV, either a Lexus, Land or Range Rover, Murray was unsure which, could be seen travelling off smoothly into the distance. Was that just a coincidence? The low wooden gate to the short path lay ajar. As did the actual door to the house. Steven Murray had experienced this often over his many years. It was nice to catch the baddie in the act, or even have the accused in custody with a healthy mountain of evidence stacked against them in advance in some cases. But today felt like one of those occasionally disappointing times. Where everything and everybody, was just a fraction late.

Murray carefully ducked his head as he cautiously entered the century old property. As much as he knew speed was of the essence, he was also fully aware of Reid's ruthless reputation and lack of hesitation for taking out police officers. So he took no unnecessary chances. He opened the door fully. The powerful stench and odour was distinctly different to the one he remembered on his only previous visit to his Chief Inspector's home. Interestingly, it was not the foul reek of nicotine in the air that Murray first became aware off, but once again a very particular brand of aftershave. The very same aroma that he had encountered at least twice before on his travels. Firstly at a restaurant in Colinton on the outskirts of Edinburgh. That was when James Baxter Reid initially appeared back on the scene after Taz Taylor's death. So although no less ruthless, it was there that he debuted his new image and persona. That particular Sunday afternoon 'Bunny' had stalked 'Ally' Coulter and had appeared totally out of the blue as Murray and his trusted Sergeant sat quietly eating lunch.

The other occasion in more recent times when that particular cologne was to trouble Steven Murray, was the very day of the raid on the ABC casino. The Inspector recognised the familiar fragrance from his concealed hiding spot behind the room's heavily lined curtains. Then thirty seconds later when the Reidmeister spoke on the phone with his unmistakable voice - all was confirmed.

Today the smell was diminishing. He was now confident that it was in fact James Reid's SUV vehicle that had just disappeared off into the distance as he arrived.

"I'm through here," was gently offered to reassure him.

Only Furlong was in the room and she appeared physically fine. Although to the experienced eye of Steven Murray, she was well and truly in shock.

"Are you sure you're okay, Ma'am?" he asked instinctively.

She nodded slowly. Possibly, oblivious to him having even entered the premises.

"I take it that was Reid, that just sped off?"

Her nodding continued, although notably more hurried than before. Her pale lips trembled as she spoke. With each syllable dropping slowly into play, she offered -

"He thinks it's one of us."

"I know Ma'am. He made contact directly with me. That is why I am here."

Her eyes shot up at this. He was here. Steven Murray was actually here, in her quaint little sitting room. He had chosen a self-imposed exile for the past two months, trying desperately to cope with his situation and the circumstances around it. But he was here. She was his enticement back to sanity! Barbra Furlong once again tried to get her head around it. Was it his loyalty to his colleagues? He had dismissed even his closest friends in recent weeks. She was aware that he had rebuffed invitations from Kerr and Coulter, and had not returned calls, texts and emails received from Joe Hanlon and others. Yet here he was. She had been threatened, her life was in danger or at least so it appeared and here he was. Why? Why would DI Steven Murray even turn up? How come 'Bunny' Reid was so certain?

"I'll tell you all about it later," her Inspector mumbled. "But first we need to get you checked over. An ambulance and fellow officers are on their way."

"But, how did you know?" she began. Before hesitatingly adding, "And anyway, you would have been too late if he had actually wanted to kill me. That is exactly what he said. If he had wanted me dead, you would have been running in here to discover a lifeless corpse on the floor by now!"

"He loves to play those mind games. I've had my fair share of that from him today myself. Let's forget 'Bunny' Reid, Ma'am," the Inspector stated assertively in a frustrated, angry and yet determined tone. "His time will come and I suspect it will be sooner rather than later. He is obviously worried," Murray continued. "So those deaths must be impacting. They must be taking their toll and actually having serious adverse effects on his daily business. Evidently upsetting his supply chain, his cash flow, his ongoing revenue stream and more importantly, his reputation. Because, that Ma'am, out of them all, is worth the most to him!"

Furlong took up the baton…

"Creating uncertainty in court, especially when you can no longer rely on tainted legal counsel. His men obviously less willing, if they actually fear they'll end up doing prison time? And with a paid up Judge now fully out of commission. How does he easily replace his contacts and influence?" She paused before continuing. "Although I suspect an apprentice or two are already on the books and taking up the slack. By now there will be at least one other unscrupulous advocate on his payroll. Someone fully prepared to step up off of one bench and deposit themselves directly upon another much more rewarding one!"

"You may well be right, Ma'am."

"**BONKING-BLONDE-BIMBOS**, Steven! Of course I'm right. Don't treat me like some second rate novice."

"My apologies, Ma'am. But with the death of several of his key players and a host of other skeletons resurfacing, he must be taking a serious hit, that is all I am saying. That in turn though, could hopefully lead him to make mistakes or take even more unnecessary risks. A prime example of which, was coming to visit with you here today in person."

"He knew that, however. So it was a carefully considered risk. However, let me reiterate, Inspector. He never came here to threaten me. In fact, he couldn't have been nicer."

Murray registered that fact and took a mental note that she chose not to call him, Steven, on this occasion.

"He came to seek help and assistance. Some much needed clarification for himself. But also to enlighten us. To point out that there is still much work to be done in putting our own house in order. He dropped several strong hints in the direction of another corrupt officer and that we have to root them out, Steven."

Ah, there you go, he thought. Now that you need my help, we are back to familiarity and first name terms again. He quietly smiled to himself. It reminded him of his childhood days, back at home in Paisley.

His slightly schizophrenic mother would constantly be on his case. She would scold or chastise him all day and then a particular refrain would begin to sound out around the neighbourhood. It was the easily and instantly recognisable chimes of a children's nursery rhyme. The melody streamed gently from the multi coloured ice cream van that had just driven into the street. With that, the mood of a young Steven Murray's mother would promptly alter. This confectionery mecca of a candy treasure trove, jam packed with assorted goodies had arrived straight out of the musical *Chitty Chitty Bang Bang*.

The mischievous, deviant child-catcher was played by a cool, streetwise, Jack the Lad character called Francis. 'Franny' to his mates. This laid back man was only about twenty-six. Yet, he was already a hero to all the male teenagers in the area. Why? Well, not only because he was brave enough to have a female name. But because he had a large tattoo of a naked female on his left forearm!

Half the young adolescent boys in the street had no money for sweets, chocolate or juice. But when the van's musical tune, 'Half a pound of tuppenny rice - half a pound of treacle,' filled the air, the hormonally challenged group used to mix with the queue of genuine customers and drool excitedly over this guy's impressive artwork. Quite literally in many cases, tiny heads bopped up and down. Bouncy perms went left, flowing fringes descended right, and often, several dipped unnaturally sideways as their trendy 1970's role model, went about getting merchandise from his crammed shelves and placing it on the counter top at regular intervals. Fizzy cola bottles, Caramacs, Bournville dark chocolate and Lee's unwrapped snowballs were always popular sellers. Snotty, running noses were then rubbed desperately against the grubby glass, as each street urchin jostled for a better view. Every local youth had their own name for this flirtatious woman. She was a sultry seductress. A vampish vixen who would live in each of their own personal fantasies for the remainder of the day.

'Steven. Oh, Steven where are you?' The matriarch of his family would cry sweetly in her best Sunday church voice. 'Would you be kind enough to get me a packet of Askit powders for my headache, two bags of Salt'n Shake crisps and a bottle of Dark Cola please.' It wasn't Coke or Pepsi in those days. Each area would carry a local brand. And in the west of Scotland, it would always be referred to as - Dark Cola. Then came the standard pause, before she finished with, 'and of course get yourself something.' That was the magical bit that the young footballing fanatic was waiting to have confirmed. He was then off like a shot, to get a good viewing spot.

Again with the Scottish Dr Jekyll and Mr Hyde. Where would one think that the Inspector inherited his Bipolar from? Well, look no further than his mother. That was certainly always, 'STEVEN,' dear Steven Murray's unconfirmed theory.

"Steven, Steven are you even listening to me? I was saying... We have to weed these dishonest officers out and hold them to account. Although Reid is convinced that it has nothing to do with a certain, Mr Scott. So much so, he wants YOU to confirm this. For some reason he has faith and trust in you. Why would that be, Inspector? I wonder!"

Murray held her gaze.

"Why Detective Steven Murray? Why you, Inspector?"

Furlong seemed to ask more with curiosity, than genuine suspicion.

"What kind of hold does this man have over you or possibly over a member of your team?"

Her colleague noticeably flinched at that last remark.

"Really, Ma'am? Are you seriously going to venture down that well trodden path? The unsubstantiated, conjecture route? The old chestnut of Steven Murray being corrupt!"

His DCI looked at him nervously. "I don't think that for one minute… about you," she later added.

He watched her. She appeared awkward, uncertain even and that was out of character. She liked to be in control. To know full well what was going on and normally to take overall charge of situations. So why the hesitancy and wavering? He pondered on that thought. Not for a minute did she think HE was corrupt, she said. So not him, but possibly another member of his team? Had she found out about Andrew Curry's brief alliance with Reid previously? Doubtful, he thought. It was a problem that Murray had successfully handled by having Curry regularly feed Reid bad info. Thus making Curry more of a hindrance than a help, to Reid's bustling empire. It was a gesture that 'Kid' Curry would be forever indebted to Murray for. He had made some bad decisions after an emotional breakup.

"I'm listening," Steven Murray said. "But be quick, the team will be here any minute."

Barbra Furlong wasted no time on that score.

"Susan Hayes," she announced.

"What about her?" Murray reluctantly asked.

"She was supposed to have been watching your place. Keeping tabs on her struggling boss," Furlong told him. "But on at least two assigned shifts, Thursday and Friday night, no less. She most definitely wasn't.

However, the fact that she blatantly lied to me about it and vouched for you, concerns me even more. It was one of our own, that was what Reid inferred."

Murray gave her a rather long lasting and disapproving look. One which clearly asked - How do you know she wasn't there? Is your information reliable?

Furlong read faces equally as well as Murray…

"Because, 'Ally,' WAS watching your place during those times, Inspector and sadly, for her sake. Detective Constable Susan Hayes was nowhere to be seen.

"But why were…"

"We were taking turns looking out for you," she abruptly interrupted. "For such a clever man, you really can be so naïve, oblivious and downright stupid at times," she scolded.

Murray felt his face instantly flush red and then recede. "Go on," he added meekly.

"You had visited me here once before, Steven, and had shared privately with me some of your ongoing challenges."

"Ma'am that was in…"

"Strictest confidence, I know! And so it has remained, Inspector. But I was concerned. As were all the members of your team. So we took turns watching your home and delivering food. Did you think that those groceries just magically appeared every few days?" A reassuring smile accompanied that last remark.

"I figured it was 'Ally' or 'Sherlock,' but not a Three Musketeers thing. A one for all, and all for one malarkey.

"For Pete's sake man. We all care about you. We all wanted to keep an eye on you. But if truth be told DI Murray," she winked cheekily once again. "I was not entirely convinced that you wouldn't get up to no good."

An innocent hangdog look appeared on the Inspector's face. Butter definitely wouldn't melt in that man's mouth. He then felt the need to respond.

"Whatever could you mean, Ma'am?" He asked straight faced.

"You know, like any unauthorised investigation taking place. One that may be tinged with some form of revenge or self-satisfaction."

She left that vague question smouldering on a baited hook. Murray on this occasion, did not succumb. He simply and firmly sealed his lips and gave her a backward tilt of his head. And although not a fully fledged nod, it was enough of a friendly gesture that clearly stated - Oh, you did, did you?

"For that very reason. You possibly, going it alone and getting up to mischief and that is putting it politely. That is why I had asked 'Ally' to keep an eye on you. To double check proceedings and that was well before our diligent, Assistant Chief Constable, felt the need to bad mouth you and stab you in the back."

By this point, Murray merely shrugged. In a dismissive manner, he added playfully...

"They'll always need a scapegoat, Ma'am. It just so happens that for the last year or so, I seem to have been their default setting. Which is good news DCI

Furlong," Murray announced generously. "Because that means, I'm keeping them from coming after you!"

A mutual smile was exchanged by the two colleagues. Murray had definite feelings for her. There was no denying it. It was just the second time since his wife had died that he had experienced those particular emotions. Jayne Golden got the better of his affections only last year. Nothing ever transpired on that front though. Apart from Golden going on the run at the end of the child trafficking case, when all the arrests were being made. This led Inspector Murray and prosecutors to question that her involvement may have been slightly more unlawful, than lawful?

When the lonely, sad figure of Steven Murray had first turned up at Furlong's cottage. Which was a week after the death of his son. Barbra Furlong was initially surprised, then delighted and finally, apprehensive and wary. Murray thought he had the strength to work through his grief. To seek happiness with a companion. To regain joy. The timing was all wrong and he chickened out. When the casually dressed, but gorgeous figure of Barbra Furlong answered her door. He played the *'I need to tell you a few confidential things about myself'* card. None of which came as any real surprise to her. She had her sources and was already well aware of Steven Murray's so-called destructive devils and demons.

"I am going to get her home searched first thing in the morning, Steven. So if you don't want to be there…"

"Sorry, Ma'am, I believe I'll be busy meeting with a certain Mr Andrew Scott." Murray quickly added. "You'll be wanting me to follow up on that distressed member of the public's concerns, I would have thought?"

"Indeed I would, Inspector. Indeed I would," she playfully agreed. "Drive carefully over to the beautiful Kingdom of Fife and give my best wishes to the BIG WALLY DUG SHUFFLER!"

Murray laughed aloud. It was infectious. It was like an early, rapid-fire spring loaded Gatling gun. It took down everything in its line of sight. He loved Furlong's non-swear words. Half the time they sounded worse and far more offensive than actual cursing. The other half, like now, were sheer nonsense, but utterly hysterical. 'You had to be there,' he would often say.

His DCI brought him instantly back to Earth with…

"You do know how the Gatling gun got its name, Inspector. Don't you?"

A shake of his shoulders and a sharp intake of breath was enough.

"Sorry, Ma'am. No time to hear that piece of trivia right now."

"I thought not," she smirked to herself.

"But one thing, however, though. Each of those murdered, so far, were single bachelors. Was that right?"

"That would be correct, Steven," she confirmed. Although she certainly did not like the, 'so far' part.

"They lived alone? With no family?" Again he sought confirmation of this.

Another steady nod was offered.

DI Murray had returned. His brain was getting back up to speed. The cogs turning faster than he could manage to keep up with.

"Then that was no stroke of luck. This had all been carefully planned and orchestrated. Exceptionally well prepared and each death executed with minute precision."

"Your point being?"

"My point being, Ma'am - is that takes a certain level of skill and an increased aptitude for patience. There was a definite, fiery determination to succeed. Coupled with a very special and specific mindset." He then paused, before blurting aloud. "Who thinks like that?"

"Normally a woman!" Barbra Furlong instantly responded with a smile. Without even a second's hesitation.

The Inspector's suspicious eyes furrowed further. His delicate eyebrows looked to embrace one another. Then a telling nod of his frenzied head followed. He had been seeking reassurance. Because that had been his thoughts exactly. 'Hanna' Hayes was now seeming even more involved by the minute. He unfortunately now had no option but to investigate his own team member. Furlong had already set the ball rolling, but Murray then had to ensure a competent and professional follow up took place.

Without any advance warning, he immediately recalled with clarity, the day that he found himself alone in a hotel room in Birmingham, England. One minute he had been happily reading the BBC News online, making facial expressions and nodding as he scanned the headlines. Then a particular line in a story hit an emotional trigger within him. Tears instantly flowed from his eyes. His decades of unhappiness surfaced. His desire to want for nothing more from this life, except to be taken home. A heavenly home far, far away from these distant shores. These days, Murray had no specific preference. Heaven or Hell? He couldn't care less. His two month hiatus had made him question so much. What was our time on Earth here really all about? Did we, or do we make the most of it? Were we born into wealth or poverty? How can any one individual accumulate untold riches, whilst others find themselves begging constantly in one form or another?

He had no immediate answers or resolutions. But was confident that with modern technology, innovative developments and the social media coverage of injustice, then surely we can at least find a better balance. His broken, emotional mind, seemed to throw up many more questions than he could ever cope or deal with. Raised with oodles of affection or uncaring abuse? Heads - Tails? Good luck or misfortune? War, starvation or hunger? Murray had never experienced any of that. Broken home or marital bliss?

Steven Murray had only known love. It was a passive, resigned, apologetic kind of love. But definitely love, nonetheless. He recalled how his parents never actually vocally expressed their love to him or to each other, but they raised him together. They never fully epitomised a loving, successful marriage. But neither one of them left the other, until death. However, he also quickly acknowledged that it was a different time and season.

Death - The actual, physical act had been a real concern for Murray in his twenties, thirties and even as recently as his forties. During those decades, the sheer thought of dying filled him with dread, anxiety and fear. He had been a churchgoer though, so was content that there was much to look forward to on the other side. In the intervening years however, more recent experiences had instilled a change in him. He had been fortunate enough to have journeyed to many varied parts of the world over the years, both alone and with family. He had met and made many new friends throughout that period of time and felt exceptionally grateful for those positive encounters. But the one thing that he never had and has always lacked - was a best friend! A laughing buddy, a fellow traveller and confidante! 'Doc' Patterson was a colleague and a friend. 'Ally' was a good friend and trusted workmate, but neither had filled that void.

In more recent years, the heartache of his personal life, woven together with the devastation and depravity he would experience regularly professionally, had become too much sometimes. His coping mechanisms would let him down and he would fail to function. Nowadays sadly, the lonely figure was happy for his Maker to take him out of his constant misery. He would be delighted and quietly satisfied these days with that. His music meanwhile would offer him temporary solace.

On the other hand, words were also incredibly powerful. Recollections of that emotive line that he once read in the Midlands, had DI Steven Murray, once again feeling vulnerable and suicidal.

Sixteen

'So she had built her elaborate home. With its ups and its downs, its rains and its sun. She decided that her work was done, it was time to have fun and she found a game to play. Then as part of the game, she completely forgot where she'd hidden herself!'

- Howard Jones

There was a small baptist church at the end of Susan Hayes' street. Twice a week you would hear them belting out some inspirational choir numbers. Many traditional gospel hymns, interspersed with a lively selection of modern pop songs. The cool, quirky and hope inspiring wooden sign on the grass verge read: *Jesus said - 'I'll be back...... long before Arnold did!'*

A cheerful, whistling postman, wearing a pair of knee length khaki shorts, gave them a confident nod as he went about his daily business. As he crossed regularly from one side of the street to the other in the early morning sunshine, he never even gave the group of police officers a second glance. He had seen it all before, no doubt. From late night party revellers, still desperately trying to find their way home. To morning glory, semi clad romps with adjoining neighbours. Like an experienced taxi driver or window cleaner, the local postie already owned the T-shirt.

As DCI Furlong chapped firmly on the stainless steel letterbox belonging to DC 'Hanna' Hayes. She sincerely hoped that there would be no further need for her, or any of their team to be back in a professional capacity at this address again. She had no personal desire to repeat Mr Schwarzenegger's famous tagline.

The long serving police officer lived in Poltonhall, a substantial residential development of the Bonnyrigg/ Lasswade conurbation in Midlothian. It was a handy, twenty to thirty minute commute each day to work. In the late 1960's and early 70's a host of homes were built in the area. Erected especially to accommodate soldiers and their families. In more recent times these had all been sold off. The stout matron like figure that answered the door that morning, Detective Constable 'Hanna' Hayes, now owned this particular property.

"Ma'am," Susan Hayes gulped. Half swallowing a piece of burnt toast, she'd been in the middle of eating.
"How can I…"

"We have a warrant to search your property, DC Hayes." Furlong stated officially. Then in a more personal, gentler and understanding tone, she instructed…

"I need you to stand aside please, 'Hanna' and let these fellow officers carry out their duties. Six unknown colleagues from a neighbouring station, then went about their business. On closer inspection, Hayes realised that she did actually recognise two or three of the men from joining up at protection duties. Events like political rallies, street cordons and the like. All well before, she moved to C.I.D.

"I don't underst…"
She was cut off in full flow.

"I need you to accompany me to the station, Constable. You are currently suspended from all duties whilst we carry out further routine investigations."

Becoming rather defensive and fiery. 'Hanna' Hayes shot back.

"Further routine investigations! I had no idea that there had even been initial ones," she remonstrated.

Barbra Furlong lifted a jacket from the rack of coats and apparel behind Hayes' back. She handed it to the mystified and bewildered officer. Then she nodded curtly to an accompanying WPC to escort Susan Hayes out to the car.

"Let's keep things civil, 'Hanna.' I am sure we can resolve this matter quickly and put all this behind us."

Hayes immediately found herself sitting in the back seat of a police vehicle for the very first time. She shook her head vehemently, as the patrol car drove across town to their Leith based headquarters. It was then, that 'Hanna' first became aware that DCI Furlong had not actually joined her, but had remained behind at her home. At that moment, a vast multitude of memories, thoughts and vivid recollections swarmed into her mind. Impressions and images of a childhood that she would rather forget, and for many years, had successfully done so. This introspection would do her no favours. It would only serve to open old wounds and allow dark, suppressed flashbacks to fleetingly filter back into her life. She blinked hard and opened her eyes widely to bring herself back to the present.

Twenty minutes of continually staring out of the misted rear windows and they had arrived. Two cyclists nearly collided as they turned into the station. A group of officers loaded equipment into the back of a Police minibus. Apart from them, there appeared to be no one else around in the car park. For that at least, she was grateful. Although several pairs of eyes could always monitor comings and goings from their vantage points high above the courtyard entrance. Having never thought about it earlier, it suddenly dawned on her. Who would she be interviewed by, if DCI Furlong was still at her place? The realization, the lightbulb moment, the full dawning of Aquarius soon filtered through. It would be her boss, her role model. Her supposed team leader, trusted mentor and friend.

"Oh crap," she let loose. However unladylike that may have been!

Whilst a certain in-depth search had taken place forty miles away at his officers home. Detective Inspector Steven Murray had headed across the Forth Road Bridge to Andrew Scott's new place of business in Fife. The man had gotten closer and closer to Edinburgh in recent years. Both in terms of the territories he covered with his endless supply of services and goods and also now in the actual location of his Head Office. Moving just over three months ago from the sleepy burgh of Kinross in Perthshire, to the bustling metropolis, that is... Dunfermline! Once the proud, historic capital of Scotland, it is now on the tourist map as the birthplace of Andrew Carnegie and the final resting place of Robert the Bruce. As well as now providing Andrew Scott Ltd, with a wonderful infrastructure of road, rail and sea networks. Transport links that will benefit and greatly enhance his range of interests exponentially.

"Hello there. Good morning Amanda." Was Murray's bright retort as he entered the new facility and slowly monitored it's interior. Stopping in his tracks and taking a second look at a rather out of place piece of colourful equipment, he felt the need to add…

"And why, my dear girl in heaven's name, do you have that in here?"

He found himself pointing at a brand new children's soft play area. Complete with netting, padded chutes and a full to overflowing ball pit.

"Bazinga!" The fresh faced, female receptionist smiled in surprise. Both at such a cheery welcome and the fact that someone unexpectedly took notice of her name badge. An added bonus on this occasion was also the fact that she could answer the potential customers question. That didn't happen very often.

"It's a children's play area!" Her voice filled with personal pride at knowing the answer.

I am neither stupid nor blind was Murray's first unpleasant possible response. But he relented and went with a happy, smiley retort instead.

"Yes, I understand that Amanda. I was more curious at how many of your big, bulky, tattooed haulage drivers or those renting industrial skips for the day, feel the desire to play in it?"

The inexperienced girl looked momentarily confused. Then sheer panic set in.

"What! No! That wouldn't be allowed. It's not for the customers, sir."

Murray's eyes indicated that he needed more than that.

"The boss has two young nieces who visit often and they'll be young enough to enjoy it for years to come. Not the truckers, you silly man," she scolded him.

"Thank you for the clarification. Most helpful and informative," Murray stated.

Young Amanda blushed slightly.

"And actually I'm here looking to chat with that very boss, Mr Scott, please."

The officer continued with the cheery, outgoing attitude. It really wasn't that difficult. Because that was his normal everyday, public persona after all. It was generally alone, at home that his 'black dog' preferred to come out and play. Maybe that is someone, that he could build a 'special' play area for. One where the overweight canine could slide down a chute into a deep pool of water, wearing only cute doggy slippers... preferably made of cement!

The rookie girl's initially friendly demeanour, seemed to change somewhat. The official, overly protective employee was soon back in place.

"I'm afraid you'll have to make an appointment, sir. Mr Scott is a busy man and his calendar is totally full for today. Sorry."

"Oh, I quite understand young lady."

She smiled. Glad that the matter had been resolved and delighted that once again she'd been of assistance.

"However," the man then informed her. "I suspect that if you let your boss know," he then flashed his warrant card. "That Detective Inspector Steven Murray is here and has a few questions for him. He will willingly reschedule his busy day and make time for me. Thank you."

Amanda considered that request for a second. But there was no need for the crestfallen gatekeeper to do anything further. For an ever vigilant Andrew Scott and his personal assistant, or bouncer more like, had watched Murray's every movement since he'd arrived. A CCTV monitor positioned on his desk, allowed him to view all transport in and out of the premises.

Today the police officer had arrived in his latest Volvo S40, a car which was already over four years old. His last vehicle had managed to travel twice around the clock with him on his murderous adventures, over 200,000 miles. This latest incarnation was a mere novice at only… 91,000.

Andrew Scott had previously operated his vast array of businesses, some legit, some possibly less so, from an old haulage company facility in Perthshire. However, as his range of services on offer increased, so had his gradual advancement into Scotland's new capital city.

As recently as yesterday, gangland bosses from Ayrshire to Aberdeen were less than impressed with the way that 'Bunny' Reid had gone after and allowed both Scott's brother and mother, to be murdered in her East Renfrewshire home in recent times. And through various sources, Police Scotland had been informed that Andrew Scott had been given the green light by a coalition of other crime lords throughout the country to cautiously redress the issue. In polite business circles, 'cautiously redress' would imply 'a stern warning,' or possibly even 'take a small liberty or two." But somehow, someone would suspect that in the business circles these two men mix - that starter's flag may signal all out warfare and a loss of life and limb on a grand scale.

During the past several days, the latter seemed to have been the norm. Even after the continued removal of key people from his organisation, both past and present, James Baxter Reid was still adamant it was not Scott's doing. But how could he be so sure? What did he know that he hadn't shared? What then, was his real game plan or motive? He'd needed Murray's help that was for sure, but why? What was the whole charade with Furlong about? That threat was never real. He was never going to cause her harm. Like he said to her at the time, if he'd wanted her dead, she would be! And no one would have been any the wiser. It would have been done quietly and discreetly and with no trace or come back to him whatsoever. Simply following the pattern of so many other disappearances that he'd ordered in the past.

This new expansive yard consisted of skip hire availability, scrap cars, waste and haulage units. Each operated as separate entities. But rest assured, Andrew Scott was in sole control. Ironically, he preferred modern, up to date, ways of operating and that was okay for high tech drug hookups and his online escort agency. But when it came to money laundering, then some of the old fashioned, rather tired, dated and possibly seen as uncool businesses were still unbeatable. In conjunction with his operations run from these premises and away from all his modern computer driven enterprises, he was also listed as an owner of a Dunfermline taxi firm and as a Managing Director of a string of tanning studios ranging from North Queensferry to North Berwick. So the six foot plus Glaswegian, had already quietly dipped his toe into 'Bunny' Reid's paddling pool in the Lothians.

A polite, yet rather pretentious voice boomed out from the bottom of a distant stairwell in the back corner of the room.

"Inspector, how are you my good man? How can I help you?"

His manners were as impeccable as Murray remembered. To go alongside that, he was trim, elegantly dressed and well groomed. His deep blue traditional denim shirt was complemented well with a beige tartan waistcoat and dark fitted jeans. If criminal activity had not been his forte, the richly distinguished features of Andrew Scott should have been plying their trade on the catwalks of Paris, Milan and London. Damn, he was one hell of a good looking man, Murray thought. Then briefly reflecting on his own rugged charms and slight tummy, he sang lightly… *'Some guys have all the luck, some guys have all the pain.'*

"What's that Inspector?"

"Oh, never mind me, Mr Scott. I was just wondering how YOU have been, since we last met? It was in the aftermath of the awful explosion at your parent's home in Newton Mearns. The one that resulted in the tragic death of your mother and brother. I was sorry about all that." Murray had felt the instant need to stir and antagonise.

Scott threw his head brusquely from side to side.

"Strictly speaking, Inspector, my dear brother was cruelly murdered before the house erupted into volcanic ash." His voice was calm, measured and only mixed slightly with a dash of polite innuendo. "Don't suppose you've had much success on catching his killer? You'll no doubt be stretched to the limit - possibly under resourced?"

Scott expected no answer. Which was good, DI Murray never gave him one. However he did respond with…

"We all know it was Shaun Scullion, sir, including yourself. So don't go giving the police a hard time."

Scott glowered down at his fellow west coaster.

"Your brother Paul had been part of a murderous double act," Murray continued assertively. "One whose signature was carving the initials SS onto their victims skin. So maybe, if you'd declined to use his partner's services, initially, sir. Never gave Mr Scullion illusions of grandeur above his Geordie, Tyneside station in life. Well just maybe, he'd never have defected to the other side in the first place and caused such chaos and mayhem. Actions which included taking your 'dear' brother out, into the bargain!"

Scott's posture, remained firm and still. Accepting the officers challenging riposte.

"By the way, sir. Genuinely, how is your young niece coping? The one that was held captive for several hours… Leah, is that right?"

"Well remembered, Inspector."

Scott was positive that he had no doubt looked it up in some file, just before he had arrived on the scene. That being the case, the crooked businessman, who, like 'Bunny' Reid prided himself on knowing all about his enemies. Confirmed that he never really knew Steven Murray at all.

The Inspector was generally very good with names, faces and places. Especially those from the past. Occasionally though, he would use this to his advantage by pretending he'd forgotten and that he had no knowledge of the incident or the individual. Nine times out of ten it was simply just a rouse to make people underestimate him, feel superior and hopefully let their guard down. Once again, normally nine times out of ten, they did so!

"We are currently having the house rebuilt, Inspector. Our intention is to then sell it quickly and put the money into a trust fund for both my nieces, Leah and her older sister."

"Leah and Chloe, that would be. If I've got that right?"

Even Scott was impressed with that. Thinking, maybe I've underestimated this man. But unfortunately he had also become bored of the small talk.

"My apologies, Inspector, but we are both busy men and I am sure you are not here to do the job of a social worker. So why the visit? How can I help you? What are you really here for?"

Murray grinned from ear to ear, much like a Glasgow smile. A term which in actual fact is no laughing matter. For as DCI Furlong could probably happily tell you - it's the ultimate in malicious wounding and is created by slashing a victim's face from one or both corners of the mouth to the ears using a knife, a broken bottle or any other extra sharp object. A saying created by the gangland culture of the city way back in the early nineteen twenties. A vicious culture that had continued to this very day Murray reflected.

Andrew Scott and his current crop of hirelings, may use modern technology and all its advantages to implement their dodgy and illicit schemes. But the enforced reminders to those who don't produce or return the required profits haven't changed. They are still carried out physically by hand.

"I love a man who says it as it is, Mr Scott. I was just saying that very thing to a colleague earlier today."

With a need to emphasize the growing bond between them, Murray threw both hands into the conversation. Animatedly his limbs gestured frantically between both parties. They indicated, 'We get it!'

"It must be in the west of Scotland water growing up, eh!" Murray ventured. "What do you think?"

"What do I think? What do I think?" the debonair businessman repeated, clearly becoming irritated. "I think. In fact I know, I have an exceptionally busy business to run. So I ask for a second time - Exactly, what do you want?"

"See! There it is again, my very point. I rest my case. Fantastic!"

Scott gave a resigned sigh.

This time his voice had been unapologetically firm and direct. No matter his words, Andrew Scott's body language spoke volumes.

"No, no, I genuinely understand sir. So here's the thing…"

Seventeen

'Disappointments weigh so heavy, leaves it's wreckage all around. Once a good man, once respected - Sorrow breaks a good man down. Had a good love, had a good life, now there's sadness all around. Dread the darkness, hate the daylight - Sorrow breaks a good man down.'

- Waylon Jennings

Back in Poltonhall, in the cramped, compact, pebble-dashed lock-up to the side of 'Hanna's' home, the search team had found a motorcycle. However, the interesting significance to the find, was that small, selected parts of its paintwork had been scorched and the muddied residue around its wheels still appeared damp and moist. That motorcycle without fail, had definitely been ridden recently. Forensics would now need to try their best to compare the soil and stone samples embedded in its tread, as well as matching the tyres themselves to those markings from the Judge's driveway. To round off proceedings unhappily for the homeowner, who was currently being chauffeur driven to Queen Charlotte Street Police Station - a bloodied Stanley knife and a bag of plastic wrist restraints had also been found. They'd been wrapped in an old cloth and disposed of discreetly behind a metal storage cabinet at the rear of the confined garage premises. The search was ongoing.

Meanwhile, in Dunfermline, Murray had paused, lowered his head and stared over at the 'eager to please' teenage receptionist behind the desk. This time Amanda made herself scarce. Well done. She was capable of learning after all, the officer thought. He then turned his gaze to the trusted 'Incredible Hulk,' positioned at Andrew Scott's side. Nothing. It then took the gentlest of nods from his master to shift the huge brute of a man. As he made his way outside, there was certainly no tail between his legs - because there was no room! His thighs were firm, muscle bound motorways. They eased graciously down to his calves, which were in turn exemplary dual carriageways of finely toned, athletic bulk. As he then, indelicately ducked all six foot five of himself underneath the door frame, he closed the trendy metallic door quietly behind him.

"So, Inspector. What is suddenly so secretive?"

"Like I said, Mr Scott, the thing is... 'Bunny' Reid's men are dropping like flies. Now at this point I wish my DCI was here," he said. "Because, trust me, sir. She loves her modern literature and the origin of phrases and all that stuff you know."

Scott appeared confused.

"So much so, she'd most likely be able to give us the full genealogy of that particular line of fly and no doubt, that also of his Uncle, the trendsetting bluebottle into the bargain!"

Andrew Scott's eyes glazed over. Was this man for real, he thought to himself. He stood easily as tall, if not taller than his now departed sidekick. Although, he was probably in much better physical shape than his bulky henchman. Murray was well aware that Scott was both a keen cyclist and walker. In fact, if his memory served him right, he recalled the so-called criminal mastermind was even a fairly advanced martial arts expert. Ju-Mitsubishi, Wan-Deid Leg, Wee Shuggie or some such combination. Scott, like most effective string pullers, always remained at arms length from any possible criminal connection. Very smart and astute in that respect. However, considering he could easily look after himself, it was interesting and intriguing that he was happy to pay a constant gatekeeper or two. The sweet and pretty to look at Amanda sufficed for legitimate clients. Whereas the more sour faced Professor Bruce Banner, worked well for his more discerning clientele.

As Murray briefly reflected upon Scott's physical appearance and workout regime. The man himself, resplendent in well polished cowboy boots and high end casual gear, now stood directly in front of the Inspector. He faced him with a definite purpose and a satisfactory smirk on his face.

"I think I may well be able to help you there, my good man." Was delivered with an elegant and upmarket Newton Mearns lilt.

A brief melody left the Inspector's lips. *"Some guys get all the breaks…"* Before being overridden. "With what exactly? And how so?" Murray replied.

"Dropping like flies."

It was now Steven Murray's turn to be bewildered. His mouth neither open nor closed.

"Excuse me?"

"When I was a young lad," Scott offered. "My elderly Aunt bought me the Brothers Grimm storybook. I clearly remember the cautionary fable, Inspector. It was of a child who easily and thoughtlessly killed numerous flies. It was called 'The Brave Little Tailor,' I believe."

Murray's mouth movement, acknowledged the offering.

"It would seem that they chose flies as being synonymous with something even a small child could kill with very little effort."

Did the DI now hear a slightly more sinister tone to the gentleman's voice? Or was he just imagining it? Had he just been on the receiving end of slowly delivered, yet well disguised threat? An informal, intimidatory warning? Interesting!

"Maybe your DCI could add that little nugget to her literary arsenal, Inspector."

DI Steven Murray gave a disingenuous shrug and confidently replied…

"I don't know about those brothers, Mr Scott? But I do know that this present situation that we find ourselves in, is exceptionally grim. And like I said previously, it would appear that Reid's men, past and present, both the powerful and the lackey, bullies of all denominations and currencies, are being taken out of circulation for good."

With a somewhat deliberate, embarrassed and rather apologetic manner, the DI could only add. "And unfortunately, sir. You are number one on our suspect list."

Scott immediately went to remonstrate. But Murray held up both hands in a gesture that indicated silence! A text message had come through. It was from Furlong. It detailed everything they had found at Hanna's home and informed the Inspector to: *get back to Leith pronto. Carry out interrogation into Hayes' conduct.* PRONTO was then capitalised and repeated one more time. He got the message.

Why though, he thought, would his DCI feel the need to use the word interrogation? He felt disappointed and rather let down in some way. He knew that Furlong was still settling in, but this was one of their own. Was she not firstly allowed to have her say and be heard? What about the old, *'innocent until proven guilty?'* Was she not entitled to the same courtesy as everyone else? The simple opportunity to offer up a defense? Susan Hayes had been and hopefully will continue to be, a trusted and valued member of his team. Murray instantly decided there and then, that he would have a 'private chat' with her. If needs be, it may very well turn into a formal interview. But there would certainly not be any interrogation. At least not carried out by himself, that was for sure.

Andrew Scott had waited patiently. He peered across at Murray, who without missing a beat, instantly carried on from where he had left off.

"Now, we are not saying you were present at the time of all the killings, sir. However, many believe they have been carried out on your orders."

Scott's eyebrows raised at that.

"Yes, and when I say many," Murray paused. "I mean the whole of Police Scotland, if that helps put it into perspective for you!"

He said no more and a quaint smile of understanding and possibly gratitude, was extended by Andrew Scott. He couldn't quite figure out Steven Murray. But he liked him. Though, he also knew life would be so much easier with him gone and out of the picture.

"I had heard about one or two of the unfortunate deaths, Inspector."

Liar. He was well aware of each and every one of them, Murray suspected.

"A judge and a top lawyer by all accounts. I never even knew they were connected to the imitable Mr Reid. Who would have guessed? How did that work?" Scott added in his usual polite, yet playfully scornful manner.

"There would appear to be several others dead also," Murray stated ruefully. "But if the rumours that are circulating are true, then you obviously don't need me to tell you who, where or when."

The game continued.

"To lose that many key players, would certainly impact on a well-oiled business infrastructure. At the very least, Inspector, it would create a lot of unwanted attention and bad publicity," Scott openly confessed.

He then tugged gallusly at the corner of his tailored waistcoat and pondered slightly. As an insightful afterthought, he continued.

"However, I'm not really sure how familiar 'Bunny' Reid, actually is with the terminology of... *a well-oiled business.*"

Once again Andrew Scott offered his charmingly gracious smile. He combined it with words from an upbringing that exemplified money, class and standards.

"Now Inspector, would there be anything else I can do for you, my good man? Because I simply don't understand how any of this is of any relevance to myself."

Another brief moment of solitude was shared between them. Neither man spoke. Murray pursed his lips and accompanied that facial gesture with a slight nod. For those that knew him - it was a number 34. Indicating the word, 'Really?' The tall so-called businessman, allowed his head to angle slightly. His solid stance, coupled with that simple movement, stated - Impasse! Scott was once again magnanimous.

"Oh, now I get it, Inspector. You fear that you have a suspected gang war on your hands. You think I am trying to railroad Mr Reid and take over his turf. Is that it? Was this visit some sort of polite warning or veiled threat, my good man?"

Scott then thought for a further second, before adding more aggressively, another interesting take on events.

"Or maybe, just maybe, it's Reid himself, who thinks I am out for revenge. That I still have a score to settle in relation to my mother and brother? But why would he think that? When, as you stated earlier, we all know it was Shaun Scullion that was responsible. That he, without a doubt, was the actual individual that carried out the fatal actions."

That may be so, Murray considered. But, both he and Scott knew that Reid gave the order. The Inspector had remained silent throughout Scott's feisty assessment of the current situation that they found themselves in.

"I hear you Mr Scott, and yet I feel inclined to make you aware of just one specific comment that a certain James Baxter Reid shared with me in the last twenty-four hours."

Scott's eyebrows again raised substantially at that. Making their owner appear nearly seven foot tall!

"It's not Scott," he said to me. "I just know, it's not Andrew Scott."

The eyebrows suddenly lowered and began to furtively narrow and retreat. They made Scott question - What was really going on here? Why did he tell me that? What gives?

In a rather baffled and bewildered manner, Murray once again shrugged, held Scott's quizzical look and asked…

"Why would he say that with such certainty, sir? I don't fully understand. Can you help shed some light on it for me? I'm at a loss."

An instant response was offered. Without hesitation, the haulage yard owner stated…

"Maybe he is simply not as stupid, as I gave him credit for!"

Murray struggled to stifle a laugh at that point.

Then as Scott arrogantly put both thumbs into the front serving pockets of his elegant waistcoat, giving the impression of being the 'Lord of the Manor.' Which in many respects he was. He then felt the need to clarify. His response was straightforward in its simplicity.

"Look around you, Inspector." He spoke barely above a whisper. "I didn't achieve this level of success in life by being reckless. If I have an issue with anyone, including a certain Mr Reid. Then I will resolve it when I am good and ready, and it'll probably begin with some low lying fruit."

Low lying fruit? Murray questioned. That was a very specific choice of words. An obscure, yet deeply troubling terminology the Inspector felt.

"However," Andrew Scott then announced in a bold, bright, unsettling manner.

"Seeing as you have been kind enough to share some of Reid's inspired wisdom with myself, maybe I could return the favour. If you would do me the honour of informing 'Bunny,' that when I start out on the path of reprisal, revenge or seeking justice and retribution, he will be the first to know all about it - Trust me! Like you said, Inspector, I like to tell it as it is. So there you have it. There will most definitely, be no sorry, misunderstanding moving forward.

It had been an interesting visit. Murray had hoped, at best, for a temporary peace treaty. But in his own unique way, he seemed to have brokered the exclusive rights to World War Three!

"Now I hope that answers your concerns and you don't feel that you have had a wasted journey, Inspector?"

As Scott turned swiftly on his three inch high cowboy heels, Murray was offered a dismissive and final... "Take care my good man!"

Eighteen

'*Shot down in a blaze of glory. Take me now, but know the truth. That I'm going down in a blaze of glory. Lord, I never drew first, but I drew first blood - I'm the Devil's son, call me young gun.*'

- Bon Jovi

DC Andrew Curry had been told to stay and operate out of the station that morning. He was also informed that his colleague Detective Constable Hayes would be delayed and that his presence would be required later to clarify some points.

At that precise moment the 'Kid' found himself with a pile of dusty old files due for destruction. The in-house shredding machine was plugged in close to the window. As daydreaming went, it was pretty intense. Curry watched as the world drifted by. Birds rested on telephone lines and airplanes left impressive contrails in the sky. A small spider scurried from one side of the window sill to the other. Then as a patrol car bumped and screeched into the car park and he watched some colleagues put final supplies into their minibus, his body froze. Did he just spot 'Hanna' Hayes exit from the back seat of the newly parked vehicle? She had been dressed in black jeans and a casual, blue cotton top. But the fact that she was being closely accompanied by two uniformed PC's was what worried Curry most. What was going on here? Why had he been kept in the dark? Had she been doing undercover work? Who had she been assigned to? What was 'Hanna' seemingly involved in? Surely it had nothing to do with all their ongoing murder investigations? The questions continued to gather in Curry's mind, as his favourite spider leapt with courage from the ledge.

When Steven Murray ventured back outdoors, a strange, slightly peculiar, although distinctly familiar smell filled the Fife air, surrounding Scott's premises. There was no denying it. It was definitely petrol fumes. As Murray walked closer to his sturdy, faithful, yet no longer Swedish built Volvo. He could clearly witness droplets of liquid all over the front bonnet. An excess had formed a small pool at his front passenger wheel. Did the car have a fuel leak he quickly questioned. Not unless the storage tank was located on its roof, *'you clown,'* he instantly answered himself. Although, he needn't have bothered, because the answer was at the rear of his vehicle. It was in the shape of Scott's trusted sidekick. Murray was having none of it.

"What's your problem big boy? Not happy at being told to shove off?"

Murray was relatively mouthy and confident, because there was still a car length between them. However, just at that, 'the mean green blubber machine' held up a tiny, blue plastic object... a cigarette lighter.

"Oh geez!" was uttered in disbelief. "Play the game my good man," Murray tried mimicking Scott's wording, but to no avail. The growing increasingly worried

Inspector, then gambled that the 'Jolly Green Giant' wouldn't set fire to his car whilst within the confines of his bosses yard. But with the odds becoming narrower by the second, he took no chances and threw himself at speed into the driver's seat. An orange flame flickered into life behind him.

"You've got to be kidding me," Murray screamed. "This is not how you go about building relationships."

That last 'Pantomime' line was hollered at the same moment a terrified Steven Murray turned the key, put his foot flat to the accelerator and sped off in search of the nearest car wash. Ironically, probably one staffed with illegals and owned by a certain Mr Andrew Scott. However, in actual fact he had only managed to travel around forty or fifty yards, before he looked back in the mirror to see the large petrol container at the man's feet. Without doubt, he was a prize buffoon. All brawn and no brain. Did he not know the chance he was taking with all that spilled...

The volume of noise and explosion was brief and startling. Murray slammed on his brakes. It was an automatic reaction. Ideally he would want to be a million miles away from any open flame. Witnessing the scene in his rear view mirror, his internal autopilot took over and the Detective Inspector immediately called for an ambulance and fire brigade. The bulky bodyguard's torso was fully alight. Flames and smoke darting high and low. His piercing screams seemed to vibrate and rebound at pace from the white ring-fenced clouds high above the scene. In fairness, Andrew Scott was first in attendance. He had run out with a fire extinguisher and was already operating it at full force. He sprayed determinedly, at least offering his employee a slim chance of survival and hope. Behind a smoked window pane, nervous and profoundly wary, Amanda remained in shock, inside. Astutely, she had chosen to watch the dramatic events unfold from a safe distance.

Within minutes the ambulance crew had arrived and surveyed the scene. They reckoned 'the green mean fighting machine' would survive and literally fight to see another day. The young female paramedic that spoke with Murray commented briefly though, saying…

"He's going to be badly disfigured, Inspector."

He was already one hell of an ugly bloke, so maybe it would be an improvement, Murray thought. However, he decided that in the emotionally sensitive, viral world that we currently inhabit. It was probably best to keep that particular counsel to himself. Ultimately, the Fire Brigade was not even required. By the time they had arrived, the proprietor and Chief Operating Officer, Andrew Scott, had more than adequately dealt with the human torch. Slight burns to his own hands, ruined designer clothing and smoke damaged cowboy boots were offered by way of sacrifice.

On the other hand, his badly injured sidekick would think twice about pulling that particular stunt again, Murray surmised. He had probably used it as a threat to others often in the past without any serious injury to himself whatsoever. Although this time, it would be doubtful if the man were to ever walk upright again, never mind return to the fold in Scott's backroom staff. The DI officially called it as a 'bad accident.'

"No need for extra police or forensics people to be snooping around your property, Mr Scott. We'll not be troubling you further today."

A surprised, yet appreciative, Mr Scott offered. "Much obliged, Inspector. Thank you."

Although, the well bred gangster, couldn't quite figure out why he was being treated so leniently. Normally the boys in blue would have welcomed any opportunity to have searched and scoured his premises. It always seemed par for the course. So how come this man's thinking was so different? Whatever it was, Scott was grateful. The Inspector knew it simply, as reciprocity. So, somewhere in Scott's subconscious, he was indebted to Steven Murray. At some point in the future, he would return the favour.

The DI gave a meagre shrug and walked back toward the area where any remnants of the plastic petrol can that exploded may have been. As expected, most of it was gone. Nearly fully obliterated. However, there appeared to be about two or three minute, tiny pieces of green plastic still smouldering in the debris. Steven Murray with blue nitrile gloves in situ, lifted one particular fragment, the largest. He studied it intensely. His eyesight was not great up close, but he had high hopes that when handed over to Doc Patterson at the lab, it's distinct shape would confirm his suspicions for him. Maybe there was an ulterior motive after all, in excluding Andrew Scott's yard from any further scrutiny. Yes, best kept off the radar at present, the Detective Inspector had concluded.

With one set of suspicions to be confirmed later, his phone pinged and a further text from DCI Furlong stated: *We need you back here now! More concealed items, including a set of keys and a burner phone were also found wrapped and hidden. Did I mention earlier, she had a badly scorched motorcycle in her garage! Where are you?*

After having just spoken with the posh Glaswegian businessman, Murray agreed wholeheartedly with 'Bunny' Reid. These killings had nothing to do with Andrew Scott. The police officer was confident of that. It certainly was a strange alliance - both of them in agreement on something. But in his often crazy, mixed-up, kaleidoscopic mind, Steven Murray was adamant that there was most definitely, something else at play here. For he also agreed with Scott, about the fact that this wasn't about a turf war. It wasn't about ruining Reid's daily business operations, or gratifying revenge attacks for the death of the Fife crime lord's mother and mentally deranged, thug of a brother. There was just something more he felt.

Murray was confident that all of those other events will eventually be avenged by Scott, but like he said directly to the Inspector - That will be within his own preferred time frame. It will occur when he is good and ready, and not before. Murray inhaled, put a finger to his mouth and sighed. So what was it all about then? Maybe, just maybe, one of the most successful outlaws in the west, did have some revealing answers after all.

Murray's fumbling fingers finished typing. His curt message read: *On my way. Have Kerr meet me there. Make sure that Hayes speaks to no one but me!*

Nineteen

'I know now where I'm going to. Not to lose now but to win. Tell me, how do I begin? I have a dream, a silver dream machine.'

- David Essex

'Hanna' Hayes was quietly seething. She had been detained for fully ninety minutes. When Furlong had eventually returned to the station, exactly one hour after Susan Hayes. She briefly popped into the interview room and told her to be patient and that currently, her DI wanted to keep things off the record. However, either way, she had no option but to suspend her at present.

"Your trusted Inspector will explain everything to you in due course. He assured me, just a few minutes ago, that he is on his way. He should have been here by now, though."

Through gritted teeth, Hayes managed a hint of a smile and a... "Thank you Ma'am."

As Furlong went to exit the room, she looked back over her shoulder, smiled and with a look of intrigue stated.

"Oh, just one more thing DC Hayes. I would have never taken you as a biker."

"It takes all sorts. *You walk three miles every day!*" 'Hanna' offered. Brusque and vague.

Even 'Ma'am,' had been dropped from that curt reply. Although she must have thought better of it, because two seconds later, she piped up… "I've never used it in months."

"Ma'am," was then respectfully added to that response.

A further quarter of an hour passed before a gentle squeak signalled movement at the door handle once again.

"Afternoon, young lady." The familiar voice continued with, "It looks like we find ourselves in a bit of a pickle. A bind. An embarrassing predicament to say the least."

"We?" 'Hanna,' exclaimed frustratedly. "I don't see any royal WE, sir, in this situation so far. And you were supposed to have been here an hour ago. Where have you been? Where were you? What can you tell me?"

Murray hesitated. With a cheeky twinkle in his eye, he proffered…

"Where I was, 'Hanna,' things got a bit heated. It's best that is all you know at present."

"Because, I can no longer be trusted?"

Steven Murray gave a considered nod. It was an undeniable number 4, which simply asked - 'Was that a statement or a question?'

"Like I said, a sticky wicket, a difficult spot, a…"

"Yes, yes, yes, I get it," Hayes interrupted his proper English articulation class! "I'm screwed! So what's next? What do I do, sir?"

"What do WE do? 'Hanna.' What do WE do? Firstly, WE clear this mess up, that is what WE do. I mean that is what WE do on a daily basis for others, for everyone else. So for you, a long standing member of our team, one that I still trust implicitly," he added deliberately. "It should be no different. WE clear up the mess. WE separate the fact from the fiction, the wheat from the chaff, the relevant from the irrelevant and WE start at the very beginning, as Mary Poppins would say!"

"Possibly, Maria? Sir. The Sound of Music, not Mary Poppins."

"Tomatoe - Tomato," Murray scoffed. "Do you want my help or not?"

Hayes smiled and shook her head in dismay. This man was often unconventional. But he was also great. He got results and of course she wanted him onboard.

"So over to you, Susan." Confidently announced. "And remember, you are not under caution. WE are just having an informal chat."

"An informal chat?" Hayes replied in astonishment. "Sir, I opened my door this morning, to my DCI and a full strength search team. I have no idea what is going on. What I have even been accused of. Honestly, where do I start?"

"My sincere apologies, 'Hanna.' I was led to believe that you had spoken to DCI Furlong and that she had brought you up to speed with what we had found," he lied admirably.

"She only asked me about my motorcycling habits," Hayes clarified dryly, shaking her head.

At that point, Murray felt the need for another song. How he loved his music. It inspired him. He took solace from it. He loved to randomly throw out an obscure lyric. It could occasionally be a random lyric.

The standing joke amongst his team was that he only knew the major line or two of any given song. Possibly he could do the chorus, but any more than that and you'd be stretching it. Interestingly though, when he eventually sang, it was almost always related to his train of thought. In more than one instance the music or in particular the song lyrics had helped him recognise, identify and solve the case. So it was always worth listening to the words. That was, assuming he'd got them correct to begin with!

Today, firstly, he went with a gentle reggae like whistle. Then his shoulders began to sway as the words surfaced… *"Suzanne beware of the devil, don't let him spoil your heart. Suzanne beware of the devil, don't let him pull us apart… don't let him pull us apart,"* Murray faded off on that line.

Susan Hayes nodded. She got it. Let's stay united in this. Don't let the temptation to lie get the better of you. She had this. Barbra Furlong looked on with great interest from the darkened interior of the room on the other side of the one-way mirror. Not quite so sure, that she got any of it.

"Moral and Union support," ventured a sturdy third voice, as the door squeaked open once again, to signal the arrival of ADI Sandra Kerr.

"Don't mind, if I do!" 'Hanna' stated with a grateful smile.

It may have sounded grammatically incorrect, but Murray got the gist of it. She was happy for another familiar face. Another to be in attendance, that she thought would be on her side. It made her feel more relaxed and possibly would even help her lower her guard somewhat. Was her guard required to be lowered? Was that why her friendly DI, had asked 'Sandy' to give him two minutes, before she came in and joined them?

Murray braced himself. "Susan, sadly this is becoming more serious by the minute. They uncovered a host of items in your lock-up. On the surface, they link you with the murders."

"What!" Hayes exclaimed. "That can't be, I don't have anything that…"

"Your motorbike, 'Hanna,' and that is just for starters."

"But like I said to the DCI, I hardly even use it these days!"

"Well someone used it. Did you know it was all scorched?"

Hayes remained silent and just shook her head continually.

"The old Judge was blown to pieces 'Hanna.' Wiring and a burner phone containing Menzies' ex-directory phone number listed on it were also found. Come to think of it, the contact details for The Doctors bar and the lawyer Ross Stevenson were contained on it also. That does not look good."

"But that is exactly all it is, sir. Superficial and on the surface."

In sheer exasperation, Hayes threw up her hands. Murray flicked open his own phone, tapped a couple of buttons and scrolled up and down a little.

"What a change from the old days, eh?" He stated. "All our fancy new gadgetry and technology. So much better."

Yet deep down, he struggled greatly when often trying to implement it. Susan Hayes remained silent. What was this self confessed technophobe doing?

"Let's take a look at the rest of this list shall we?"

He pushed across his phone, so that the poor woman could read the text for herself. *Motorcycle; Bikers boots and helmet; Plastic restraints; Burner phone; Bloodied overalls; Stanley knife; Roll of cling film; Box of black and white photographs; Large syringe and as yet, an unidentified set of keys.*

The scroll of items seemed never ending. It was intensive. However, lots of checks and analysis would need to be done of course. But the female officer may well have a much lengthier wait to resolve her 'bind,' as things currently stand. Than had first been previously thought.

His friend felt nauseous. Her stomach churned at this cruel twist of events. The detective was in her early forties. Forty-three to be precise. She had served fully for eighteen years. She had a healthy pension and retirement pot to look forward to. This just didn't make any sense. Her normally cheerful, bright hazel eyes, today offered a more reflective, subdued and resigned look. A sense of tiredness, an uneasy acceptance of what life had conjured up and thrown randomly her way in recent times. The dazzling, glowing embers of a fire that once burned so brightly back in those early years, had gradually been gently extinguished over time. Now it has been replaced with an understated contentment and acceptance of life. She had been generally happy serving as a Police Constable all these years. She had never gone in search of a promotion. She thoroughly enjoyed her role supporting, correlating and training. She never wanted to be in charge. She had no burning desire for that responsibility and the extra baggage it brought with it. This long serving officer was more than satisfied with what she had achieved. She, like her boss, was highly thought of and well regarded by all. In the main, that was because 'Hanna' Hayes was firm, but fair. She knew the ropes and was a straight talking, solid, dependable individual. One, more than capable of sorting out the valuable from the worthless.

After several years at college, she had worked in the advertising world briefly, before joining the Constabulary at the tender age of twenty-five. Now the unique strength that she had tried so hard to build up, garnish and foster over nearly two full decades was being eroded. Gradually piece by tiny piece, her reputation and character, were not only being called into question, but being torn down rapidly and destroyed forever.

Literally only yards away from his colleague, 'Kid' Curry had eventually ventured downstairs to the interview suite. When he had witnessed his partner earlier enter in through the back door to the station with her two minders in tow, he had wanted to go down immediately. However, more experienced fellow officers had persuaded him otherwise. Frustrated at his inability to help, he had tried to placate himself by sitting for a few moments to reflect on what he really knew about this woman. A woman that he trusted with his life each day.

At average female height, stocky and slightly overweight, Detective Constable Susan Hayes always maintained a pearly white smile. She had most certainly never been a so-called 'dolly bird.' There was no fake tan, extended lashes or pretentious, overly long fingernails. Hayes was secure and content with the public image that she portrayed to the wider world. She had nothing to hide. At least that was how it had always appeared to her colleague and co-worker, these past two years.

Andrew Curry had been fresh out of police training when he began his probationary period alongside a 41 year old female Police Officer. At that time she already had a full decade and a half of experience behind her. Her partner had noticed early on, that she never spoke much about her own personal past or upbringing. As a young, inexperienced, yet well mannered police officer, Drew Curry was never going to broach the subject. So he had always stayed well clear and it was never an issue. In fairness to DC Susan Hayes, she in turn had never inquired about his home life, unless he himself had opened the door on the subject. The 'Kid' had naturally assumed that she simply liked to keep her personal life separate from work.

Today though, he was now questioning that assumption. It was the late, tainted DCI Keith Brown that first called her, 'Hanna.' It was short for Hannibal. It came from the 1970's TV show that Brown had grown up with as a boy: 'Alias Smith and Jones.' It was an imported American programme, where the two lead characters were lovable cowboy outlaws. They went by the names of Kid Curry and Hannibal Hayes. Next time Andrew Curry was interviewed by the DCI, his Chief Inspector referenced him as 'Kid' and the new pairing of Hayes and Curry was born and officially sanctioned.

As Drew Curry sat pondering all the angles. He was now privately convinced that his partner was being investigated over this series of vicious and alarming murders. What else could it be? He couldn't quite get his head around it. There was no way that 'Hanna' could ever do this. Or be involved in anything to do with it. It was impossible. It was preposterous and silly, he had thought to himself. Not even worthy of consideration. But sadly, that was all he could think about, as he sat impatiently waiting to be called to help out with their enquiries. Again, he re-emphasized to himself that his trusted colleague wasn't like that. Or was she? There it was! He had given in. He had briefly thought about the other side of the coin. He then suddenly began to quickly recall the many occasions, scenarios and events where he had witnessed Susan Hayes instantly draw upon her training and expertise. Images of suspects being dealt with uncompromisingly came vividly to Curry's mind. Prisoners being crudely handcuffed, thrown against walls and or hastily manhandled and taken down to the ground. Never without good reason or excessive force it must be said. Again though, he paused to insert a… Or was it?

DI Murray got the best out of his team members, there was no doubt about that. Curry and his fellow professionals understood and appreciated it. Susan

Hayes was no different. She had been well trained and would not hesitate if confronted with a challenge, either verbal or physical. She had become a master of her craft. She was an exemplary example of an experienced, long standing police officer. Yet persistently niggling at the back of his mind, was her continued reluctance to ever talk about her background and presently, that concerned him greatly.

Unfortunately the more DC Andrew Curry dwelt on his friend's abilities, he began to fully realise one thing. For sure, Susan 'Hannibal' Hayes was absolutely more than capable of having the skill and the stomach to carry out those heinous, unprovoked attacks. Thankfully - He just didn't believe that she did.

Twenty

'Feel the rain like an English summer. Hear the notes from a distant song. Stepping out from a backdrop poster, wishing life wouldn't be so long. Ah-ah, we fade to grey. Ah-ah, we fade to grey.'

- Visage

By now DCI Furlong had witnessed Curry, 'loitering with intent' in the corridor. What that looked like, she was confident even he didn't know! She quickly instructed him that his presence would be required soon. But that currently DC Hayes was helping Murray and Kerr with some sensitive enquiries. She then encouraged him to meet up for a while with DC Hanlon in the canteen, and wait there until he was called.

With a disappointed and somewhat frustrated sigh, Drew Curry ran his fingers uneasily through his greasy hair. He scratched relentlessly and nervously at his forehead and ultimately resigned himself to obeying his Chief Inspector's counsel. Within thirty seconds, he took the elevator to the appropriate floor and found himself instantly following the wafting smell of cooked food. An aroma that lingered in the old sandstone corridors from morn until eve. There, sat two tables in from the doorway, was 'Sherlock.' He had only just returned with Sandra Kerr from the Judge's five acre countryside retreat. Currently, grasped tightly in his hand was a cheap, disposable ballpoint pen. He had never yet taken up Steven Murray's example - A quality pen, purchased and placed in all his suit jacket pockets. 'An invaluable addition to every detective's armour,' the Inspector would often quote. OCD, many others simply thought. However, whatever its merits, Joe Hanlon was using this cheaper alternative to clean out the deep, rubber soles on his fashionably green wellies! The lady serving the food at the hatch had scowled at him on more than one occasion in the last five minutes. In fairness to Hanlon, he had then wisely put a large supermarket 'Bag for Life,' down below his feet. Its sole aim was to catch the remnants of soil or stones that had taken route in his rubberised allotment.

"I must have walked easily two miles backwards and forwards around that estate," Joe Hanlon said, with exhaustion in his voice. His arm gesture invited Curry to take a seat, as he determinedly dug deeper and proceeded to scrape and scratch more unknown muck, dirt and grime onto the canvas bag below.

"No plastic bootees on?" Curry queried. "How come?"

"Oh no, Drew, I had them and the suit on previously. All throughout my investigations inside the badly demolished home and even outside, where we followed the trail of the blast into the front lawn and gardens."

'Kid' Curry nodded. But the tilt of his head, the squint of his lips and one closed eye, suggested he was even more dumbfounded.

"This was from later on," Hanlon enlightened him. "From when I went to inspect the paths, yards and enclosures at the rear of the main building on my own."

Yet again, another couple of inches of ground-in ash and grit were deposited. Although by now, 'Kid' Curry could not contain himself any longer. He had no real interest in his damned boots.

"What's the score with, 'Hanna,' Joe?" He blurted out nervously. "She was escorted under police guard and is now being questioned privately by the Inspector and ADI Kerr? You must be in the loop. You must know what is going on."

"But, I don't," 'Sherlock' said calmly. "Sorry."

Joseph Hanlon then weighed up Andrew Curry.

The two men were brought up on different sides of the tracks and although colleagues, they never mixed socially. Joe knew that his fellow Constable had gone through an emotional break up in the last six months. It was a separation that had in turn impacted his work. A dishevelled appearance, tardiness with his timekeeping, coupled with heavy drinking had all taken their toll. However, in recent months Drew certainly seemed well on his way to being back to his normal self. 'Sherlock' suspected this had more to do with a certain DI, other than solely the 'Kid' himself.

Again Hanlon repeated, "I honestly don't know."

Curry sat silent and still.

"But I do know one thing." Hanlon then gave a considered pause before continuing.

"Firstly though, can I ask you something, Drew?"

"Of course. Anything. Fire away."

"Well it's quite simple actually. Has Detective Inspector Murray ever done the dirty on you?"

Curry thought for a brief second. Was this some sort of underhand move? What did Joe Hanlon think he would say? Had he previous knowledge about something? How was this supposed to play out? Was he possibly being recorded, monitored or watched? Or had he himself, just become totally paranoid?

"It's an easy question, Andrew. I didn't think you would struggle with it. I'm not trying to trick you."

Hanlon offered it once again, this time with an added caveat.

"Has Steven Murray ever sold you down the river? Or has he always had your back?"

"He's always been there for me." The 'Kid' answered swiftly, without any hesitation or delay.

"So why would you question him being in there with your partner? Wouldn't you think he was by far, the best man for the job? Who else would you rather have looking out for her?"

Joe Hanlon left that question hanging. He really wanted it to sink in and resonate with his colleague. He had wanted that knowledge to reassure and convince him. 'Sherlock' had witnessed his mentor do this on numerous occasions and it seemed to work for him. So he was sure it was worth a try.

Two mugs were then raised to parched lips. One contained coffee - That one was filled to the brim. The other, tea. It sat at the half empty mark. Suddenly, after a brief two second lull in the conversation, a volcanic eruption of dark liquid was sputtered out from Andrew

Curry's mouth. His shirt, trousers and the surrounding floor at his feet were drenched. His anxious, animated stare however, never flinched from it's spot. It was fixed firmly at the base of Hanlon's chair. His alarm and immediate attention was fully focused on the small mound of debris that had been scraped from 'Sherlock's olive green wellington boots.

Heads turned quickly. Faces lifted from conversations. What was going on? Security issues were always at the forefront of people's minds and thoughts in any aged police station. The 'Kid' immediately tried to put everyone at ease and reassure them. He spoke clearly and loudly.

"Nothing to be worried about, folks. But let's just try and remain still until I deal with a potential piece of vital evidence."

His calm, assertive manner was impressive. Murray would have been pleased with him. Hanlon on the other hand was just keen to find out what all the fuss was about and had remained statuesque for the past ten seconds. Andrew Curry slowly lifted a plastic teaspoon from the table. A fresh napkin was used to wipe it dry again. He carefully crouched down at Hanlon's feet and extended a nervous arm toward the small piece of earth that had been removed unwittingly from Judge Menzies' estate. The flexible, white utensil then gently made its way under the surface, of what on first sighting, was a tiny, minuscule item, shaped like a rugby ball. The 'Kid' scooped up the oval shape and placed it gingerly onto a spare napkin. Joe Hanlon had placed it out into the centre of their table. It rolled and wobbled once or twice, before gradually coming to rest and sitting perfectly still. Both men gave each other an intense stare and never blinked. Which in itself was ironic. Given that positioned carefully between them… was a detached human eyeball.

Unaware of those eye opening scenes going on only yards from their intimate discussions, Murray had encouraged 'Hanna' to furnish him with some further knowledge regarding her teenage years growing up.

"My teenage years? Of what relevance are they?" Hayes was sharp and abrupt.

"I know it was a while ago, 'Hanna,'"

Hayes rebuked him immediately for that comment, with an insolent stare. A sensitive nerve had obviously been touched.

Murray rolled his eyes like a winning fruit machine, indicating that he still did humour.

"Well, I need you to have a little faith in me. Remember, Constable you are not under caution. But run with me here. Help me out."

She seemed to consider his words for a second or two, before coming to a decision. Begrudgingly, she began to reminisce.

"During my High School years I studied most of the time. I was always reading, revising and preparing for tests and exams. My parents had split up. I was being brought up by my father."

Her DI smiled and offered a positive dip of his chin. "Go on," he said. "Anything else you think may be helpful?"

"None of it's been helpful so far," Hayes protested. "I don't really see what you think you'll learn from this?"

"Carry on 'Hanna,'" Murray encouraged. "What did your father do? Was he an influence on you?"

"This is a waste of time. And with respect sir, I suspect, you of all people, already know what my father did."

Kerr turned her attention momentarily to her boss. What did she not know? What hadn't he told her about Susan Hayes? The Inspector knowingly ignored her pleading eyes.

"Please trust me, Constable." Murray said sharply. He now felt the need to pull rank and firm up his tone.

"He was a nightclub manager, if you must know. In fact, he supervised the running of three clubs, altogether."

A nightclub manager, Kerr thought. That wasn't so unusual.

"Three establishments?" Steven Murray exclaimed. He was intrigued. "How did he manage that? Actually, do you possibly remember the name of the clubs?"

"It was thirty years ago sir, and like I said I was a swot. I was only interested in getting good grades and passing my exams. So no, I don't recall their names."

She hesitated, as if afraid. Before continuing on her nostalgic trip down memory lane.

"But I do recall that we travelled from club to club in the back of a vehicle during those busy academic years. I was picked up directly from school and we would then drive on to whichever location my father was based in that evening."

"And your schoolwork?"

"My homework, Inspector. Was normally carried out in whichever dark, dreary and thinking retrospectively, sleazy, smoke filled room was available and free."

"You mentioned that your parents were separated. What role did your mother play?"

"None!" 'Hanna' said dismissively. She had noticeably grown tired of this line of questioning. "Inspector with all due res…"

"We are nearly done, Constable," Murray interrupted, before adding, "And you have been a great help."

That was exactly what she had been afraid of. She knew that her DI was capable of going on a relatively innocent fishing expedition. One where most people in the world would catch two pilchards, a red herring and a week long cold. But no, not him. Not Detective Inspector flamin' Murray. He, on the other hand, would eventually land a basketful of delicious fresh salmon!

What had she said? How was it of any use whatsoever? He was just getting into her mind. Who was he kidding? And surely, if he was really trying to help, would he and Kerr not be out there proving her innocence? Currently, she thought she was definitely going to be made the official scapegoat and didn't see much light at the end of this particular tunnel.

"Your mother?" The Inspector reminded her.

Susan Hayes revealed that her mother had left the family home when she had discovered her husband's gangland connections. Sandra Kerr recoiled slightly at the unexpected revelation. Steven Murray - not so much. So 'Hanna' was absolutely correct Kerr guessed.

Steven Murray was acutely aware of her father's background. Interesting.

As Hayes continued to speak about her mother, it became blatantly obvious that the woman had integrity and standards, and was most probably a good person in the eyes of the world. Even the Detective Inspector reckoned that she had no other viable way of financially supporting her young daughter at that stage in her life, and was more or less emotionally bullied into leaving her in the care of her philandering father. Murray further suspected that his daughter was being rather kind to him with the *'Cheeky Chappy,'* style description. Hayes was in full flow, however. Cajoled by a few more interesting and relevant questions from both Kerr and Murray. She spoke for a further twenty minutes.

The Inspector had observed her carefully throughout the delivered monologue. Light and shade, he thought. Definitely light and shade. There were elements of her story that made her come alive. That alluded to great dreams, goals and aspirations for the future. Aspects that had notably enriched and brightened her life at that time. It was during the times when she spoke about studying, homework, academia and school in general that she lit up. Other chapters in her upbringing that she had shared and related, carried a rather more intense darkness. Shades of her young life that she gave the impression that she would have rather forgotten. Grubby, grey areas that Murray suspected that she had wished she'd never experienced in the first place. Those surfaced mostly, when she spoke about taxi rides, night clubs and her low-life, part-time father.

During her sentimental teenage commentary, Susan Hayes stated that her life had changed forever back then. She had never elaborated any further on that comment, or made it more specific. Except to say that she had been badly scarred. At that moment in time, her Inspector had no desire to pursue it further. Although he was now mindful and fully aware of it and would store it away safely for future potential use. He did also immediately send 'Ally' Coulter a quick text. It was a solitary, single line enquiry that had come to mind. One straightforward question that he was desperately keen to have answered.

His long term, retired buddy had been unable to meet with him personally over the past couple of days. *'Too busy'* was all his texts said. Obviously his Private Investigator work must have been flourishing, because his ex-colleague seemed to have had a very busy appointment book over the past 48 hours. Good on you, 'Ally,' Murray thought as he pressed send. Further thoughts serenaded him like - I know I can rely on him to provide an answer for me by the end of the day and it will certainly save me time going through official police channels. Especially as you never know who may be presently monitoring those official channels, according to DCI Furlong's recent internal concerns. Then a firm knock on the door sent all those previous thoughts scurrying for cover. The bang on the door had preceded the pretty face of a smiling WPC.

"It's the T'inker, sir," she said brightly. "Doctor Patterson. He says he has something that you will want to learn straightaway."

"What is so important, Constable?" 'Sandy' asked.

"Please tell us? Or is he on the phone?" Murray questioned. "Have you got a copy of the information? What?"

She smiled innocently. "No, he is actually out here in the corridor, sir. He just needed someone brave enough to interrupt you. It would appear that I was the only one fool enough to volunteer!"

"Thank you, Constable." Sandra Kerr responded and gestured for her to close the door.

Murray had been left open-mouthed. Gobsmacked even, that he was thought of as so unapproachable.

"Let's take a break there 'Hanna' and see if the Doc is able to help us clear some things up. Oh, and I'm going to have a short chat with DC Curry before I come back through."

Again, 'Hanna' reckoned, if this was as informal as they made out, then why not say, 'The Kid' or Drew? Why his official rank? Everything was going haywire. She was second guessing everyone's actions, thoughts and deeds. She was certainly not under arrest, but it felt like just a matter of time.

"Let's go and get a bite to eat together," 'Sandy' said to her.

On my own was never going to be listed as an option either, Hayes surmised. And off they both went to the canteen. They walked past DI Murray and Doc Patterson. Both of whom by this point were already deep in conversation. Sandra Kerr mouthed the word, 'canteen,' to Steven Murray and pointed upward. It was located on the second floor. She instantly received a visual thumbs up from the DI as confirmation of the message being received. However, when the lift doors opened seconds later, the whole eating area had been sealed off. It looked very much to Kerr - that members of the Forensics team, Hanlon and Andrew Curry were all heavily engaged in the mix, one way or another. Hayes and Kerr quickly retreated back into the elevator before they got embroiled in anything and went to inform their Inspector that DC Curry may be a while.

Twenty One

'Why does it feel like night today? Something in the air's not right today. Why am I so uptight today? Paranoia's all I got left.'

- Linkin Park

Doctor Thomas Patterson had informed Murray that there had been minuscule traces of a coloured metallic substance found on the inside rim of the baseball cap retrieved from his Constable's garage.

"I was able to test it at t'e scene, Steven."

"So what is it when it's at home then, Doc?" Murray asked sternly.

The Inspector would normally always have a bit of banter with Patterson and his playful Irish accent. But today there was no playful fun with t'istle, t'anks and t'ats amore!

"It is a biodegradable glitter made from eucalyptus tree extract," the Doc stated. "It's metalized with aluminium and can be coloured. Most eco-scientists will tell you t'at it is 40% softer and more delicate on t'e skin t'an conventional glitter and it decomposes in soil or water."

"So ideally worn by someone hell bent on saving the planet then, Doc?"

The 'T'inker,' gently pursed his lips and nodded in agreement. His smooth Irish lilt more prevalent than ever.

"T'at would t'ertainly t'um t'em up, Steven," he smiled.

The Detective Inspector knew exactly one person, that would describe to a tee. However, she was currently on the run from the police. The glitter was what had apparently given her away before. So she knew full well that Steven Murray would discover it and hopefully come to a conclusion. The conclusion being that, this wasn't so much a clue, but was indeed, a very important tip-off!

"T'anks Doc. I t'ink t'is will be of great t'ignificance."

The Doc smiled and shook his head. Murray really just couldn't help himself.

"You do?" Patterson asked with genuine scepticism.

"Oh, I really do Tom! I have no idea exactly how yet. But I'm fully confident that I now know who wore it and I trust it will be helpful in a major way."

"I t'ought it might be. Just like the last time," Patterson remarked.

Then he offered a hand gesture that intimated, he would say no more.

Jayne Golden's background may well all be false. But Murray wondered why she would be involved at all. And what then, was her real story? What part did she ultimately play in the bigger picture? How had she managed to become entangled in yet another web of deadly deceit and danger? Recently she was wanted in connection with the people trafficking. So why would she risk everything and come back out of hiding now?

Then it dawned on him - No way! It couldn't have been, could it?

He thought back a few weeks. He reflected upon that solemn day at the church. He fast forwarded and replayed edited highlights in his mind. He rewound, paused and finally pushed play again. A lump came to his throat.

"It was, wasn't it?" He mumbled aloud.

His voice grew in confidence. The clarity of the stilled image in his mind had become crystal clear.

"It was her at the funeral. The woman in the red hat. He remembered that there was an impressive ribbon tied around it. A brightly coloured ribbon. In fact it was a *'Golden'* ribbon!"

At that precise second, Murray must have hit the pause button again. Everything stopped. Including his heart momentarily it felt like. 'Doc' Patterson was still present. He had been privy to the mental recognition and accompanying dialogue, but said nothing. Even although, he also would now have most certainly accepted that there must be a definite link with that elusive femme fatale. A link that if that mysterious and seductive woman was involved in, must be highly valuable and most probably extremely dangerous!

Straightaway the Inspector text Kerr: *Get Hayes back in the room and you track down Jayne Golden. SHE IS BACK!* Some female help and thinking was required on this, Murray had decided. That was inevitable. Then right on cue, the lift door reopened. As Murray raised his head, slightly mystified, he watched both his officers make their way back into the very room that they had just vacated five minutes previously. In turn, he was equally surprised to see that the T'inker was still there by his side.

"Sorry, Doc. I thought you were gone and that we were finished."

Patterson hesitated slightly. He then made the age old side movement of the eyes, coupled with the head tilt. Both together indicated he wanted Murray to step over and talk privately. 'Can I have a quiet word?' Would have worked equally as well, the Inspector smugly thought. Especially spoken in Tom Patterson's sparkling Irish brogue and without the need to arouse everyone's suspicions in the corridor with the cloak and dagger stuff.

"You told me a few weeks ago t'at you shared some of your back story with DCI Furlong."

Murray nodded tentatively. He remembered that he had deliberately left out the part about actually having romantic leanings toward his immediate superior.

"Did she perchance share any of her recent, intimate back story with yourself?"

The Inspector stood bolt upright. He looked seriously concerned. It wasn't like his friend to invade people's personal space without good reason.

"Is she alright, Doc? What is up with her? How can I help?" All three questions were rattled off, in what seemed like a tenth of a second.

"Calm yourself, Steven. Sure she is fine, Barbra Furlong is fine. It is just t'at I t'ought if you had opened up to her, certain memories triggered may have made her reciprocate."

"You mean about my Bipolar?" A heavy sigh of realisation then interrupted his comments. Murray was becoming agitated. "You mean she suffers from serious depression, Doc?"

"You know, I cannot and would not talk to you about someone's PERSONAL medical condition."

Heavy emphasis on personal. Murray took the hint. So a close family member or loved one. But how would The T'inker even find out, unless…

"You said recent Doc. Were you involved in a case that affected her? That brought this to your mind? Why pull me aside if you are not going to include me?"

"It was about a year or so ago Steve. Before t'e demise of Keith Brown and before she joined your team. She was still in North Berwick at t'e time. T'e old derelict farmhouse in Pencaitland. T'ere had been…"

"A suicide!" Murray stated strongly. "I remember it. DS Kerr covered it. But 'Sandy' said there was nothing suspicious about it."

"Oh and she was spot on, it was a definite suicide. T'e man had hung himself right enough. T'ere was no foul play, whatsoever. However…"

The pathologist left a deliberate pause.

"Who was he? I don't remember his name."

Patterson remained sombre and silent.

"Was he Barbra's father, her husband, her lover even? For goodness sake, help me here Doc. Shoot me or put me out of my misery."

His words were spoken with great urgency, a genuine need to know and real concern. His friend had also taken a mental note, that that was the first time he had heard the Inspector refer to his senior officer as Barbra. Not something he would have done lightly.

So the Doc, relented slightly. "Dennis 'Denny' Furlong was in fact her younger brother, Steven. Married less t'an five years at t'e time. T'ey had two tiny angels under t'e age of t'ree. He held down a respectable job, and everyt'ing in their garden appeared rosy. T'ere had been no signs, no indication t'at he was unhappy. Nothing at all. He had left a note for his wife at t'eir marital home and one for his sister in his car at t'e scene."

"I had no idea. We never got wind of this, Doc."

"Which is t'e way it should be, Inspector.

"Agreed." Murray nodded. A definite number 19. The single figure tears that now lay seeking solace and comfort on his cheek bones, beckoned the question - 'Why the hell am I still doing this job?'

Grateful for the heads up, but now wholly unsure what to do with it. Detective Inspector Steven Murray walked dejectedly into the other interview room. It was there that young DC Andrew Curry had been patiently waiting. On leaving later though, he was now more determined than ever to have an evening, without his 'black dog' as company. One that involved no rope, stool, high wooden beams, or the crashing of cars! One where there would be no late night driving with the intention of finding a suitable brick wall! But an invaluable night to reflect on the good things in life. The many blessings, that he was lucky enough to enjoy and the wonderful memories that he should cling too. Especially if he had a desire to make hundreds, if not thousands more of them in the future.

Firstly though - How could he save the faltering career of Susan Hayes?

Twenty Two

'I ran away today. Ran from the noise, ran away. Don't wanna go back to that place, but don't have no choice, no way. It ain't easy growing up in World War Three.'

- Pink

After giving his statement alongside Joe Hanlon, with regards to the gatecrashing 'eyeball' at the canteen, 'Kid' Curry met up with his Detective Inspector before Murray re-engaged in discussions with 'Hanna.'

 Steven Murray's experienced and recently fading gut, told him that it would be beneficial. But rather than in a formal interview setting, where he would normally search and probe for information on his partner. He thought he would share with 'The Kid' some important facts that would most definitely come up when he next met up with 'Hanna.' And by the time that particular chat with Susan Hayes was over, he needed and expected Detective Constable Curry to have carried out an interesting and productive, fact finding mission of his own.

"So you think Harry Hayes got off on a technicality then, sir?"

"I don't know for sure, 'Drew. Though, usually with *'Not Proven'* verdicts that is more often the case. Ultimately though, that is where you come in. Because

'Hanna' has not mentioned this yet. She has not spoken about her father in any depth. But I desperately need you to give 'Sherlock' a run for his money when it comes to unearthing things today. Borrow all his various helmets for this one."

Steven Murray was loud and passionate.

"Put on his explorer's hat and dig as deep and as fast and as furiously, as you possibly can Constable."

All the 'Kid' heard was, that it had a competing element to it and he was in. He liked competitive sports. Murray was giving him a real opportunity here to prove his worth. He knew that Joe Hanlon was fully deserving of 'Sherlock.' But 'Kid' Curry was keen to earn his stripes and receive a proper nickname. One that got you respect amongst your peers. An honest-to-goodness name that attested to your talents and abilities. In his relatively short time in the force, the Constable had noticed that it normally went one of three ways regarding tags and pet names.

Firstly, like Murray, you never had one.

Secondly, it had been well earned and like Hanlon's deserved, 'Sherlock.' It elevated you and gave you a certain gravitas.

Then of course, there was the third and final option. The one he was the proud owner of currently. A dismissive moniker. An overtly loving terminology that either made fun of you or was cute, cuddly and affectionate. Certainly Curry was well aware that his, was the latter of those two descriptions and fortunately, not like their newest team member, Detective Sergeant Linn. Because his, was most definitely the former. Most people thought that his 'Baldy' nickname was simply a play on the fact that instead of being *'as bald as a coot'* up top, he actually had a full head of blonde hair. In reality, that was not the case. After chatting with him recently in the canteen, DC Curry had discovered that his Sergeant's actual Christian name was Mitchell, and although people normally referred to him as Mitch, that forename is where the true identity of his term of endearment came from. It referred to the 'bald' tread on a tyre. When ran together, Mitchell Linn soon became 'Michelin' - and so 'Baldy' was spawned by his ever kindly and considerate colleagues at his old station. To lose his friendly, 'Kid,' label and earn a more self respecting nickname, Andrew Curry would have to go some. Because with the surname Curry, he was certainly asking to be shot down in flames!

Murray shared with him his considerations on the case......

"I believe Harry Hayes had carried out a contract killing on behalf of Kenny Dixon. From thereon he had no chance. KD owed him and initially by way of payment, reward, call it what you may. He was given three established clubs from the crime lord's Edinburgh empire to look after and manage. It was guaranteed, steady work. No doubt he was well compensated both financially and in kind. But I suspect his limited parenting skills, if he ever had any in the first place, were put on the back burner indefinitely and his daughter's upbringing suffered somewhat to say the least."

Curry was all ears. Trying desperately to absorb everything that his Inspector had told him. Murray was even angry at the thought of the life that man had immersed his impressionable daughter into back then. All for the prestige, greed and power. That's what the whole seedy life of organised crime is all about. Harold George Hayes would have been no different. He would have had visions, or more likely in his case, great delusions of grandeur. Dreams of moving up the pecking order, becoming a trusted right hand man and eventually taking over the world. A little bit like the hundreds of thousands of budding actresses throughout the planet. Each one innocently auditioning to be the next Julia Roberts, whilst sadly plying their trade night after night, in some sleazy dance hall, pub or gentlemen's club.

"Eventually," Murray continued, "Harry Hayes, himself, was found murdered."

Curry's mouth fell open, but silence. He was gobsmacked. He had no idea that his partner's upbringing was one extra long, Scottish edition of *'Taggart meets the Godfather.'* No wonder, as a serving police officer, she did not want to discuss her past.

"Fair play to him," Murray continued. "He did manage to last a quarter of a century. However in recent years he was obviously deemed surplus to requirements. Perhaps still seen as a loose end, so his time was up. Enquiries uncovered that he had fallen out in a major way with Kenny Dixon."

"Would it or could it," Curry warily started with. "Have been conceivable that he was still in possession of evidence that credited Dixon with the initial hit, sir? Maybe it had surfaced or he had unwisely made someone aware of it."

"Who knows?" Murray said. "But that was a very logical and believable scenario, Drew and a good question into the bargain. Well done"

Curry blushed slightly. But would take that as praise, no matter how small.

"Ultimately, during that time it would have been his trusted lieutenant, James Baxter Reid, who would have dispatched with any worker surplus to requirements and that may have to have been 'laid off!' Needless to say and unsurprisingly, no one was ever caught or charged with her father's murder.

"James Baxter Reid. Just to confirm, that would be our very own Bunny?"

"Indeed." Murray clarified. "Sadly though," he continued. "For 'Hanna,' no matter how you look at it. Her father was not exactly a pillar of the community. He was a 'bad un.' It's a little wonder that her mother left. The poor woman may well have loved her child dearly, but was most likely afraid for her own life and unfortunately had no structured, long term way to support her young daughter.

"She's done alright for herself though," 'Kid' Curry added.

"Maybe so. But trust me, that's a challenging upbringing."

"Possibly, exactly why she joined the force, sir?" The young DC wasn't sure if he had stated that as fact or question.

Steven Murray carefully considered those words. Had it really become too much of a burden for Susan 'Hanna' Hayes? He had tried to imagine briefly what it must have been like. All those years of keeping her relationship with her father bottled up. Constantly avoiding questions about her upbringing and background. The visits from social work. Her mother's constant black eyes, bruising and verbal abuse. So, she sought out a life in the Police Force. However, had that simply become an overwhelming need for closure? An opportunity to firstly take some of those dishonest and dishonourable individuals off the streets of Scotland's capital? That 'Not Proven' ruling, never gave the poor families of the deceased justice or closure and it allowed Harry Hayes to pedal filth and drugs within those seedy clubs he managed for many, many years afterwards.

But why now? What was the catalyst? Hayes had maintained her innocence. However the evidence was continuing to mount up against her. She had lied to the DCI about her whereabouts, thus giving an alibi to DI Murray. Then there was the motorcycle, Stanley knife, keys, restraints and phone. It didn't look good.

Murray re-entered the interview room where both Kerr and Hayes were sitting in silence. Except for the infrequent tummy rumblings emanating from two stomachs that had lost out on a much needed bite to eat.

"Did you find out what all the shenanigans at the canteen entailed?" Kerr asked gently, reminded by another random murmur from below.

The puzzled expression on Steven Murray's face said it all. He had no idea what she was talking about. And in all his nervousness and fluster, Andrew Curry had never even mentioned it. The 'Kid' had assumed that the Inspector was fully up to speed with everything. Now comfortably sat back down though, DI Steven Murray signed back in for a reality check. He firstly shook his head. He'd watched and worked closely with 'Hanna' Hayes these last few years. She was not stupid. She would have never left a footprint, if her motive for being there had been an unlawful one. So her reason for being there must have been legal and relevant. Because, Murray had concluded that she had most definitely been there. The key question - Why? To that, he currently had no answer.

However, there was no way a member of his team (because they were each cleverer than that), would have ordinarily wrapped up the alleged murder weapons inside old overalls. Especially ones like those worn by the carpet fitter and then thrown in the baseball cap for good measure. She was being set up. That had always been his assumption right from the start. 'Hanna' would have undoubtedly known the place would be searched thoroughly. Including, every floorboard lifted, every storage unit emptied and every DIY container rummaged through and carefully scrutinised. So he was equally convinced, that Detective Constable Susan 'Hanna' Hayes was not the transgressor here. She would have been totally oblivious and fully unaware that these items had been stored or planted there. Her motorbike could easily have been stolen at some point and then put back without her ever realising it was gone. That certainly wasn't hard to do if you went about it in a professional manner. And this had clearly been carried out in a very professional way. Indeed, it looked more than likely that currently as things stood and like she had said herself, she was about to be the official scapegoat here. Or even more likely was Murray's more recent theory - That she was just being used as a minor distraction to take their eyes away from the real culprit for a few hours. Thus allowing themselves, even more time and freedom to carry out some further unfinished business.

Twenty Three

'I'm in the phone booth, it's the one across the hall. If you don't answer, I'll just ring it off the wall. I know he's there, but I just had to call. Don't leave me hanging on the telephone.'

- Blondie

Murray was waiting for forensics to get back to him, although he and Hayes were running out of time, if this was to remain informal and no charges were to be made.

"It has been confirmed, 'Hanna.' It was your boot print in the flower bed," he stated solemnly.

Kerr sat upright. Hayes remained impassive.

"They also found prints on the intercom buzzer," he gambled.

"Sir, what is going on here?" 'Sandy' offered by way of Union representation. "These are serious accusations and 'Hanna' has no lawyer present. Why would you do this?"

"Well," Murray hesitated. "That would be, because I believe Susan was actually outside the premises on her motorbike."

Both sets of shocked female eyes glowered at him suspiciously. What had he meant by that comment?

"Now whether she's the mystery motorcyclist seen fleeing the scene, that is another question entirely."

"You think?" Kerr remonstrated.

'Sandy' was becoming most uncomfortable with the situation. She knew Steven Murray could be a bit unorthodox and nonconformist at times, but this was now becoming unacceptable. Had he breached and crossed the line yet again?

'Hanna,' sat still and said nothing. She just watched with intrigue, the contrasting exchange between her two superior officers.

"DC Hayes, I recommend that you ask for a lawyer immediately," Kerr stated assertively.

'Sandy' then stood up and added aggressively…

"I can't understand, sir. Especially since he went after the DCI, why you can't see that this is some crazy sadistic power struggle, between Reid and Scott for control of Edinburgh's illicit sidelines."

Murray shook his head in disagreement.

"Why would 'Bunny' imply it was one of our own, sir? If he had not already put things in place to frame the individual and lend substance to his outlandish claims. It's obviously a set up and these things have been planted. It has been far too easy, sir, and you know it!"

Impassioned rant over, the flame haired Sandra Kerr remained standing. However, she sat almost immediately when Susan Hayes eventually did decide to speak.

"But it was my footprint," she said suddenly. "It's okay, 'Sandy,' I'll take it from here."

Kerr's mouth flew open, as she dropped instantly to her seat. Mutual disappointment seemed to be shared briefly between Kerr and Murray.

"Can I explain, sir?"

"I always hoped you would."

Kerr remained in shock. She felt deceived and let down. Although she had not yet heard the Constable's version of events and how everything came to be.

'Hanna' Hayes reached into her back pocket and produced her mobile phone. She had never been formally arrested and was just helping with enquiries, so it had remained untouched on her person until now.

"I did not want to have to play this card. But it would appear the only way to help justify why I was there and to clear my name." She paused before adding, "Because I had nothing whatsoever to do with his death."

Both other officers were relieved to hear her say that at least. But they also knew that she needed more than one text message or picture to chase away all the other circumstantial evidence.

"Let us see it then," Murray requested.

"Oh, it's not visual, sir. It's an audio recording that I received on Friday evening."

Murray found himself even more intrigued, yet perplexed. Kerr looked on, unsure of what she was witnessing play out before her. Anxiously 'Hanna' scrolled forward on her phone and then pushed play. The sound had clearly been digitally distorted to hide the callers real voice. But the six words were perfectly clear and audible. Sounding robotic, it affirmed - *'I know who ordered the hit.'* Hayes stopped it there. Feeling rather defensive herself now, Sandra Kerr added.

"Sorry 'Hanna,' but you'll need to let it play on."

She did so.

'Meet me at Judge Menzies home at 10pm Sunday.'

Again Hayes paused it.

"The hit being the Judge himself or did it mean Stevenson?" Murray asked.

"It could even be referring to Johnny Johnson, sir," Kerr added. "We have no actual clue as to what murder it is referencing with any real certainty."

Murray looked genuinely hurt when he glanced across at DC Hayes and spoke softly.

"But 'Hanna,' why would you go? And especially not confide in me? Or at least, in one of us?"

In sheer amazement, the frustrated Detective Constable raised her voice and spoke candidly.

"Would you have taken my call, sir?" she asked politely. "Because you have never spoken to any of us in weeks. We've all tried you numerous times on the phone. Only to be ignored and get your voicemail if we are lucky!"

Sandra Kerr's facial gesture, indicated that 'Hanna' had made a fair point.

Hayes continued. "However, that is because as always it was all about you, sir. All about our Inspector. His state of mind, his feelings and his well being. Always, it's all about Steven Murray."

Kerr tried to interrupt… "That's unfair, 'Hanna,' you know…"

But Hayes was having none of it. With her voice raised and her hackles up, she let rip.

"Yes of course I know, 'Sandy' - HE was grieving, HE'D just lost his son, HE suffers from depression, HE needed our support and ultimately - HE'D be back soon! Well, I've heard it all before," she said dejectedly. "And look where it's got me. Sitting here for hours on end being interrogated as a murder suspect… Fantastic!"

A full three seconds of silence filled the void. In a less aggressive and much calmer voice, Hayes then led with…

"But you know what, sir? Maybe some of us, were genuinely still thinking about YOU. Maybe some of us were still trying desperately to protect YOU. Even to the detriment of our own careers."

Murray and Kerr turned sharply toward each other. What had they missed here? 'Sandy' reached out for Hayes' phone. There were still a few seconds of the recording to be played. She held it directly out in front of the emotionally charged Detective Constable. Susan Hayes frustrated as she was, reluctantly pushed play. The final disguised remark, was much edgier and threatening. The bounce and tweeness had gone. The quirky voice had now transformed somewhat. The last few seconds stated menacingly…

'Or I reveal details of your father, to Murray.'

The recording stopped. Murray's face fell. That was unexpected. Alert to the situation, 'Sandy' took up the slack.

"So they had attempted to blackmail you in a warped kind of way to ensure your presence," Kerr said. "And all the other stuff we found, 'Hanna.' I assume that was all planted?"

"I already told Furlong and the officers at my home, that of course it was. It definitely must have been. I don't know exactly what was all recovered. But I am sure if we go through it all, I can clear my name fully."

Murray had sat quietly contemplating. It had been all about him, right enough. His bipolar was now crossing over into his effectiveness. It had caused personal sacrifices and extra workloads for each of his team and he'd begun to deeply regret his recent actions. Misguided, but well intentioned, he called out with regards to him shutting himself away.

"I just wish one of you had told me sooner."

Daggers and looks questioning his parentage, came thick and fast from both females in the room. All three sat still and reflective for the next 5 minutes. Before, eventually, Susan Hayes broke the ice.

"I had never fully realised just how convincing you two were, when you played out against each other. You know, the Good Cop - Bad Cop scenario."

Kerr and Steven Murray raised their eyes.

"There is no way that any boot print would have been processed that quickly. And I most certainly never touched the intercom with my bare hands," she said. "Although that was a reasonable attempt, sir."

Murray smiled through gritted teeth.

"And encouraging me to seek legal counsel so convincingly, that was a nice touch. Well played, 'Sandy.' A damn good effort."

"I've no idea what you mean," Kerr said indignantly.

"Do you really think you would be on my team, if I did not already know about your father?" Murray questioned.

"I always suspected that you would probably have been aware, sir. But I had faith that the others didn't. And I certainly did not want it to become public knowledge."

"I understand that, 'Hanna.' But I also think the more we know about each other, the more we can look out and protect one another."

"That is an admirable comment, sir," interjected Kerr. "But you do realise it has just been made by the most secretive and private member of the team," she said bluntly.

"I do, 'Sandy' and that's something I promise I am going to work hard to change, moving forward."

"My father, sir?" Hayes enquired. "What do you actually know?"

"Do you want me to leave?" Kerr asked.

"No, like I said, I think it would benefit us all, to hear at least the condensed version."

Hayes and Kerr both nodded in the affirmative and Murray prepared himself, to offer up his brief take on the controversially bold, Harry Hayes.

In the Scottish Crime Campus laboratory at Gartcosh, one of the forensics team was busy sending an important text to DI Murray. That particular individual had just confirmed a theory for him.

Beep! Murray scanned the text briefly, his mind already preoccupied elsewhere.

'So Harold Hayes Esquire. Go on, sir," his daughter encouraged.

"Very well, 'Hanna.' I know that your father got involved in a street brawl approximately thirty years ago and was charged with murder."

Sandra Kerr looked across the room at DC Hayes with concern. "Are you sure about…"

"Go on," 'Hanna' repeated. "Continue. Don't stop."

"Very well," her Inspector said bluntly. "He was found, 'Not Proven' and ultimately released," Murray announced. "From that day on, he ran three night clubs like you said. Interestingly though, you omitted to mention that they belonged to Kenny Dixon at that point."

'Hanna' was then, reticent to either confirm or deny her knowledge of that fact. She was barely in High School and surely would have been forgiven for not knowing her father's ultimate employer.

Murray finished with, "That was up until his disappearance and subsequent find five years ago."

"What!" Kerr exclaimed.

"He had gone missing." Hayes informed her. "And then six months later, his murdered body was discovered by workmen. He had been buried in a field."

Murray's nod (a number sixteen), was confirmation of that statement.

Kerr simply stood rigid, devastated by those recently revealed facts. She had then thought for a second about how little, she actually did know about her fellow officers and their respective lives. The wide and varied roads they had each travelled together and the bittersweet experiences they'd each gone through. In relation to who exactly had gone through those painful encounters, her final impression was probably the most accurate of all. She'd simply concluded - Haven't we all? A tenderhearted tear was shed between the two women. Then Hayes once again spoke up.

"You know, all those years ago when I was left to study on my own at the clubs. One of the premises, I can't remember which, had a rather cheesy and long winded plaque on the wall. At least it seemed cheesy and corny at the time," she reflected. "Today however, it probably has more relevance to me than ever."

Her colleagues remained silent. Sensitive to all that she had gone through today.

"I can still remember the words clearly," she said. "It read - *Real isn't who is drinking and dancing with you when you make it to the top. Real is who helped you walk again when you were at rock bottom.* Thank you both for today," she offered sincerely. "I may not quite have hit rock bottom, but I was certainly heading there."

All three, content with that outcome. Went to exit the room.

'Hanna' Hayes paused slightly. Before finally taking one last, concerned look at DI Murray. On witnessing her uneasy attention, the Inspector rubbed at his freshly shaved skin and offered up.

"Out with it, 'Hanna.' You've not held back so far."

Sandra Kerr smiled at that acknowledgement of Hayes' forthrightness.

"It's just," she began...... "And you two, take a different slant on it. But I, I actually thought - '*I know who ordered the hit,*' was in reference to your son, sir," she said bluntly. "That was why I turned up. I wanted to help relieve your pain and bring them to justice."

The Inspector, emotional at her comments, seemed to mull over the notion briefly and then headed directly out the door.

Once outside, he chose to ignore the theory and privately updated Sandra Kerr on what he required of her. They walked and talked all the way to the front door of the station. Kerr's vehicle was parked directly across the road. They had just entered through the main foyer, when the duty Desk Sergeant shouted them over.

"We were just about to send this up to you, sir."

Rather dumbstruck, the Sergeant pointed hesitantly at the far end of the counter to what looked like a rather oversized cake box.

Kerr became nervous. "Sir, don't you think we should…"

"For me?" Murray immediately questioned. "From who and when?" Quickly followed.

"A nervous delivery driver dropped it off two minutes ago. He just said it was for Detective Inspector Murray."

The DI tapped it gently. He then carefully rubbed at its sides and anxiously studied the outside of the box for clues. He could then witness that the poor, overworked Sergeant on duty was looking decidedly guilty about something. Murray's eyes caught his.

"Sergeant Simpson, do you have something that you wish to share with us?"

"Apologies, Inspector. But we've done the security part. We've already looked inside!"

DI Murray glared harshly at the man and broke into a strong west coast, Glaswegian accent and offered… "Aye, very funny, ya big tube!"

The Inspector then firmly lifted back the lid to unveil a trendy, rather up market, ladies scarlet red hat.

Unsurprisingly, it had a beautiful golden silk ribbon tied around it. Murray couldn't figure out what she was up to this time. But Jayne Golden was right back in the thick of things. This time, however, the Inspector had some of his minions on the case as well as himself.

The card inside read: *Picked up a slight injury. Otherwise I would have been there with you.* It then went on to list what hospital and ward she was currently in.

"Tell no one, 'Sandy.' But I need you on this. I need her background to be one hundred percent accurate this time. She'll wait and we'll go when we are fully prepared for her. Let me know as soon as you have something solid."

"Why are you not sending, 'Sherlock?'" she asked, slightly intrigued.

In recent months, Murray had always relied upon Joe Hanlon to do his digging and to source accurate facts and figures. Her boss's rather slowly delivered and sheepish reply, certainly failed to convince her.

"He genuinely has to keep a low profile from the DCI at the moment, 'Sandy.' Plus, he's just finishing something else off for me. A somewhat delicate matter and if I'm honest," Murray stated more confidently. "I genuinely think this might need to be seen from a woman's perspective. Remember she had me totally fooled last time around."

At that, Kerr delivered a blow well below the belt.

"Fooled? I think I may have opted for the word, 'smitten,' myself."

On that note, Sandra Kerr opened the door and exited sharply. She never bothered to look back.

Twenty Four

'No more carefree laughter, silence ever after. Walking through an empty house, tears in my eyes. Here is where the story ends. This is my goodbye... Knowing me, knowing you.'

- Abba

In July 2010 Ellen McCann had just resorted back to her maiden name. She was drinking heavily and her upcoming divorce was taking its toll. After seven years together, the couple had been forced to sell their luxury three bedroomed home in Broxburn, West Lothian. Unfortunately for them, it had little or no equity in it. They had purchased it at the height of the property boom, only to see it lose a third of its value, two years later. At that point, she had barely enough available funds to put down as a deposit, to rent a one bedroomed flat in Edinburgh's Easter Road. Literally a stone's throw away from the Hibernian FC stadium. She could only afford that, because she would no longer have the one hour train commute each way, to and from the bustling world famous Waverley Station. Now on a good day and after a brisk walk, she could be sitting at her desk in the city's council offices by 9am. It also allowed her, two extra hours each day to be productive in some way shape or form. Or on the other hand, it gave her another ten hours per week to reflect on her life. A full working day's worth of anxiety and stress, based on her continually deliberating over her failed marriage, her current living quarters and her vast pile of mounting debt. With all that going on in her life, in early December 2010, the 30 year old clerical officer had the bitter misfortune to be introduced to a certain Mister Kenneth Dixon.

The author Robert Frost once wrote: *'Two roads diverged in a wood, and I, I took the one less travelled by, and that has made all the difference.'* At a low ebb and extremely vulnerable, this civil servant was ignorant to the dangerous, murky and ultimately fatal path that she was about to choose to venture down. Kenny Dixon had already been the top man in Edinburgh's criminal underworld for a decade by this point and had served a five year apprenticeship at Her Majesty's pleasure, previously. Over that Christmas period, KD ensured that his right hand man, 'Bunny' Reid, was more than generous to their new 'trainee.'

Heavily laden with financial obligations, Ms McCann was grateful for the support and the initial helpful backing. Throughout the month, she was to be showered with several theatre tickets, weekend flights to Brussels and Berlin to experience their wonderful Christmas markets. And if that was not enough, she was then treated to a champagne gift hamper, jewellery deliveries and a £2,000 cash bonus to make her festive season go with a swing. By the time Santa came to pay a visit, Ellen McCann was reeled in - hook, line and sinker. Ho, Ho, Ho!

They had their insiders in several high profile, important locations throughout the city. And they certainly had high hopes for this woman and the lofty heights of influence that she could reach. This was very much an investment in the future being made by Kenny Dixon. In fairness to the individual, she soon buckled down, worked hard and was most helpful on many dubious projects over the intervening years. In fact 16 years after her messy, complicated divorce, she was now the proud owner of a luxury penthouse flat in Edinburgh's prestigious city centre. She had always continued to work diligently and progress up the ladder. So much so, Ellen had been promoted several times over the years and although she still worked at the Planning and Development Department. Ms Ellen McCann was indeed, HEAD of the District Councils Planning and Development Committee.

The gruesome discovery of her body, or at least half of it, was made at the ancient Portobello swimming baths. She was a well known public figure in the city council and at least two police officers recognised her facial features. Outside of the historic premises they had a ceramic lifebuoy embedded on the side wall. That morning attached above and below the red and white porcelain swimming aid were two unofficial additions. With sturdy, industrial, twelve inch nails, two naked appendages had been positioned in place. Two bodies. Well actually, in fact, only half of two bodies. As the young, anxious Constable had informed Murray and Hanlon, the top half belonged to a female and below the lifebuoy, the bottom half, was of a male from the waist down. There was very little blood at the scene, which certainly implied the bodies had been dismembered elsewhere and simply brought up to

Portobello for display purposes only. Both Detective Sergeant Linn and DC Boyd had arrived at the scene.

Industrial rods had been fired into the dead flesh of the individuals. Like using a nail gun, only on a much grander scale. It was a dreadful sight. Although, to DS Linn it appeared as abstract art.

"It is hard to feel emotional, Allan, don't you think?"

Boyd nodded. His ginger hair blowing wildly in the heavy breeze from the nearby sea.

"I know what you mean, Sarge. There is no life present. It could easily be two pieces of modern sculpture. Given the contrast between dark and light, you could feel like you are at a Tracey Emin or Damien Hirst art exhibition.

The male half had been held in place by three rods. One had been fired through each of the victims thighs. The other, rammed down deep, directly through his scrotum. Both officers agreed there had been no actual need for that final one. They were adamant that the two fired through the thigh bones would have supported the weight fine. A black man was still very much in the minority in Edinburgh.

"Identifying him will take time," said Linn.

"Normally, I think you would be right," Boyd agreed. "However, based on what the DI told us in relation to the other victims, with the whole Reid and Scott situation, I've got an idea. Leave it with me."

Allan Boyd pulled out his phone and dialled, or pushed a button or two, would be a more accurate description.

"My dear Boydy. How are you doing?" Police Constable Christopher Carruthers said, on answering.

"Hi Chris. Aye, I'm fine. I was just wondering are you on shift today at all? Because we are on a shout in your neck of the woods right now. Portobello Swimming Baths to be precise."

"As luck would have it, I am only a few streets away, DC Boyd. Brighton Place in fact. What's up?"

"I think we could do with your help."

Linn looked on tentatively. Curiosity had certainly gotten the better of him.

"I'll be there in five."

And both phones were instantly put away.

"PC Carruthers is one of six local community officers we have here in Edinburgh. He is also married to my young cousin."

His Sergeant nodded.

"Chris covers east of Leith, right up to Portobello."

"That is some LOCAL area that he is asked to cover," Mitch Linn commented. "It's certainly not quite old style community policing, with your local Bobby on the beat, if that is what they were trying to replicate."

"No, I don't think it is Sarge," Boyd replied. "But it's reasonably reassuring for a fair percentage of people in the area, just knowing that he is around. Many of the shopkeepers, traders and business people have his direct number to call should they need help or assistance on matters. Also, he travels up and around his beat by nipping on and off public transport. So in many respects, he may well be more consistently visual than many of the previous officers from years past. Anyhow, the important thing is that …"

"His beat covers Kenny Dixon's old yard!" Linn jumped in to offer.

"You have got yourself well up to speed with everything, Sarge. Well done," Allan Boyd remarked, mightily impressed. "Yes, the very same lock-up and storage area, that 'Bunny' Reid continues to operate out of currently."

It was nearer the seven minute mark, before community cop, Chris Carruthers, arrived at the scene and offered up his own suspicions about the identity of the dead man. He had instantly recognised the highly distinctive tattoo on his thigh.

At their historic Leith HQ, Murray had made his way back upstairs and met up with 'Sherlock.' As they chatted quietly in the corridor about writing and wrapping up the 'Fake News' deaths and suicides, they were approached by a new, fresh faced male recruit. One noticeably sent on a specific errand. These physical duties and assignments were still mainly only done, to give these individuals interaction with senior officers. To allow beginners to put names to faces, etc. Because in this day and age, no matter who you're looking for, information required or knowledge forwarded - We have instant messaging, texts and alerts all done in a nanosecond. There is actually no need to have some poor newbie, walk half a mile from one end of a decrepit old station to the other. 'Ah modern technology,' Murray could hear himself whisper under his breath.

"Sir, sir, DI Murray. There has been another suspicious death. Well, two in fact," the out of puff Constable announced. "DCI Furlong instructed me to let you know, as a matter of urgency"

"She did, did she?" Murray grinned.

"How suspicious?" Hanlon queried.

"It would appear the body has been cut in two."

"Well, yes, I suppose that is rather suspicious," Steven Murray smiled. "And what about the other one?"

"The other one?" the young Constable questioned.

"You said a couple of deaths! Don't you remember?"

"Ah, well, yes. M'mm, I think this may be the suspicious part, sir."

"Come on young man," Murray encouraged. "I've heard it all before son, but for the benefit of our esteemed colleague here. For Detective Constable Hanlon… spit it out!"

"Well, the thing is, sir. The top half belongs to a woman," he stated hesitantly. "And the bottom half…"

"Yep okay, son. We get it. Two deaths - and mighty suspicious right enough," Murray bellowed.

"Murders, more like." Hanlon said confidently. "But why us?" Joe turned to his boss. "She knows we are all hands on deck with the Stevenson, Menzies and Jo-Jo enquiries. Not think we have enough on our plate?"

Inspector Murray, noticed that it was the young Constable's turn to gently smirk.

"Again, out with it, son."

Firstly, he handed over an A4 sheet. "All the details you need are on there I was assured. DCI Furlong also said that, she'd be surprised if one of you didn't mention or question - Why you guys?"

Both officers looked sheepishly at each other.

"So, she also asked me to pass on to you vocally, that the male, the bottom half was 'Bouncy' Reid's finance guy. That is all she said. I hope that helps. Also that, she had already assigned Linn and Boyd to investigate. Because she KNEW, how busy you two were already."

All of which was stated and delivered with a huge self-satisfactory smile.

"Thanks," Joe Hanlon offered on behalf of them both. "James 'Bouncy' Reid, that certainly seems less threatening than, 'Bunny,' and we all know just how wholly inaccurate that particular statement is."

Murray was already rubbing and scratching furiously, at the three days of growth on his stubbled chin.

"And so it goes on. The demise of 'Bouncy's' inner circle," he smiled.

"Hey, Constable," he then shouted after the departing officer. "Remember, to be sure and tell DCI Furlong, that it was 'Sherlock' here, that questioned her. Thanks very much for that. Much appreciated."

The Constable's pocket-sized smirk, instantly turned into another fully fledged grin.

"Will do, sir. I'll certainly do just that!"

Hanlon could only shake his head and look bemused.

DI Murray spontaneously burst into verse. Just as any normal sane person would…

"Their bouncy, trouncy, ouncey, pouncey, fun, fun, fun, fun, fun. But the most wonderful thing about Tiggers…… isssssss…… that I'm the only one!"

Twenty Five

'Child, you don't know, you'll never know how far they'd go to give you all their love can give. To see you through and God it's true. They'd die for you if they must... to see you live.'

- Freddie Aguilar

Murray nodded. Things on the surface were beginning to fall into place and make sense. This woman that had won over the Inspector's heart last year, before going on the run, was once again causing chaos. She was in her own flawed, unique way, trying her best to scatter remnants of helpful clues along the path. Or at least that was what Murray was being led to believe. That it wasn't 'Hanna' Hayes, but the larger than life persona of Jayne Golden that was quite literally offering her head up on a plate, considering the various fibres and scrapings that they had retrieved from the baseball cap. He was mindful though, that they had also gotten plenty of hair belonging to DC Hayes as well. Although 'Hanna' had previously acknowledged owning a similar cap. At that point she had no idea that it was indeed her headgear. The very same hat that she kept on the handle of her motorcycle when she'd do work on the bike. She would simply throw on the baseball cap, turn it around, and it worked a treat keeping her lengthy hair out of her eyes.

Murray had to once again remind himself that he never honestly thought for a second that Susan Hayes was guilty. However, the mounting circumstantial evidence against her was always going to be problematic and she had never helped matters initially by remaining silent. Ultimately however, Murray's decision to have her remain at the station proved the correct one. As did, unfortunately, his hunch that it allowed the real culprits the freedom, time and opportunity to go kill again without scrutiny or fear of reprisal. Having been asked recently to leave their fully independent reviews on the Lanarkshire countryside, on TripAdvisor. The travelling, gypsy throng of experienced journalists, TV cameramen and radio news reporters were now busy jostling each other for an ideal spot, on the classic Victorian promenade at Edinburgh's Portobello Beach.

In the relative privacy of the gents toilets at QCS station, Leith -
"So delicately in the background and without your DCI's knowledge you were working on and closing the file on three suicides?" Murray asked.

'Sherlock,' put down two of the aforementioned case files at the sink in front of his Inspector.

"Well, I wouldn't quite put it like that, sir. It was kind of more joining up the dots and putting them together into one appropriately condensed file."

"Even, I know they are all on the computer, Joe." Murray smiled. "So no real difference in width then."

Hanlon shrugged his shoulders to at least concede that point. But pointed at the files in front of them.

"This was done old school, sir. Remember, I learned from the best."

Murray beamed slightly at that. But what he also knew was that, what 'Sherlock' actually meant was - He didn't want DCI Furlong checking that he'd been on the computer at regular intervals ascertaining facts, figures, times, etc. So he printed off one copy and between that and Radical Lizzie's in depth report, he had foraged enough to be going on with.

"From what you've told me Joe, I assume you picked up that piece of slime Christian Blear, or at least put the fear of God into him with a severe reprimand, threat or warning."

"Each of those very methods would have been applied, sir. If only I'd had the chance."

Murray seemed mystified.

"Let me briefly update you. Things seemed to have backfired big style for our Mr Blear. Because whilst 'Bunny' Reid's associates were getting bumped off right, left and centre. Several key individuals that Blear had attacked on social media here in Scotland, had looked to turn the tables on him in a serious way." "I'm listening, Constable Hanlon. But I'm not sure I like where this might be heading."

Hanlon frowned. "In the last several days a story about a certain Mister Christian Blear, himself being a paedophile has been circulating."

"What!" Murray exclaimed.

"Stick with me, sir. During the first afternoon alone, six people turned up at his door whilst the blogger was out. They were willing to babysit the Blear children, as advertised online. They eventually left after Mrs Blear threatened to call ourselves. But the seeds of doubt and uncertainty had been planted in her mind. Just as planned."

"Go on Joe, you have my full attention."

"Well with perfect hindsight after the event. We believe that the callers were actually actors portraying rather sick, perverted individuals. They had been watching the home and on instruction, once they saw the man of the house leave for the shops, their devious role-playing began. However, after they'd been threatened with police action and dispersed, Blear's wife's curiosity got the better of her and she opened up some suspicious looking folders and documents on his computer."

The DI smiled with a nod. It was a grin that reckoned this man was about to get his due, deserved comeuppance.

"Pornographic images of children began appearing," Hanlon continued. "She was stunned, shocked, sickened and disgusted in equal measure. She knew that her husband had recently bought a gun on the dark web. Mainly because some of the many threats against him had become increasingly worrying over time. Generally he had just laughed them off, but for piece of mind, they now had a small revolver kept loaded in their bedside cabinet. At that moment his wife immediately retrieved it and brought it closer to hand."

Now indeed, it was Murray's turn to frown. "This can't end well, Joe." he said. Before slumping forward in his seat.

"When Christian Blear returned later in the day. He found his front door locked and a screaming, distraught wife terrified of him, at the other side of it. She wasn't willing to allow him access to their marital home or to their children. Although, thankfully the older child, the daughter was still at school and never saw any of this."

Steven Murray now apprehensively held his head in his hands between his legs and thought to himself - Any of what?

"Her husband denied all of it, sir. He had no idea what his wife was going on about."

"What people? What childminding? Someone is setting me up," he protested.

"Yeh, right," she lambasted him.

"And what dodgy images of children? You must be mistaken? I love our kids, I would never try to access…"

"I have your gun Christian, stay out," she shouted.

He attempted again to unlock the door with his key.

The Inspector's head was now shaking desperately in despair.

Joe Hanlon continued to read extracts from witness statements of neighbours, from the remaining file in front of him.

"The husband continued to twist and turn at the lock. Eventually, he managed to gain access and was heard to shout - 'What is wrong with you woman? - This is all complete nonsense! A complete fabrication of lies.' He looked at her empty hands. "I thought you said you had my gun?"

"I didn't say, I was holding it," came his wife's hysterical reply.

"You know it's loaded at all times though, right?"

"Of course I do. That is why I went to get it."

"But if you don't have it," he said in an alarmed manner. "Then where did you leave it?"

Both parents held eye contact with one another. At that, an almighty blast went off from their nearby sitting room.

"No, dear God no," Blears cried. "Not our child!"

"Two further gunshots were fired that afternoon, sir"

"Just tell me what happened, Joe." Murray pleaded.

Before Hanlon could respond, the toilet door flew open. It nearly broke clean off its hinges. A livid, beetroot faced, Detective Chief Inspector stared directly ahead at her two skulking officers. She then furiously began to let fly with a string of newly invented expletives!!!

"You two **SHAKESPEAREAN SARSAPARILLAS! TEST ACKLE MOJOS! And BANJO PLAYING BUNION BUSTERS!**" She yelled at the top of her voice.

The less experienced officer simply nodded, as he stepped forward to hide the case files. He then tried to add, "Ma'am. I think you may have lost your way. This is in fact the…"

"Your genitals are already hanging on a shoogly peg, boy." Furlong let rip. "So don't test me any further," she rattled off in double quick time. "Understand?"

'Sherlock' crossed his legs and winced at the very realistic and vivid image his superior had conveyed quite concisely to him.

"It was my fault entirely, Ma'am," Murray jumped in.

The Detective Inspector then held his head in shame, as he began.

"I should have told you that I'd left DC Hanlon here, strict instructions to tie up all the loose ends in those suicide cases. Especially, as I was photographed in one of the images. I didn't want any journalists looking to dig up dirt. Thinking that we maybe had something to hide. Sorry Ma'am, I should have reminded Joe to tell you. But he was trying not to bother you with all the Reid and Scott gangland mafioso stuff going on."

'Sherlock' felt his peg may just have firmed up slightly. Thank you, sir. He thought to himself.

Furlong also, appeared to have been won over. Pleasantly taken aback by her west coast Inspector's honesty and forthrightness. Although she was well aware that the blunt Glaswegian style was very much, 'tell it as it is,' and 'to hell with the consequences.' Her direct manner eased slightly and her overall body language relaxed. However, even a confused passersby in the corridor outside could see that she was still not wholly convinced. Her demeanour was now down to one, of a stern headmistress delivering a telling off to two unruly schoolboys. And maybe their busy colleagues would not have been too far off the actual mark with that assumption! Steven Murray was reluctant, but he also knew that there was one final little thing that could possibly swing the deal in their favour. So he took a long, deep, protracted breath and added.

"Once again my sincere apologies...... *Barbra!*"

At that, a slightly flushed DCI backtracked and quickly accepted her Inspector's apology and reasoning. Her exit from the gents was nearly as swift as her entry. DC Hanlon looked at Murray with a cheeky, devilish glint in his eye.

"You're welcome," his boss said. And both men broke down into tears of laughter.

"Watch out for that shoogly peg though, son!" Murray offered in a bold, west coast drawl.

Hanlon walked out from the Gents, with both hands in his pockets uttering - "Houston, we most certainly, don't have a problem!!"

Within ten minutes a level of somewhat maturity had returned. They sat back at DI Murray's desk to clarify the FAKE NEWS suicides. It was then that Hanlon finished off the awful story of Christian Blears.

"So when they got to the sitting room," 'Sherlock' began. "They found their four year old in possession of the gun. One of the computer screens was busy smoking and hissing at having taken a bullet."

DI Murray felt relief upon hearing that it was only a monitor that had been the target.

"Yes, sir. However, in sheer panic his mother ran to retrieve the loaded revolver."

"No, no, no!" Steven Murray wailed. "I don't want to hear this." He shook his head and ran anxious fingers frantically up, down and all around his upper body. "No, don't go there Joe, seriously."

"We don't know for definite, sir. But based on the timeline of the shots, the position of the bodies, neighbours statements and forensics. It would appear that the youngster was probably startled or frightened. As a combination of one or both of those emotions, he fired off another round. This time it hit and fatally killed his mother. It was a bullet to the forehead, sir. Death would have been instantaneous."

Murray sat numbed. He thought about his own immediate family challenges and the future ahead. He had lost a wife and now more recently, his youngest son. How was Christian Blears going to cope knowing that his son was going to grow up with the guilt of killing his own mother? And would he even question his role in those circumstances? When would the youngster eventually find out? How would you go about breaking that to the poor boy? The timing would be all important. Otherwise someone else may inform him erroneously. He'd ask questions and friends, neighbours or other family members may feel pressured into spilling the beans! Would this divide the family? What about his older sister? How would their relationship develop from there on? Oh my goodness, what a can of worms the Inspector thought. This was horrifying. All those questions and dilemmas. How heartbreaking. Finally, after several minutes his detective's brain clicked back into gear and he returned to reality. DC Hanlon had remained silent throughout. However, Joe fully recognised the fact that Murray was back on course and had had sufficient time to reflect on how the events eventually unfolded.

"But you had begun all this by linking up suicides, Joe. Plus you said three shots were fired?" Murray needed confirmation.

A tender nod was offered by his young colleague. It was a slow, succinct, movement from 'Sherlock.' One that said - you must know what happened next, sir. Murray's croaky voice was empty and coarse, filled with empathy and despair of tragic experience.

"The man would have been engulfed in darkness, Joe. Regret, guilt and shame would have instantly kicked in. Whatever raw emotion overcame him. For definite, in that split second, he saw no future in this life. I have no doubt what I would have done, Joe. I would have foolishly picked up the handgun, turned it on myself and fired one deadly shot through the side of my skull."

After a minute of complete silence and solace between the two men, DC Hanlon was first to speak.

"When the armed response boys got there, sir. Three bodies lay still on the floor."

Murray's eyes flickered with incredulous alarm. Had the troubled father somehow taken them both out at the same time?

"Much to the relief of the first firearms officer on the scene," Hanlon continued. "He suddenly saw the youngster's torso steadily rise and fall."

Murray himself was relieved at that particular news.

"With rising panic and fear outside, doors had been broken down to gain immediate access." Hanlon continued, "There would be nothing FAKE about the

'Breaking News' that went out from Christian Blears home that day. A young boy, now sound asleep, cuddled warmly into his deceased mother. Several feet away, lay his dead father, with his brains blown clean across the carpet."

Within ten minutes, Murray had returned to the room with the shoogly peg. He suitably freshened up and then went back to the business of catching a murderer or two. That is what you have to do. Who knew?

CCTV footage had been found of a motorcycle heading through Larkhall Main Street at 10.04pm on Friday night. It was unclear who was driving. It looked like Hayes' bike, but the grainy image was unclear and would never be good enough for them to use in court. A group of officers involved in the case gathered around the screen to view an enlarged image. It appeared to give them renewed optimism. Because, although the registration plate was unsurprisingly covered only. To the left hand side of its letters and numbers, you could just about make out a small symbol or logo. This time when made bigger, it clearly represented capital letters… S. H.

"Susan Hayes," someone cried out.

Murray said nothing. He just shook his head and smiled. He knew whose door he was about to chap at next. Then he spoke.

"Someone is playing silly beggars with us, Joe. We should have figured it sooner."

Twenty Six

*'In Scotland's story I read that they came. The Gael and the Pict,
the Angle and Dane. But so did the Irishman, Jew and Ukraine.
They're all Scotland's story and they're all worth the same.'*

- The Proclaimers

'Bunny' Reid was busy reflecting on the fact that a
further two of his 'employees' had been victims
somewhat. Their top of the range vehicle had all its
tyres slashed. The pair were out and about, collecting
retail insurance payments. Good old-fashioned
'protection money,' in other words. It was only their
second stop of the day when this occurred. Both men
were in the store premises. No one had spotted anyone
loitering or walking about outside. The 'collecting
agents' had literally been away for only two minutes.
That last fact had intrigued James Baxter Reid. Because
that was surely no coincidence. He pondered and cast
his mind back to a portion of the words that he'd so
eloquently delivered previously to DCI Furlong.

"This is one of your own!" He had said.

Were those words coming back to haunt him? What if
that was exactly what it was? One of HIS own. Up until
now he had suspected a police insider. One of Murray's
crew possibly. The perpetrator certainly seemed to
know individual locations, pick-up times and exact car
details. Someone had definitely been expecting them.

Someone knew their precise route. They even knew what specific shop they were going into and roughly what size of window they had to work with, before either of the men returned. But who? No one individual was that close to me, Reid reckoned. Or were they? He then ran through mentally in his head his personal diary for the last week or two. It was during that time that all the chaos, disruption and noise had begun in earnest. He replayed his daily routines. His early and late rises. There appeared to be no steady pattern to them. No familiar routine or continuity that even he could pinpoint or figure out. They were still very much spontaneous. Breakfasts, meeting schedules with 'area reps,' 'leisure breaks' and 'policy decisions' with key associates, etc, etc. All mixed and varied.

Something concerned him though. It was slight, a very small lingering doubt. The awareness of one potential thread. A link or common denominator that did briefly enter his mind. Initially he dismissed it as silly, irrelevant and a definite non-starter. Then however, he gave much needed further consideration to the option. He became less dismissive and thought more thoroughly about all the various roads (the pieces of information) required to cause severe damage to the smooth running of his operation. He assessed it even more fully and in depth. He began to contemplate the two recent fires that had broken out at separate luxury flats he owned. Well equipped apartments that were used for his escorts to operate from. Both had initially been put down to carelessness. One Reid thought, maybe! Now on further scrutiny, he'd concluded that they had not been accidental at all. Numerous numbers of drug delivering drones (an idea he stole from Andrew Scott) had been found to be faulty and stopped several important dealer drops from going ahead and taking place in recent weeks. Once again, impacting his business. His cash flow had suffered greatly. His ability and reliability to deliver his merchandise on time came into question. His good name and reputation was and had been, taking quite a hammering. His buyers were going elsewhere. Word was beginning to spread. His lack of dependability had gone viral.

Now all this earlier turmoil and disarray had escalated substantially in recent days to the callous murder of several key people in his organisation. After dismissing from his mind several other crime lords from throughout various parts of the country, including his latest, most recent rival, Andrew Scott. That was when 'Bunny' became convinced that it was a police officer. Not a retired ex-cop, but a current one. Someone that he had wronged or embarrassed previously. An officer that he had probably made look stupid in court. Yet another detective that had failed to make a charge stick and was now out to seek justice in another way.

He was wrong though. The aging gangster had figured it out. Crazily it was the only thing that seemed to make any sense. The only thing that ticked all the boxes and joined up all the dots. Having allowed each of those hectic daily schedules from recent days to be played back and reviewed in his mind, he once again nodded. With a look of conviction, he continued to shake his head in disbelief at his sheer gullibility. The Reidmeister was now fully satisfied that he was correct in his assumption.

"You stupid old fool," he shouted. Disgusted at himself.

When Clark and Co. amalgamated with that other significant name in Paisley at the time, J. & P. Coats. It made the newly created J. & P. Coats Limited the largest thread manufacturer in the world. The company employed thousands in the Paisley area and exported to millions of people across the globe. Today as Sandra Kerr travelled into the forgotten mill town, she offered up a nostalgic smile, as she gently stroked the edge of her Paisley patterned silk scarf.

She had discovered that Andrew Scott's father had enjoyed a brief affair in the early years of his marriage. His wife had forgiven him. But only years later did it surface that his mistress had given birth to a child. It had taken her nearly ninety minutes to travel from East to West, along a busy M8 motorway. But 'Sandy' had tracked down Scott's only aunt. Ms Marion Connell Scott was his late father's sister. The short, thinly built, silver haired, seventy-three year old spinster, stayed in the Hunterhill area of Paisley. Literally, within five minutes walking distance of the old Anchor Mills and this particular *'Paisley Buddie'* turned out to be a gushing font of knowledge. In the old Scots vernacular, she was, *'A wee sweetie wife!'* - Someone that spoke incessantly. A woman that knew everyone's business. A purveyor of fine gossip.

What a find she had been for both 'Sandy,' and for the case itself.

The woman had never married and had only been made aware of the other sibling, when the child reached teenage years. Her brother had confided in Marion often over that time. He assured her of how he'd made regular payments toward the child's upbringing and kept constant tabs on their personal welfare, safety and wellbeing. It had only been in the last four or five years of his life that all three children were first made aware of each other. The trio would meet up regularly according to the aunt. In actual fact, in recent times they had all grown to be very close. Although their own mother had always thought that they just shared a close friendship.

Sandra Kerr found that last comment rather hard to swallow. Everything she had discovered about the late Jean Scott told you that nothing got past her. That she was one sharp cookie. A ruthless, domineering matriarch. Someone switched on with every aspect of her family's lives. ADI Sandra Kerr was convinced that she would have known about the situation fully, but that it was in everyone's best interest to just look the other way and allow the others to have their so-called secret sister.

A sister that throughout her adult years had gone by the name of surprise, surprise... Jayne Golden. As soon as Marion had divulged the name, 'Sandy' contacted her Inspector straight away.

"You knew didn't you?" Kerr asked.

On the other end of the line and with only a slight hesitation - "I had my suspicions," he confirmed. "But like I said earlier, 'Sandy.' I genuinely wanted a woman's perspective and solid clarification. Thank you for both. You now need to return A.S.A.P. We are heading out with Furlong in tow and I want you there with her. You've got ninety minutes to get back here." He hung up.

Murray had started to do a Rubik's Cube in his head. Which was impressive, because he had never managed to finish one in real life! The dots, or at least the colours on this occasion were beginning to match up. Scott and Golden were family and that made all the difference.

Steven Murray now suspected and without too much overthinking, that Andrew Scott had planned deliberately to infiltrate and demolish Reid's established empire from a long way back. Possibly even from the year before, when Kenny Dixon was still in charge. Andrew Scott had a good head on his shoulders. He was very much a long haul player. A strategist, a planner and a visionary when it came to moving his business empire forward. His recently discovered step-sister, needed to be carefully positioned within the inner sanctum of the ABC casino. Scott, through his connections, made that happen. The new 'crime lord on the block' had been fully aware through his various dubious sources that Sir Gerald Anderson and his son Cyrille were involved with 'Bunny' Reid in some underhand way. So he needed to get someone close to the action. That someone turned out to be Jayne Golden. Sadly Steven Murray got even closer to her and things took on a whole new dynamic. Golden had never been involved in the human trafficking, but was well aware that it was going on. So she was actually happy to help DI Murray, without compromising her own position, bring 'Bunny' Reid to justice. That in fairness, turned out to be a plan which would also have been a very acceptable outcome to her brother. It was no wonder though, that the mysterious woman had never been found, Murray thought. She was ultimately, directly connected to Andrew Scott. The current heir apparent to Scotland's underworld throne. From that moment, she was always going to be securely hidden. With her trail and tail, well and truly covered. Murray, on receiving Kerr's update, assigned two extra officers to guard Jayne Golden at her hospital bed until he got there. Within quarter of an hour, Joe Hanlon and himself had visited with her briefly, got some interesting worthwhile information and then drove off again at an alarming speed toward Fife. Murray thanked her and promised a full catch up later, but currently, arrests had to be made.

The Inspector's understated, Volvo saloon had screeched noisily along the rural streets of Fife. He'd accelerated and was going wide to swing in left through the gates of the yard. He'd obviously had dreams of being a lorry driver when he was young, Hanlon thought. But actually there was a much more deliberate method to his madness. It had actually allowed him to slam on the brakes and block entry to a dark SUV attempting to turn in from the right hand side of the road. Murray had recognised the vehicle coming towards them, as they both approached Andrew Scott's premises from totally different directions. The Inspector told Joe to remain inside the vehicle. Once out, Murray slammed his door shut and turned to face the sinister looking beast of a motor before him. Its engine purred gently and a delicate indicator announced its desire to turn right. The Detective Inspector stood fully upright, then boldly and confidently folded his arms, with his legs slightly apart.

The driver's electronically controlled darkened window, slid down with ease. Beyond the growling exterior of the newly employed sidekick, who was obviously, temporarily filling in for 'The Sizzling Hulk,' sat a much more recognisable face. Murray could tell he had only just beaten James Baxter Reid to the punch. Why else was 'Bunny' here? He'd figured it out also and knew exactly where to find the culprit. Steven Murray's stance weakened. He turned chauffeur-like and opened his back door. Reid furrowed his eyebrows. He strained in front of his new driver to look more clearly at the unmarked police car. Yes, as suspected, the back seat was empty.

"It's the only way you are getting an invite to this party tonight," Murray shouted across. Gesturing toward the interior. "Are you coming, or not?"

Reid and his Latvian, Ukrainian or possibly local Stenhouse thug exchanged glances. The man behind the wheel continually shook his head. His thought and message was loud and clear. But the man in the passenger seat was ultimately the one in charge. He was the individual that was currently having his kudos and bravado openly questioned in public. Murray had now blatantly challenged him to a duel and a public dual at that, nonetheless.

"Get in and tell your new pet to pull up across the way and stay there, until we're finished."

Slowly 'Bunny' Reid surfaced. For a limited time only - unguarded and unprotected. Willing to make his way into the lion's den. In fairness, he probably thought that having DI Murray for company was protection enough. If only he knew how little the Inspector would have done to keep him safe? In a dark two-piece designer suit, with extra deep pockets, and after a slow confident walk across the newly resurfaced roadside, Reid dipped his head forward, bent his knees and slid effortlessly into the middle of the back seats.

"Not the first time you'll have ridden in one of these then, sir?" Murray politely offered.

"I'll let you close it yourself!"

A gruff, ungodly growl from the rear could be heard as the door was reluctantly pulled shut.

"You're a funny man, Inspector. That's what I like about you."

His grating, cast-iron voice sent a chill immediately throughout the interior of the vehicle.

'Sherlock' questioned at once. "Do you think this is a wise move, sir?"

His own high pitched voice was exceptionally nervous and seemed to tremble at the end of each word delivered. Joseph Hanlon had never actually been in the Reidmeister's company before and the gangster's unique sound, up close and personal, was even more intimidating than he had anticipated.

"You mean with James Reid and Andrew Scott in the same room and at the same time." Murray then paused for effect, looked over his shoulder at 'Bunny' and cheerfully offered up - "I can't for the life of me see what could possibly go wrong, Constable?"

DC Hanlon simply rubbed his forehead and sighed.

The frenetic, pulsating day continued back at the station. Chris Carruthers early suspicions on who their dead Portobello male may be, proved to be correct. Allan Boyd had just had it confirmed to him and instantly texted Murray the details. The community officer though, had never doubted himself. He was confident that he had been correct all along. Based solely on the fact that the dead man had an unusual reputation for someone living in the east of Scotland. Which was?

He was renowned for wearing sports or cargo shorts and treating every day as if he lived in a tropical paradise. *Ah, sure you can take the man out of Birmingham,* Carruthers thought. But the dead man's tattoo of the world ran like a globe, stretching right around the top of his left thigh. Pinpointed and highlighted in red it stated: The Bahamas. Each month the much travelled individual would then have other locations highlighted that he had just recently visited. He was a money man after all.

The reason Carruthers knew all this was straightforward and simple. Because he'd often been in the man's company. Regularly he'd pop into the Portacabin that he operated from. As black as the ace of spades, John Samuel was a Birmingham born child of the seventies. Originally of Jamaican descent, with high, glossy cheekbones and tight curly hair. This well built body builder was indeed......... 'Bunny' Reid's accountant. He was his financial wizard. A job that was well rewarded, as his top of the range Mercedes testified to. His premature death would put yet another spanner in the works of the Reid empire. Cash flow - New person required - References - Capabilities - Industry Aware - Trust - Trust - Trust!

Allan Boyd had just messaged his boss to confirm the identification and give Murray a brief, although exceptionally helpful rundown on the background of Ellen McCann also.

Mitch Linn nodded. Even the new Sergeant felt that things were beginning to fall into place and that some hard and fast lines were about to be drawn under the whole sad, sorry state of affairs.

Twenty Seven

'Underground, overground, Wombling free, the Wombles of Wimbledon Common are we. Making good use of the things that we find. Things that the everyday folks leave behind.'

- The Wombles

Murray and Hanlon had driven the final fifty metres accompanied by their extra passenger. The Inspector's own car was followed through the gate by two further unmarked cars. One of which heralded the arrival of DCI Barbra Furlong and her female partner for the day, ADI (although soon to be Sergeant again) Sandra Kerr. 'Sandy' had only made it back to the station by the skin of her teeth. Their vehicle had caught up with Murray, while he'd had his Mexican stand-off at the front gate. Two further officers were behind them in a third accompanying car. DI Murray was not taking any chances here in Scott land. Six full-time police officers and currently one member of the public in tow as an observer - A shy retiring fellow, a local Rotary Club member, who went by the name of James Baxter Reid!

The Inspector nodded when he saw the impressive Volvo XC90 parked directly outside the doorway to the foyer. A slightly concerned and rather worried look, was then added to his demeanour. As he prepared to enter, he saw two young girls bouncing, laughing and playing in their own personal play area. An interactive structure, purchased and installed courtesy of their favourite deranged Uncle. In fact their only Uncle. Cuddly, friendly Uncle Andrew. The tall, kind, always smiling, greed infused, no-nonsense... psychopathic killer! Murray opened the reception area door and quickly scoured around to see who else was in view. He then questioned... How was this going to play out now, with all the family in tow?

The innocent smiles and infectious laughter of Scott's two gorgeous nieces would and should have been reward enough. Murray offered a clipped wave to Amanda. The young clerical worker certainly seemed more ideally suited to caring for children, than being a genial gatekeeper for...... Murray tried hard to once again gather up a few appropriate words for her employer in his mind. Oh yes, he recalled some - A sadistic mobster, a murdering scumball, a friggin' law unto himself. Or in DCI Furlong terminology...

A WINKY WONKING TUNNEL TICKLER!

With the commotion of the cars, the sound of raised voices and no doubt monitoring it on his own personal CCTV. It wasn't long before the lengthy legs of Andrew Scott came into view. Today, he was kitted out in Armani jeans and a tailored, cornflower blue jacket, with a delicate crimson pinstripe displayed at regular intervals. The pure wool garment stated quality and class.

"What the hell is he doing here?" Scott boomed out.

Pointing at the only non police officer in their group. Having left the comfort of his upstairs office suite behind, the wealthy businessman continued his tirade of derogatory remarks, as he approached the halfway mark on the stairs. His new, ultra modern, bespoke premises were one million miles removed from those of the old guard. Ironically, since 'Bunny' Reid had taken over from Kenny Dixon, his whole modernisation program for the Portobello criminal hub, consisted of putting up a mirror, buying toilet roll and upgrading from white to brown sugar for the tea!

"Again," the increasingly angry voice yelled. Each word, delivered independently. "What-is-that-man-doing-on-these-premises?"

Whilst, Scott was now on a level footing with his guests. His outrage palpable. Murray continued to stir things up...

"I had no idea that you knew Constable Hanlon, sir. Let me formally intro..."

'Sherlock,' recoiled somewhat.

"You know fine well, who I am referring to Inspector."

"Alright, big man." Came the fiery, rasping taunt from the spawn of Satan himself. A dirge delivered directly from the depths of hell. "This heart to heart has been a long time coming *my good man*." A satisfactory smirk, accompanied that last lingering remark.

That was a very interesting turn of phrase to use on Andrew Scott, Murray acknowledged. 'Bunny' Reid was very well informed, wasn't he? 'My good man this, my good man that' - That was all Scott had previously seen fit to refer to Murray as. That day, he had mistakenly looked to belittle the Inspector and that was usually not a good idea. It was normally often something that came back to bite the initial instigator. As this meeting here was about to prove.

"You need to leave. All of you. You need to go." Scott's arms flapped wildly as he walked away from the stairwell and approached DI Murray.

"Would this help appease you somewhat, Mr Scott?" Stepping forward the female officer continued to speak. "I am Detective Chief Inspector Furlong," she purred as she approached Reid.

"Ma'am," 'Bunny' nodded. As he ogled the woman up and down, like a hostile dog in heat. He then stretched out his tongue in a sleazy, suggestive manner and......

'Whack,' first on his left cheek. Then a no less resounding, back-handed 'whack' to his right side.

Everyone froze. Andrew Scott was stunned in amazement. Hanlon in terror. Kerr in utter disbelief and Steven Murray, in sheer admiration. 'Bunny' Reid's cheeks slowly reddened with pain. His eyes with blind fury and his head with delayed anger. His first response was to reach into his suit's extended pocket and live up to his nickname. That was where his 'Rambo' style blade was kept inside a soft toy hand puppet. One in the shape of the Duracell Bunny! Reid thought better of that idea. Instead, in a self satisfied manner, he looked around the room in a more considered fashion. His arch nemesis was present, it was his home turf. He himself, had no bodyguard to lookout for him and he was surrounded by six serving police officers. Strangely, none of which were currently in his pay. What was he to do? What would be expected of him?

Everyone remained motionless. Each individual was on high alert. The Reidmeister's action however, surprised them all. Probably including himself. The aging villain took a slow, deep intake of breath and uttered...

"So, did that appease you, Mr Scott? Can we all stay now?" He rasped. "Cause I can tell you, that's certainly not happening a second time."

He glowered at Furlong. A visual scowl that was intimated in his vocal follow up.

"Because for one, the DCI will want to keep her remaining fingers, I'm guessing! And secondly, if it was repeated, there would definitely be no more walking 'three miles' in the evening ever again. That's for sure."

As the DCI pondered the threat to her pet's safety. Reid surprised her by concluding...

"And Ma'am, that's got nothing to do with your dog. It's simply - that you'll have no legs!"

Furlong held his gaze. She was unflinching and unrepentant and not afraid of his 'bully boy' tactics.

The impasse was broken by a trembling, yet attentive, teenage office worker.

"I'll take the girls to their mother, shall I?" Amanda announced and questioned loudly.

"Well done young lady, good thinking," Murray acknowledged. At that, the frozen spell that seemed to have taken effect over this cast of pantomime characters automatically lifted.

"Good idea," Kerr shouted toward her, by way of extra encouragement.

Both of Scott's nieces had also been rooted to the spot. Each mesmerised by all the unusual amount of extra commotion, activity and noise. This was their exclusive, private playpen, remember. Normally it was just them and either Amanda or their mother. Speaking of which, the svelte figure of Tracy Scott was now holding an upstairs handrail. She looked as glamorous as ever at the doorway to her brother's office, at the top of the stairs. Dressed in purple, tight fitting denim jeans and a chunky cream Aran sweater. The classic image portrayed, was a shining example of a definite homely, girl next door.

The unassuming woman had witnessed everything. If her good looks were anything to go by, then the mother of two certainly seemed to be coping well with motherhood, once again. Her catalogue pose was rounded off with shoulder length, shimmering blonde hair, bright red lipstick and low heeled, virginal white pumps. An upmarket mummy look, if ever there was one.

"I'll take them home now, Amanda." Tracy called from the stairway. "If you would be kind enough to get their jackets on, we'll head off."

She glanced down toward her sibling.

"Will you be okay to deal with all this interruption on your own big brother?"

She gave Andrew Scott a rather resigned look. One that said - It's not something you've never dealt with a million times before. Miss Scott was not the only one distributing philosophical looks. 'Bunny' Reid was now at the base of the modern stairway. He had checked out the sister carefully. Furlong and others had certainly found him to be a rather lecherous and lustful individual. He slowly began to ascend each step.

"Bunny," the Inspector cried out. "Leave it alone man. I will deal with it."

"Aye, right," was muffled from below the ruthless man's breath.

The others in the room seemed to be rooted to the spot. Including Andrew Scott, whose mouth opened widely, but remained silent. Realising he had left his sister unprotected. Reputations were riding high on this series of events. He gradually went to move, but DCI Furlong gently tapped his forearm and shook her head.

"Let it play out," she whispered.

Sergeant Kerr, the rank 'Sandy' had already resorted back to, was very much aware that Scott's sister seemed to be rather embarrassed by the whole affair. Her cheeks had flushed and she had deliberately tried to keep her head down and remain out of view for as long as possible.

Her voice certainly seemed fresh, perky and polite, Murray thought. Yet his experience also told him, that it was plainly tinged with a slight undercurrent of the blues. He'd observed a definite sadness. Not wholly surprising one thought, given all the recent turmoil in her life. As Reid reached the top step, he stood only an arm's length away from the doting mother. He observed her closely. He examined her from every conceivable angle. His head turned, strained and maneuvered at will. With the exception of Steven Murray, no one had any idea what he was doing. He gazed into her eyes, carefully considered her stance and then began to peer closely at her hands. Initially by way of distraction, Murray called out.

"Is that your Volvo outside Miss Scott?"

Although there appeared to be a particularly real, authentic and genuine interest in his voice.

"It's a lovely looking car," he continued. "Spacious I'd imagine. Ideal for the kids. I'm a Volvo driver myself. Have been for many years. Don't imagine at my age I'll ever change now."

Waiting until Murray allowed someone else to get a word in, Tracy Scott was still beaten to the punch by her brother's subtle, but firm tones.

"It's actually a company car, Inspector. Strictly speaking it belongs to the business."

"Yes, I see. I understand, sir. Tax reasons and all that. Oh, and I love your company logo on the number plates. A nice personalised touch."

Andrew Scott shrugged in a very matter-of-fact way and nodded.

Inspector Murray then turned to a rather, red faced 'Bunny' Reid. The look on his snarling face, said that he knew exactly what the diligent and experienced officer was trying to do. Contemplating Reid's next move, the DI raised his voice and offered...

"It's always good to have a reliable and trusted accountant. Isn't that right, Mr Reid!"

But that was a mistake. Reid witnessed recognition in Tracy's face and in that instant, he had his confirmation.

DCI Furlong lurched forward and instantly grabbed Andrew Scott's arms, thrust them up his back and securely attached a pair of handcuffs.

Reid looking down from above, was slightly confused and baffled by those events.

"There you go, 'Bunny.' We have Scott in custody and we'll sort out all the paperwork at the station," Furlong cried.

Reid and Murray instantly exchanged glances.

A slow shake of Murray's head was not enough to appease Jimmy Reid.

An unnerving smile, flashed across his face. "You never even told your boss, Inspector. Oh, how I love you," Reid coughed. "You are some man!"

It was now DCI Furlong's turn to stare intensely at Steven Murray.

"Inspector?" She quizzed. "What exactly did you omit to tell me? And it had better be good."

"Ma'am. We are all good. It's all good. I told you we were going to Fife to take Scott into custody for questioning."

"That you did, Inspector. So what do I seem to be missing here?"

Everyone on the periphery, continually turned their heads, as if on Centre Court at Wimbledon. On this particular rally it was now time for Murray's match winning return.

"Yes, well, Ma'am. It's just that you have handcuffed, the wrong member of the Scott family!"

"What!" Furlong gasped.

Then, seeing his chance, 'Bunny' Reid reached out toward the young woman's face. Tracy Scott flinched immediately and stepped back. On first impression, she appeared to catch her foot on the edge of the top step and tumbled at speed down the modern wrought iron staircase. Murray and others ran toward her as her body twisted and turned. Her face and forehead cracked against the metal on numerous occasions, before assistance arrived at her side in the form of Sandra Kerr.

Amanda and the two children screamed. An ambulance siren, echoed and sounded through the gates and into the yard. How did that work? Joseph Hanlon it appeared, had already called it in as soon as they entered the premises. He'd just had a bad feeling about how things would turn out. Murray would owe him one for that, for sure.

Andrew Scott, still handcuffed, bellowed: "I'll get you for this Reid."

Now with everyone's attention focused on him, the Reidmeister stood with his hands in the air pleading his innocence. Even more interestingly than that, their combined gaze was fixed at the end of his outstretched right hand. For there, held tightly in his grasp, was a shimmering, shoulder length, female blonde wig.

Twenty Eight

'Too many Florence Nightingales, not enough Robin Hoods. Too many halos, not enough heroes coming up with the goods.'

- The Housemartins

Tracy Scott had taken over Jayne Golden's exact hospital bed. As well as having an officer stationed outside her door at all times, she also presently, to her surprise, had the luxury of company inside as well. The soft, apologetic cough from the shadow of her quiet room interrupted the silence. The injured woman turned her bandaged head slowly. A head that had been half shaved for weeks and well disguised under her 'Marilyn Monroe' hairpiece. As she desperately tried to focus, gradually she began to recognise her guest, as he eased himself toward her.

"Morning Miss Scott." The voice was softly spoken and non-judgemental. "It would appear that your devastating trail of destruction has caused quite a stir young lady. Social media loves you." With a troubled smile, he continued with, "Our press boys are busy creating headline after headline about you. *The Vigilante Killer! The Peacemaker! Angel without Wings!* Hey, the general public are even 'Crowdfunding' to build a statue in your memory and put each of your kids through University."

The slightly taken aback Ms Scott had no idea whether to believe him or not. Heck, even Murray no longer knew what to believe on social media, in print or on TV. Spoiler alert - Fake News! The Inspector then calmly paused, before adding cheekily with a wide grin…

"And whilst all that is going on - Crime figures in the city have fallen to an all time low! It would appear that most of Reid's associates have taken the hint and either kept their heads down or ran for the hills." He laughed gently. "You've most definitely made an impression. Ever thought about being a gangster's moll?"

The woman grimaced with pain as she attempted firstly to giggle and then to sit up straight. A simple manoeuvre that was made more complex by the fact that her left wrist was currently handcuffed to the metal bed rail. After her headline grabbing stumble, her natural good looks still shone through. A knowing, understandable smile was directed straight at Steven Murray, alongside a careful determined shake of the head.

"I couldn't let him get away with it, Inspector." Her voice was calm and polite. "Taking a hit out on my mother and allowing one of my children to be taken by his goon. Even finishing off, that waste of space brother of mine. Let's be honest, it was only good fortune that Shaun Scullion came to his senses in time and ensured my daughter's safety from the fatal explosion."

"In fairness, Ms Scott. I don't think 'Bunny' Reid ever targeted your daughter. That was all Scullion's stupidity and lack of brain power, that brought about that course of events."

Tracy Scott gave a tentative shrug of her shoulders. She knew in all honesty, that she couldn't really pin that on Reid. Steven Murray then remembered only too well that recent January afternoon. The day they discovered too late, that Scullion had jumped ship for *'thirty pieces of silver.'* The Geordie hardman had clearly been lured from Andrew Scott's employ by the promise of a better deal. An attractive offer that included a team of his own and a specific location to develop, build up and rule the roost over in the coming years. In return, Scullion, who had killed plenty over the years, ended the life of Andrew and Tracy's brother Paul. Before needlessly blowing up their mother in a car fire in the garage of her luxurious Newton Mearns home. Paul had been the only loose end that could tie him to most of his previous kills, as they carried them out together. So it made sense to take him out, before he transferred sides.

This currently detained mother of two, had cruelly and instantly, had her mother, the grandmother of her two daughters taken away from her on that day. A distinct feeling and emotion that Detective Inspector Steven Murray, only days later, was to experience with his own youngest son. And although Reid was thought to be definitely behind the hit put out on Tracy's family. As always, no actual proof was found to tie him to the specific crime. But she had been determined to create a plan and see justice carried out. This matter was never going to be settled in the normal course of events through the courts. But what better way to impact

Reid's existing business than… through the courts in a more unconventional manner!

She had gotten close to him. Through her shaved head and biker gear, she ensured that 'Bunny's' normal one night dalliances were a thing of the past. She had worked her magic on him. She had charmed him into letting her stay over on several occasions. Pillow talk ensued and slowly but surely facts and information were gradually extracted over the coming days and weeks. She had cleverly made a pact with the devil. 'Bunny' Reid, on the other hand, had slept with the devil! Gender played no part in anything these days.

Getting caught on camera in Larkhall was the clincher for Murray. That was when the Inspector realised that the initials on the bike, never stood for Susan Hayes. 'Hanna' had no ego that needed boosting with personalised number plates or the like. No, the S.H. was part of the corporate branding. It stood for Scott Haulage. Tracy's Volvo, parked outside his premises in Fife, had the exact same lettering under the registration. She may not have fully recognised the fact these past few weeks. But Tracy Scott had for all intents and purposes been, 'that gangster's moll!'

After speaking with her for over thirty minutes, Murray decided to open the door and take a quick peek into the hospital corridors. Then, when finally back in the confines of the room, he once again shook his head. Outside a significant queue had gradually formed. A long line of genuine well wishers. It consisted of many individuals who wanted to openly applaud and thank Tracy Scott. And again, although it wasn't the normally done thing, nearly every police rank in the force seemed to be represented. Assorted family members let down by Judge Menzies, waited patiently to show their support and appreciation. Several leading prosecutors that had figured Stevenson was a *bad 'un*, from day one. Were there making a stand and taking a stance. It was a PR and social media influencers delight. This would have been a dream come true for Christian Blear to put a crazy spin on.

 Throughout this case Murray had been disappointed in certain people's actions. Actions he felt he could have possibly prevented, if he had only acted sooner. He recognised what was still required and ultimately, he blamed himself. He had not been there when key members of his team truly needed him and he would now have to live with that knowledge. He was fully exhausted by purely watching the effort and energy his colleagues had been able to muster up, to get this result. Although he knew one more piece of the puzzle was still to be slotted into position. All being well, it would be fully resolved later that afternoon. Just in time for the scheduled press conference, Steven Murray had hoped. Someone was diligently searching for that remaining piece for him, whilst DCI Furlong was working on the media angle.

"We'll be moving you to the station in a couple of hours, Tracy."

With that as a brusque parting shot, he quietly closed the door and set off for yet another informative rendezvous. One that he hoped would help join up all the dots in this mad hotchpotch of a case.

Twenty Nine

'Mother's Pride on the table, Batman on TV. A Man in a Suitcase, Daktari and Skippy. Jimmy Clitheroe, Colin Stein, and Lulu selling tea. Going to school in the dark, in the winter.'

- The Proclaimers

They'd arranged to meet in the staff car park at the Inspector's relatively new, but second hand Volvo. Murray saw 'Kid' Curry approach him, as if floating on air. This should be interesting, he thought as he exited his car.

"How did you get on Drew?"

Both men remained standing at the front of the vehicle. Curry hopelessly tried a *'calm down, calm down'* expression with his hands. It involved him spreading his fingers wide and gently beckoning both palms to rise and fall to the ground simultaneously. He repeated it three times. Sadly, the young man appeared more like a constipated pianist, than a Police Constable. 'Cool' would never quite work for Andrew Curry, Murray decided that day. However, he was about to be blown away by his ever improving investigative skills.

"Three decades ago, a murder charge brought against Harold George Hayes was found *'Not Proven.'* But we knew that, sir" Curry mumbled. "We also knew that 'Hanna,' had lived with that secret most of her life."

His Inspector was gracious and nodded patiently before adding, "And we also know that her father's life was cruelly taken in the last few years, Drew. Murdered. His body was found buried in fields on the outskirts of town."

"Yes, sir. Indeed we did! Do!" The 'Kid' stated slowly. As if to ask, are you telling this story or am I?

"I'm intrigued," Murray said. Passing the baton firmly back over to his enthusiastic Constable.

"Well, all those years back. Thirty to be precise, like I said. The individual he was accused of murdering went by the name of Alexander James."

Murray listened intently.

"He was some sort of financial genius, sir."

Occasionally, 'Kid' Curry would refer to notes. But he had obviously been exceptionally thorough, because he retained much of the finer detail in his head. Again like Hanlon, he'd had excellent tutelage.

"The man was aged 44 and he had started up his consultancy, slash investment company, straight out of University," Curry told him. "So he had built up a respectable portfolio of clients over those two decades, sir. Plus a mightily impressive pot of cash one might also add."

Drew signalled that last fact by rubbing his thumb and forefinger together.

With Murray's grasp of songs gradually coming back to the fore. The musical 'Oliver' leapt instantly into his mind and he tried desperately at that moment, to restrain himself from singing - *You've got to pick a pocket or two boys, you've got to pick a pocket or two.*

He'd been off his game recently and his musical references and singing opportunities had been restricted to say the least. Today though, he could visually picture Andrew Curry with hat, scarf and fingerless gloves on stage in the West End of London, doing a very impressive Fagin!

"Are you even listening, sir?" Curry asked brazenly. Spotting his superior's seeming lapse in concentration.

"Absolutely." And as if to confirm, "I knew nothing about this man Alexander James," he said.

"That's because, he didn't actually exist, sir."

Murray remained silent and allowed 'Kid' Curry to continue explaining all. He was currently competing with Joseph Hanlon for the 'Sherlock' shirt badge!

"Interestingly, Kenny Dixon's name cropped up on more than one occasion back then. Although that was not wholly surprising, given what we've come to know about him over the years. However, the really interesting point that I was about to tell you, Inspector, was that the deceased man never actually used his full name in connection with his business ventures."

Still silent, yet growing even more inquisitive by the minute, Murray pulled his lips together in anticipation.

"Office staff and colleagues from the early days talked about how 'their,' Alex always preferred to just use his forename and middle name," Curry continued. "He felt it had a more prestigious ring to it and gave his enterprise elevated gravitas."

It also seemed to certainly backup Curry's nickname theory.

"At least that was what the owner felt, sir. So he went through a few viable options before settling on: Alexander James Financial Analysts."

Murray's face was nonplussed.

"I know, right! Not very original. Even three decades ago."

Murray's lips moved briefly. It was a motion that indicated, 'Whatever!'

"So now as I conjure up a pretend drum roll, DC Curry, you are going to reveal his actual surname I assume."

As the Inspector's hands started beating a rhythm by his chest and his tongue protruded at regular intervals from his mouth. He definitely looked and sounded more like Skippy the bush kangaroo, than a middle-aged amateur musician.

Drew Curry enjoyed the moment, captured it on film and allowed Murray to reach a crescendo...

"Trrrrrrrrr," the impressive combination of snare drum and marsupial brokered.

And then the unveiling began. "The impressive finance company was owned and operated by one..."

'Kid' Curry gave him sufficient time to join up a few dots. To consider some of those involved in or on the periphery. With a gradual turn and lift of the head, Murray's gaze met the name on the sheet of paper that his young protégé held up in front of him.

"You have got to be kidding me?"

Curry shook his head vigorously. "It was you that put me on to him, sir!"

"I know, Drew, but a small part of me wanted to be wrong."

"Well, a big part of me wanted you to be right," Curry said with a huge smile.

"And you are certain of this Drew? You are sure that it is the same man?"

"Positive, sir. Checked, checked and triple-checked."

DI Murray then proceeded to throw both his arms into the air and bellow out a fairly accurate impersonation of a certain female colleague.

"Burning - Black - Belly - Warmers!" He yelled.

"I know, right!" Curry chortled. 'Our 'Barbra' is going to go absolutely ballistic."

Thirty

'Misunderstood, overlooked and jaded. Falling in front of unfamiliar faces. Funny how the jigsaw falls into place. Even if I could, I refuse to change it.'

- Ryland Rose

Barbra Furlong was deep in discussion with ACC Martin. On her arrival he had been busy preening himself for the TV cameras. Running through his speech word for word, monitoring his delivery and presentation. Role playing in front of his office mirror, he tried desperately to make it sound natural and authentic. From what little Furlong had observed and heard, he was having very little success. The Assistant Chief Constable seemed set on his decision.

"There is no chance that man is getting any exposure during a live television interview DCI Furlong, of that you can be quite certain."

The Chief Inspector watched the man spit each word from his lips.

"I for one, believe him to be corrupt and exploitative."

His arms swung lazily, like an overweight baboon on barbiturates.

"He may have you all fooled over in Leith. Where like a group of subservient lemmings, you follow him around all day and cater to his every whim."

"Really?" Was all that the DCI could respond with. As well as an exasperated sigh.

"Although, I aim to ensure he is gone by the end of the year. Trust me on that."

Barbra Furlong could not quite believe what she was hearing and she certainly wouldn't trust this slimy, hypocritical individual one inch. But she was certain about the part where he intended on getting rid of Steven Murray, as soon as was humanly possible. So this may well be the Inspector's last chance to impress, she thought. With that in mind, the Chief Inspector took a deep breath and began to implore and petition her ACC to reconsider.

"You fully deserve the spotlight Paul, we know that. But he was the one that figured things out and those fine boys and girls of the local press will push to know where he is and why he is not present. They'll think you are covering up something or heaven forbid, looking to have the spotlight all to yourself!"

Martin seemed to consider this for a brief moment, looked himself up and down in the mirror once again and then uttered…

"No! Sorry, afraid I can't take the risk, Barbra."

A negative response, one would think. But he used my first name. So he has weakened slightly was Furlong's current assessment of the situation.

"You know how the TV, newspaper and media guys love an exclusive, sir? Something that has not yet been revealed to anyone else or went viral already. Literally, breaking news live on air, as it happens. Wow, how do you think they would react to that?"

"What has this got to do with…"

"Murray has one. That is what I've been trying to tell you, sir. He would not even reveal his information or source to me," she lied. "He says it is a vital piece of the jigsaw. That is why he asked me to plead with you to allocate him some time to reach out to the hundreds of thousands who will be watching live. Let's be honest, it must be an extra special revelation, for Murray to want to put himself in front of any cameras."

Now that part, absolutely resonated with ACC Martin. Whereas he loved the attention, the media hype and Q & A sessions with the journalists. He knew full well, that DI Murray did not hanker after any of that nonsense. The Assistant Chief then began pondering on the new merits of this plan. If it was a good inside story, the press would love him for long enough and trust him moving forward. On the other hand, even if the information is newsworthy and well received, Murray may still come across as an incompetent clown during his delivery, and that, possibly even more so, appealed to Assistant Chief Constable Paul Martin.

"On reflection," he announced calmly. "I do value that each of our stalwart officers get an opportunity from time to time to be recognised for the fine job that they do. And in that respect, there is none more stalwart than Detective Inspector Steven Murray," he rounded off.

Of course you do Furlong squirmed. She felt a description coming on.

"We shall give the Inspector, one final swansong in front of the cameras," Martin added. "He deserves that at least," he lied through his teeth.

Her vocal chords delivered, "Perfect, I'll let him know, sir." When the voice in her head impolitely screamed: **You Friggin' Big Basketball Rambler!**

Two hours had come and gone. It had turned out to be a very productive day so far, for DI Murray and his team. When the Inspector entered the interview room there were definitely two polar opposites in attendance. Sat stone-faced at one side of the table was a fully endorsed police officer. An individual, that Murray had felt had excelled himself thus far on the case - Andrew 'Kid' Curry. Sat directly facing him, the good looking woman in Murray's eyes, was still very much a grieving child herself still. Although she was also an over anxious, worried mother and how could one say it nicely - A cold hearted, manipulative, bare-faced murderer. A well loved one at that, mind you. Murray figured he would have his work cut out.

"Still waiting for your brief?" the Inspector asked wearily.

A feeble nod from Andrew Scott's sister was offered.

At the front desk in the Queen Charlotte Street premises, PC George Smith was under strict orders to delay the aforementioned lawyer. So far he has succeeded. Murray had just under three hours before the media people would be expecting their promised statement. ACC Martin had ensured that Police Scotland's public relations team were on the ball.

"Detective Constable, I'm sure this young mother would welcome a cup of extra strong coffee right at this very moment in time."

Murray gave him a knowing nod. One that the fresh faced Curry recognised, as a number 64 - 'Take your time, young man.'

"Black. Two sugar," Tracy Scott felt the need to yell out. It was complemented with a rather quieter and possibly more reluctant, "Thanks."

No recording devices had been switched on and the cheap, ancient looking door swung tightly shut behind Andrew Curry, as he casually made his way to the furthest vending machine in the whole building. It would easily take him ten minutes. Hopefully that would be long enough for Steven Murray to work his magic, Drew thought to himself. Pulling his chair a little closer and clearing his throat, Murray began with…

"So my intention is that I intend to speak up fervently for you, Tracy."

The woman uncrossed her legs and eyed the Inspector warily. Suspicious of his intent.

"I can believe that you were naturally devastated at the loss of not only your mother, but also the untimely death of your brother and have never fully recovered from the shock of it all. Especially with the brief kidnapping and disappearance of your beloved daughter also. All of that would naturally impact a person's personality. The need for revenge and for justice, would have seemed absolutely normal, given that set of circumstances."

Scott's 'girl next door' clothing had been ripped and damaged during her fall. Now in possession of a new set of her own clothes, her legs under the tight black leather trousers were once again crossed. This time she went to sit upright in her chair. These were words she needed to hear. The experienced Murray was pushing all the right buttons so far. But he also knew George Smith could not delay her lawyer much longer and that 'Kid' Curry would be back in the next few minutes. So he had to work hard and fast and get her onboard quickly.

"Those horrendous circumstances had festered away at you. They'd eaten you up," he said sincerely. "No doubt your sleep pattern was irregular and your ability to care for both of your daughters had become deeply affected," he continued.

Once again, the shaven haired female gazed upon DI Steven Murray with uncertainty. However, she remembered that her brother always spoke positively about this man. As much as they may well be adversaries, Scott had accrued a high level of respect and admiration for the Inspector. He had done his homework on him and had mentioned to Tracy on more than one occasion that he was a solid cop. One that could be trusted, if he gave you his word. So she was more than willing to hear him out.

"I'll offer up my testimony, under oath, at what you must have been going through Tracy. The combined stress, pressure and daily fear that you lived in."

Murray spoke faster and raised his voice an octave or two, as he continued his dialogue.

"I'll confirm the perceived danger and continued harassment, that many of Reid's foot soldiers regularly put you through."

The female biker liked where this was heading. She rocked forward, remained silent, but continually nodded positively. Murray suddenly sat back and sighed.

Instantly she responded with, "What is it? What's wrong, Inspector?"

He pursed his lips, went to speak and then restrained himself. His head began to shake.

"Just tell me," she said. "I can take it."

"I'm sure you can, Ms Scott. Actually, I've every confidence in that fact. However, there is just no way I can sugar coat this."

She stuck out her chin, waiting literally for the sucker punch.

"Then don't!"

Murray then spoke in his best apologetic voice. His tone and cadence, both caring and understanding.

"No matter what anyone says," he began. "Now are you listening to me? Anyone!" he confirmed. "For remember, you are going to be locked up behind bars for a substantial period of time. There is just no getting away from that Tracy. Can you fully get your head around it? Understand it? Live with it even?"

Her eyes fell. Her mouth cascaded open, before gradually closing like a reluctant drawbridge. All her inner emotions were now in turmoil and that was when Murray played his hand.

"With all that said, young lady. I suspect that you still want to play an active part in your children's future."

Her ears pricked up at that potential promise.

"Well, I believe that you can do so. We can make that a reality."

Again, her eyes lifted and brightened at that news. The Inspector added confidently...

"I never got to experience that special bond with my youngest son, but you most certainly can with your girls."

Tracy Scott pulled her lips back with her tongue and nervously stroked an earlobe with her right hand. She had been made fully aware of Murray's own personal situation during one of her intimate chats with her brother. It would have been back around the time when her daughter had been taken captive.

"I would have given anything Ms Scott, and I mean anything, to have been able to have made amends. And I think you would too Tracy. Actually, I know that you are being given that very opportunity. Your cooperation, your admission of guilt to these murders, your willingness to throw yourself at the mercy of the Judge, will all count in your favour. It is your chance to redeem yourself and be a real life heroine to your small family."

Murray, then paused slightly, before taking his enthusiasm down a level or two and letting his more pragmatic and practical voice continue...

"Plus a positive statement and glowing recommendation from myself, could make all the difference between never being released and a reduced sentence. Hopefully one with time out early for good behaviour."

Tracy Scott was listening intently to those words, as Murray's delivery continued.

"That would be in time Tracy, to see both your gorgeous daughter's graduate High School. It would allow you to witness them attend a prestigious University, based on the education fund that your kind-hearted brother has set up for them."

Murray knew this made Andrew Scott appear like some modern day Robin Hood philanthropist, rather than the crooked, opportunistic, crime lord that he really was. But needs must, for the greater good, the Detective Inspector thought wistfully. In conclusion, he yet again played to the woman's ego.

"The people are still on your side. They love you and all that you stand for," he echoed passionately. "When they found out it was a woman, especially one that had been wronged, that was the so-called guilty party. The newspapers and media lapped it up. So did social media for that matter. The headlines would continue to write themselves."

Andrew Scott's long term, biological sister, bobbed her head from side to side. The Inspector certainly had a point, she thought to herself. This may well work in her favour. The reporters and journalists had all held Tracy Scott up as some sort of Sainted action hero. A rare breed. A cross between 'Kill Bill' and 'Mother Teresa.' Tracy couldn't help but laugh out loud slightly, at the thought of that warped description.

"Only Ed Sheeran is trending higher than you are currently," Murray declared with a smile. "You bagged a crooked lawyer, a celebrated judge on the take, an unscrupulous *Master of the House*. A dodgy, financial sleaze ball and a long term corrupt district councillor. Each had looked to unsurprisingly line their very own deep pockets. With that said, who could forget all those years ago, the taxi driver who was actually acting as a pimp and a crafty drugs mover and shaker in his day. In fact," Murray questioned. "Who knows what else that guy got away with back then? A man whose actions went unchallenged and undetected for so long, that he was now able to live in relative obscurity and genuinely work as an honest everyday Uber driver!"

Tracy Scott had always maintained that she had no involvement in that last death. But she had allowed the Inspector to tell her a rather interesting story that accompanied the cabbie's brutal ending. Murray knew he had to be brief and to the point.

The true story involved a young schoolgirl who never stood a chance against a sexual deviant. He had molested and abused the young girl on numerous occasions. Her father had been paid to turn a blind eye. Against all odds the girl survived throughout her teenage years, got a good education and is now in a steady job. But all these recent deaths were linked to this man and memories of her horrific attacks had flooded back. She snapped and eventually succumbed to getting her revenge on her attacker after all these years.

Tracy Scott sat numbed by his heartfelt remarks. She knew what he was asking of her.

"How would you have reacted, Tracy? What would you have done if Scullion had interfered with young Leah? Would she have ever recovered mentally?" he asked softly. "Would you, for that matter? As it is, you sought retribution."

She once again listened carefully. Then pondered deliberately and thoughtfully over all of Murray's previous remarks. One had to remember that this female was not stupid. This was not some immature, downtrodden, sad, single mum lacking in strength and self-confidence. This was a bright, articulate woman. A well educated individual, that had simply desired for a long while to be a mother. That was why she was single. She was financially comfortable and had no need for any man in her life at present. Except that was, for this man. The one stood directly in front of her right now. This middle-aged detective spoke a lot of sense and seemed to offer her real hope. She continually reminded herself that her brother had said he could be relied upon and that was important to her. That one thing more than anything else right now, was what she needed to know. She desperately needed someone to put her trust in. Someone that could tell her the best way to do as little jail time as possible. Enabling her to return and quickly re-establish her vital role as a nurturing mother in her family's long term future.

Suddenly the door opened and there stood DC Andrew Curry, with one cup of lukewarm coffee. He had caught the mutual expression that was being shared between the room's two key occupants.

"Everything okay?"

At that, the female voice politely asked, "Where do I sign, Inspector?"

Murray cautiously and with grateful relief, looked up at Curry and answered his question.

"I believe it will be now, son. It will be now."

He then graciously smiled at Tracy Scott and nodded.

The Inspector knew he could trust her. Not once did she look to blame others or infer that someone else was in it with her and that was impressive.

Thirty One

'I've been checking you up, I've been tracking you down. Funny all the things that I've found. My camera never lies. So I'll put you in the picture and cut it down to size. My camera never lies anymore. 'Cause there's nothing worth lying for.'

- Bucks Fizz

The body on the M8 overhead gantry had been identified. It belonged to one Chrissie Cardwell, Reid's estranged sister. Cardwell had been on the run with a quantity of Scott's product and money these past few months. All because, she had started dealing under the radar on his turf previously. The misguided enterprise ended in getting her own daughter sadistically murdered into the bargain.

In fairness, she had lasted longer on the run than anyone, including Murray, had initially anticipated. So much so, the Inspector had never even bothered trying to track her down. She had betrayed both 'Bunny' Reid and Andrew Scott. It really was just a matter of time. There was no way, long term, that she could have evaded both of their networks in this tiny home patch...... that we all call Scotland!

There had never been a close relationship between Chrissie and her brother. Reid and Cardwell had grown up in the badly damaged and fractured foster system. They had been split up since they were young. There had been no bond, no lingering brother and sister connection. No solidarity existed at all between them. It was nothing like the deep, loving kinship that existed between Scott and his sister and her two girls. However, over the years that had had its own difficulties. For whenever anyone she dated found out that she was related to Andrew Scott (MoBstEr). Their awestruck interest in her seemed to cool immediately. The bubbly, fun and laughter they had enjoyed getting to know one another, was quickly replaced with fear, trepidation and worry. Mainly about their two kneecaps being irreparably damaged. Both her beautiful, fun loving daughters had come about through short lived relationships with different men. By which point Tracy Scott had simply been desperate to be a loving mother and parent.

When Shaun Scullion had set about (under orders) to execute her mother and brother in Newton Mearns. He had no idea that the family Matriarch, Jean Scott would arrive home early with her oldest granddaughter in tow. In their linked garage Scullion ensured that the homeowner was trapped in the backseat of her vehicle, after having earlier placed the child securely in the boot. This was merely seconds before he brazenly set alight to the fifty thousand pound car. At the very last minute however, possibly because he discovered that he had a conscience after all, he changed his mind. He quickly rescued the girl from certain death and ran at great pace from the garage. The almighty explosion rocked the quiet, leafy, suburban neighbourhood. The Geordie fugitive then held the girl captive for several hours.

Presumably at that point, he weighed up his options, whilst putting the child's mother through hell and anguish. Given that her own mother had just literally been blown to pieces, that in itself should have been sufficient to deal with. The harrowing thought of what Scullion had done, was doing, or may be about to do to her oldest child was simply unbearable. Mental torture in the extreme. It was the unseen scars from that afternoon, that had indelibly left their mark on both mother and daughter. Tracy and Leah were both changed forever that day. Revenge was always on the cards. Probably, just not from the Scott family member that everyone expected.

The whole squad had been gathered up in an adjoining room, ten minutes before the official press conference was due to start. A few more bodies, including senior ranking officers, some curious hangers on and one or two others, who simply loved to be in attendance at a Murray rundown on a case. Amongst those in attendance were new boy Sergeant Mitchell Linn, Joseph Hanlon, DCI Furlong and Andrew Curry. Then, ACC Paul Martin unexpectedly entered the room. Quite what for, no one knew. Presumably to keep his disdain for DI Murray simmering nicely on the boil. Given his rank however, no one felt to question him or remove him. Murray always enjoyed privately playing to the audience and the more the merrier. So he was actually delighted to see the man present. It got his bravado up and he decided to throw caution to the wind by announcing…

"We're just warming up, sir. Waiting on your prophetic words of wisdom!"

"My prophetic words, Inspector, predict that you and no doubt several of your gathered cronies here. Will be out on your ear in double-quick time, if I ever get my way. You're a joke and a disgrace to the force," he shouted. Before deliberately slamming the door on his way out. A large united, "Oooooohhhhh," was sarcastically offered in his absence.

"A certain someone had waited a long, long time to get some so-called justice, fitting revenge even, on James Baxter Reid and his team." Murray informed his officers.

"Absolutely and now Tracy Scott will serve her time for it, sir." Sgt. Mitch Linn offered.

Murray's head tilted from side to side. His lips pulled back like a slingshot. Puzzlement or agony crossed his face.

"Are you saying it was not Tracy Scott, sir?" 'Kid' Curry questioned with surprise.

"Well it definitely wasn't her brother, either then?" Allan Boyd proffered. "Because he's a relatively new kid on the block."

At that, the Inspector heard the room door either open or shut. Barbra Furlong immediately noticed that it was in fact, Joseph Hanlon going out. He had been instructed to accompany and lead two bodies into the waiting Media room.

Back inside, Linn quipped, "Suggesting then, it was one of their old territorial enemies."

Murray's head, as in the old children's song lyrics, had *'travelled this way, that way, forwards and backwards over the Irish Sea,'* with all of those previous speculative assumptions.

A gentle female voice then quietly interrupted. "Like you said, someone has waited patiently over all these years. An individual seeking redress. Because actually their grievance stemmed from way back in the day when Kenny Dixon was in charge."

One or two audible gasps were heard at that. DCI Furlong was surprisingly teasing those others in the room with cute, compact clues. Murray smiled at her willingness to get with the program.

"Decades had long since come and gone," she added. "Yet that lingering thirst for divine retribution had remained with that one person to this day. Isn't that right, Inspector?" Furlong concluded.

As if to deliberately keep the mystery going and with perfect timing, a well mannered PC appeared at the doorway and announced…

"They are ready for you next door, sir." His remarks were directly addressed to DI Steven Murray.

The normally adequately sized training room was bursting at the seams. The police station with its make-do Media room, was housed in the old Leith Town Hall, which was built around 1827-28. From the Queen Charlotte Street entrance, punters and officers alike are greeted by a grand ceremonial stairway that leads to the magnificent old Council Chamber. Today the historic walls were trying their best to fit in all the 'sardines' it could. Intimacy of the highest order was in play. Individuals could literally check out how much their respective neighbours had in pocket change, such was their proximity to each other.

Murray's whole team had all been encouraged to be there. To witness this and be an active part of this, whatever THIS was. Hanlon had escorted Radical Lizzie and Sarah C. into the press room also. Lizzie wore a tabard giving her Press privileges and the right to ask questions. That is, had it been the correct accreditation and not one that stated Joseph Hanlon was a competitor in the recent Glasgow Green 10k race.

Boyd, Linn and Curry had all moved room and were in situ. They were even joined by one very tired and drained looking, 'Hanna' Hayes. 'Doc' Patterson had been given a heads up by text. He hoped it would all be worth it. Having taken a special detour on his way home from the Gartcosh premises. Murray's brief message earlier, had encouraged the T'inker to be in attendance. But he gave no indication as to what to expect. On the other hand, Sandra Kerr who had only just arrived, felt certain that something major was about to kick off. She knew Steven Murray's style and mood swings. She could tell by the tunes he was whistling and by the spring in his step, that something of note was about to go down. Even she began to hum to herself - *'Home, home is wherever I'm with you...'*

Kerr, now officially returned to the rank of Sergeant from Acting Detective Inspector, stood smartly alongside DCI Furlong at the back of the bustling room. The atmosphere was intense. The TV, press and social media journalists were hyperactive. An unexpected, bizarre rumour had been circulated. Confusion reigned and clarity and order required to be restored.

Furlong herself had been locked away for the past hour or so. Busy making personal calls to news editors, TV connections and the like. Encouraging them to ensure they had someone covering this press conference.

"You'll owe me big time," was all she told each of them.

"Is that the Chief Constable himself, I see seated at the front, Ma'am?"

"It is 'Sandy.' That took a bit of personal persuading, let me tell you." Furlong smiled.

She had personally persuaded the head of Police Scotland to be in attendance. What was really going on here? 'Sandy' began to question. Then it slowly dawned on her.

"You know, don't you?" Kerr yelped. "You know exactly what's about to go down, Ma'am, don't you? You and the Inspector have concocted something, haven't you?"

"It's certainly extra busy here today, Sergeant," Furlong said. Choosing to deliberately ignore the loaded question.

Wow, hearing her lower rank spoken aloud once again was a bitter blow to Sandra Kerr. She always knew that it was only temporary, up until her boss had returned to work. But the title felt good. It had given her fresh hope and optimism for the future. And it certainly did her self esteem, no harm whatsoever. She'd suspected that her work in recent months had plateaued. Possibly like thousands of other working mums, that her career had stalled since coming back to work after the birth of her twins. This recent promotion had reminded her that people still had faith in her and in her capabilities. For that, she desperately wanted to repay them. To show them that she was more than able, and not just in the short term. DCI Furlong had continued to monitor Kerr's facial expressions as they spoke and as if able to read her thoughts, simply put a reassuring hand on her forearm and stated:

"You did a fantastic job, 'Sandy.' Especially given the unusual circumstances. It won't be long, you need to know that. Trust me on that score."

Sandra Kerr pursed her lips and smiled appreciatively. Suddenly a hush of anticipation spread across the historic room. Fidgeting and unnecessary chatting, stopped almost immediately. Cameras flashed into action, people stood up trying to get better vantage points. Microphones and mobile devices were instantly switched to recording mode, and we were off…

Thirty Two

'We don't need no education. We don't need no thought control. No dark sarcasm in the classroom. Teachers leave them kids alone. Hey, teachers, leave them kids alone. All in all it's just another brick in the wall.'

- Pink Floyd

ACC Martin appeared cool and relaxed as he entered stage right. That demeanour altered substantially though, as he spotted his superior, Scotland's Chief Constable. He was already suited and booted next to where Paul Martin would be seated. The head of Police Scotland had entered stage left two minutes earlier. Both men exchanged respectful glances, but the ACC was far from happy. He was no longer the sole star of the show. Especially as he had already given up some of the limelight and conceded time to Steven Murray at the behest of…

Before he could even finish that thought, he soon realised that it was his, *'Barbra,'* DCI Furlong that had set him up and had played him at his very own public relations game. He glowered toward the back of the room, where a flirtatious finger or two, were being waved by a suitably experienced female officer of rank!

Refocusing his attention, Scotland's second-in-command quickly composed and suitably reminded himself of what was at stake today, of the potential riches that lay ahead. This man's inflated ego really knew no bounds. Even from the back of the busy room and with her hands now both by her side, Barbra Furlong could witness clearly that this self-absorbed individual was currently in his element. His narcissistic tendencies to the fore. As he stood up to take the floor - God help us, she thought.

"Ladies and Gentlemen of the press - Good afternoon."

There was a deliberate pause. The ACC waited for a response. The assembled journalists must have wondered if they had just stumbled into a matinee performance of a local pantomime, or had returned to Primary School, as they all at various staggered stages and assorted tones responded with…

'Good afternoon, sir.'

The Headmaster then reconvened proceedings.

"It is with much relief and delight that I, Assistant Chief Constable Paul Martin (in case the large, clumsy name card in front of his seat was not significant enough). That I can inform you that we have in custody, the individual we believe is responsible for the recent spate of murders in and around Edinburgh and Lanark. Responsible for the deaths of John Johnson, Ross Stevenson, Ellen McCann, John Samuel and retired Judge, Gordon Menzies. The remains of one other individual have still to be formally identified."

Furlong looked on with fascination.

Martin had paused this time, to look studiously to his left and then head nodding to his right. To take stock of the assembled press pack and also one would guess, to allow ample opportunity for flash photography. Head shots and side angle pictures that would adorn local and national newspapers and their accompanying websites by the close of day. DCI Furlong and DI Murray were also confidently hoping that would be the case, but for a very different reason entirely.

"Investigations are ongoing," he continued. "But we are fully satisfied that due to the diligent efforts and nature of how Police Scotland officers went about their duties, and in conjunction with the help and support of various members of the public, we have achieved this positive outcome."

DI Murray had respectfully followed Paul Martin out to the waiting table earlier. He was now sitting quietly to his left. As the ACC turned admiringly to him, only Steven Murray could witness up close the sheer insincerity in his eyes and his reluctance to give up the media spotlight.

"Detective Inspector Steven Murray helped lead the investigation," Martin offered up through gritted teeth. "In actual fact, he played a major part in discovering the true identity of the accused."

Those words must have really stuck in his throat, Barbra Furlong acknowledged. A gentle smile simmered across her face as she continued to monitor proceedings from afar.

"At this point, I am sure the man himself would be delighted to answer any questions that you may have for him."

ACC Martin then turned his whole body ninety degrees and gestured toward the Inspector sat by his side. You have got to hand it to him Murray thought.

He just simply had oodles and oodles of self proclaimed 'Smarm!' Steven Murray had never been officially informed by his Assistant Chief Constable that he would be required to speak, answer questions or be unexpectedly thrust into the lion's den. However, the Inspector was not inexperienced in this man's ways. So much so, that he had fully anticipated it, was waiting patiently for it and in actual fact his plan would have been derailed if the invitation to speak had never been extended to him.

"More than happy to do so," Murray said confidently in low tones.

Several hands shot into the air. Including one belonging to a particularly healthy 10k athlete!

"Inspector, is it right that the suspect is female?"

"I can confirm that it is a female that is in custody, correct."

More hands and microphones jostled for position.

"What seemed to be the motive behind the attacks, Inspector?"

Murray considered his answer to this one carefully. He couldn't very well say that - *she was trying to get her own back on a nasty piece of scum. A man that never gave a toss about authority in his life and had a hit carried out on the accused's mother and brother. Oh, and by the way the brother was already a murdering thug in his own right.*

No, Murray stalled, played it safe and opted for...

"We are at a very early stage of uncovering exactly what was behind it all. But I think it would be safe to say that the woman sought revenge on a particular individual. However, rather than take it out directly on them, she decided that through a third party would be the better option. At that juncture the 10k runner spoke up loudly…

"No one was getting in her way for the next question.

"It is nice to hear from the Inspector," she said rather dismissively. "But ACC Martin, YOU have helped bring this case successfully to a conclusion."

Oh, Paul Martin's ears pricked up at that and he smiled graciously, gave a fleeting nod and accepted the kudos that accompanied the remark. Acknowledging the wisdom of this so-called blossoming reporter, he quickly recognised that this cute journalist had obviously wanted to speak to the organ grinder and not his monkey!

He retook the reins.

"So what can I answer for you, young lady?"

Heads, cameras and the potentially unnerving spotlight duly returned quickly to Radical Lizzie. Standing quietly by her side, Joseph Hanlon thought that her innocent, fresh faced look, coupled with her abounding confidence must enable her to breach all sorts of security on a regular basis. He, alongside Murray and Furlong, were the only people that knew the really hoped for outcome of this press conference. And so far, everything was going according to plan.

"Was this all done single handedly?" Lizzie asked. Others couldn't resist and spoke over one another.

"Was this woman solely responsible?" A voice from the front row screamed.

"Was anyone else involved in the murders?" The dishevelled reporter from the Evening Courier asked boldly.

"Well actually…" Murray went to respond.

"No, no, I have this Inspector," ACC Martin confirmed arrogantly.

"But, sir. I think you'll want me to…"

"I have it, Inspector." Martin once again stated dismissively.

Of course you have, sir, Murray smugly thought. And he had no need to be told a third time. He swiftly held his hands up in mock surrender. A clear nod was then exchanged between him and Furlong at the rear of the room. It was a short, brief interaction. But one that was not only spotted by 'Sherlock,' their accomplice. But also by Detective Sergeant Sandra Kerr.

She abruptly turned to her DCI.

"Seriously? Even DC Hanlon is in on the act. What is going on here, Ma'am?" she asked with a knowing look.

"Patience, Sergeant Kerr," Furlong grinned. "Enjoy the special moment, it should be a momentous occasion."

'Sandy,' simply sighed and shook her head.

" … so yes, ultimately the accused was acting on her own." Martin's sentence tailed off. But he soon followed it up with. "We are happy and one hundred percent confident that no one else was involved in the planning and carrying out of these atrocious and heinous acts. That if and when the individual is found guilty, then the sentence handed down will reflect the serious nature of these savage and heartless crimes."

Murray definitely regarded that last line, as an added bonus. Their ACC was certainly getting into the swing of things. His juices and prejudices were overflowing. The man was continually thinking about all of those viewers and households that were tuned in and listening to his every word. He even concluded with…

"The individual involved will feel the full force of this country's justice system. You mark my words, there should be no fear on that score."

Nods of overall approval and a few outright cheers, greeted his stirring political speech. The man on his right, should and could have felt threatened by his supremely arrogant remarks. They were quite obviously made to stake a claim to be the next Chief Constable of Police Scotland. Even the current incumbent appeared wholly embarrassed by the inappropriateness of several of his over the top comments. Suddenly a loud, correctional cough, came over the public speaker system. It came unexpectedly from DI Murray.

"What's wrong with you, man?" His obnoxious superior asked him quietly. Guardedly covering the microphone with his left hand.

"So, let me be clear," the female voice cried, in her quest for quiet. "You did not know this individual personally, Assistant Chief Constable?"

Lizzie's loaded question, now had others scurrying for calm amid the commotion.

Scotland's Assistant Chief Constable appeared to suddenly see this reporter in a very different light. Gone were his rose-tinted glasses that only seconds earlier had seen her as a wise, blossoming journalist, with a promising career ahead of her. With his face flushed, anger began to infiltrate his thoughts and he was now struggling to find the right words. The country's news media spotlight was most definitely still on him. There was to be no hiding place at this moment in time. Especially with the one man who currently outranked him, sitting by his right shoulder.

"What? No! Of course not," were the first words uttered from his mouth.

He had lost all his composure. Paul Martin did not do well when unprepared. A fact that over the years DI Murray was aware of. And he had hoped today, to use that fully to their (Police Scotland's) advantage.

"I had never even heard of the young woman, never mind met her," the ACC replied defensively. By which point he wished he'd never entered back into the fray at all.

Murray coughed aloud a second time. If his first signal had been missed, then this one had certainly not been. The large HD monitor that had sat patiently behind the three men in relative obscurity and darkness, now burst vividly into life. The gaze of all three men at the top table swivelled around. Recognising instantly, where it had been filmed, Paul Martin made to switch it off. A resting hand on his shoulder from his Chief implied - Sit still!

"Is that her?" One of the male journalists shouted. "Is that the accused?"

"It is. It most certainly is." Steven Murray, happily confirmed over the PA system.

There had been no real need for the clarification, except for the personal satisfaction that it no doubt gave the DI. Because there, on screen, in Andrew Scott's new modern premises and in full glorious Technicolour for everyone present to witness - 'Beauty and the Beast.' DC Boyd and the other team members struggled to contain their shock. Thousands of their fellow officers would be dancing in the streets at this piece of filmed recording. 'Doc' Patterson simply shook his head in amazement. How his friend had pulled this off, he did not know. What would happen to him next, regarding disciplinary action, he dreaded to even think about. But fair play to him and hats off for doing so. A massive, satisfactory grin shone like a radiant summer sunset, lighting up his friend's normally sombre face. However, Radical Lizzie's role was not yet complete. She jumped in once again and her 'Best Supporting Actress' nomination was in the post.

"Wait a minute I know her," she said, stirring her imaginary pot. "Is that not the alleged gangster, Andrew Scott's sister? And who is that with her? If I am not very much mistaken, sir - Is that not your own lovely, clean cut, distinguished features? ACC Martin you seem to be having a rather in depth conversation with the woman that one minute ago, you claimed never to have heard of? Never mind, met in person!"

The room went mental. Everyone was on their feet. A barrage of questions ensued. Photographs and mobile recordings of every sort went viral. Commotion, commotion, commotion. Christmas had come early for those gathered reporters today.

"Why are you with the accused?" Several yelled.

"Is that timestamped before the first murder?" Another spotted and asked.

"So, you did know the accused! Why would you lie?"

That one - was one final stir of the pot from Lizzie. She had thoroughly enjoyed the last five minutes. Now though, both her and Sarah C were being escorted at speed off the premises by DC Joseph Hanlon, just as other shouts, queries and accusations were being hurled in Martin's direction.

"The full force of the law?"

"Will that still apply?"

"Really!"

"Disgraceful, disgusting."

"Shame on you, Murderer," and "Scum," were some of the other opinions still being freely aired.

Suddenly, as quickly as the room had erupted, it fell silent. You could quite genuinely have heard a pin drop as Police Scotland's Chief Constable rose from the table. He turned briefly to watch a further few scenes of the security footage unfold in front of him. The white haired man never spoke, he just nodded brusquely at his Deputy. The arrogance and self confidence were long gone, as Paul Martin began to slowly and steadily rise up. He knew instantly that everything had imploded. In some respects as DCI Furlong watched from a distance away, she fleetingly felt sorry for the once proud man.

Now ashen-faced, head bowed and shoulders slumped, he faced years behind bars. A career down the toilet and no legacy whatsoever. The experienced officer knew the drill and reluctantly placed his hands behind his back. His boss unhesitatingly offered yet another curt nod. This time its intended recipient was Detective Inspector Steven Murray. He like many of his fellow colleagues, had been continually hauled over the coals and made to look stupid and inferior so often in the presence of the ACC's bullying ways. So here was one man that did not need to be asked twice. He was rapidly up on his feet, had the handcuffs attached promptly and stared Paul Martin straight in the face before DCI Furlong could cry: SCOOBY DOOBY DOOOOO!!!

Thirty Three

'Heaven is a metaphor, the lovers of the world reach for and truly you may find the occasional angel. Mostly when we get up there, far above the city air, all we have for company is crows, ravens and rooks. Crows, ravens and rooks.'

- David Rotheray

One of Murray's few strengths throughout his career, was getting close to the workers at the coal face. Treating so-called underlings well and with due respect. His yearly Christmas gift to his local lollipop men and women, being a perfect example of such. With regards to gleaning information over the years. He never ceased to be amazed at the amount of individuals on the periphery of his social circle, that were more than happy to share helpful information, tips and background details with him. In the main, they trusted the man because he treated them fairly and was honest with them. Ultimately he made them feel valued and of worth to their community and to their surroundings.

It was in the little things that he excelled. Asking after them and their families, about their aspirations in life and then more importantly, following up on that information and retaining it for future use. Just like the way he remembered the names of Tracy Scott's two daughters when speaking with their Uncle Andrew. That impressed the up and coming gangland boss. The wayward, ruthless and dishonest outlaw had mellowed toward him that day. They may well be on different sides of the divide, but Scott has since developed a healthy respect for Steven Murray. Both the man that he was and what he stood for. He recognised integrity and the aura of a man that cared. A man that could be trusted. A man that led by example, a listener and a genuine man of and for the people. All that respect was borne out of a seemingly insignificant fact - remembering those two girls names.

One of the people that he had tried recently to find out more about was young Amanda. The Scott Haulage employee that was treated like a general dogsbody. Given no official title - Yet her job included being secretary to all his businesses, legal and otherwise. She made the tea, dealt with clerical work, answered multiple phone calls and in addition to all of that, she was expected to be an unpaid, part-time nanny and crèche worker to his frequently visiting nieces.

Amanda Campbell was seventeen years of age. Her hair was short and bobbed. A tiny silver piercing, shimmered in her left cheek. She had left school last summer with little in the way of qualifications. She'd been too busy messing around and being a fool. At least that was what she had told the Inspector. And there, directly in front of her that day was her partner in crime. A serial joker in his teenage years. A man that could relate one hundred percent to that type of behaviour at High School, on the rare days that he prepared to visit that was! She, like Murray, was regretting it now. Needless to say, just like many kids do, she lacked the maturity to fully understand and appreciate the benefits for her in later life. However, she'd been grateful to have been taken on by Mr Scott, seven months earlier.

Interestingly, if the bold Andrew Scott had never deliberately kept DI Murray waiting that day when he had initially popped in to his new Fife premises. His sister may never have ended up in prison facing a life sentence. *Circumstances and timing,* Murray thought. *Circumstances and timing!* Chances are the boys in blue would still have been out searching fruitlessly for the killer and Murray would most likely never have linked ACC Martin with any crime whatsoever.

As it was, that day in the office, Andrew Scott left Murray to stew. So in turn, the Inspector made good use of his time and found out more about the childhood life and times of Amanda Campbell. Including the fact that he was only the second police officer that she had ever spoken to in her entire life. Interested in hearing more on that subject, Steven Murray automatically asked the inevitable…

"When was the first time, young lady?"

The DI had asked genuinely. Expecting probably that it was in Primary School. Possibly on a day when officers were visiting talking about 'Road safety' or 'The danger of strangers.' How wrong could he be? He remembered her reply, verbatim.

"A couple of weeks ago!"

"Really!" Murray's eyes lit up at that little piece of intriguing information. "Tell me more," he had asked slowly at the time. Quickly followed up with a… "I don't suppose you have CCTV here do you?"

The rest as they say… is history. He had given her his card. Written his 'personal' address on the back and instructed Amanda to send him a copy of the footage from the day when the other officer visited. He recalled the conversation vividly.

"I don't think Tracy even knew about the CCTV," Amanda remarked. "But Mr Scott insists that we have it running 24 hours a day, 7 days a week," she informed the Inspector. "Seems like a pure waste of money, if you ask me?" she then added.

But thankfully you are not an extra cautious crime lord running twenty percent of Scotland's drug money, Murray mulled over. Those specific thoughts remained carefully in his mind.

"A full month of recordings are stored, before we wipe over them," Amanda added.

Murray had been in luck, by six full days. Their private deal was concluded and her boss knew nothing about their personal arrangement. Amanda was fine with that part and smiled even more when Murray handed her fifty pounds in fresh, new notes.

"You never know how much the postage might be? Maybe send it Recorded Delivery," he grinned.

"What age are you really?" she smiled. "I'll send it attached to an email. That will mean no cost whatsoever. So does that mean you'll want these back?" she asked flirtily and winked. Reproducing the five, crisp tenners.

It was then Murray's turn to reply with, "No, you're good." And return a wink of his own! At that moment, the obviously exceptionally busy and elusive Mr Scott appeared at the landing outside his upstairs office. Curiosity had gotten the better of him. Thinking - What could they possibly have to chat about?

There would probably have been some limited damage caused to Martin's reputation if Murray had released the footage sooner. But there was no solid proof of his involvement. Although it would have definitely muddied the waters and possibly saved the lives of Ellen McCann and John Samuel. By this point however, the others had already gone to their celestial glory or more likely and hopefully, Murray figured - A twenty four hour cesspit of burning flames and continual torture. At least that was the wishful thinking, on the Inspector's part.

He knew Paul Martin would have pulled out all the stops, made his excuses and desperately covered his back. As for poor, if one can call her that, Tracy Scott. She would have taken the fall and carried the can all alone. Because she was no 'Grass!' As Steven Murray had witnessed personally in recent days, this woman was not giving up ANY other names in relation to those killings. Fully aware that he himself, had made some interesting arrangements in the last few days with multiple people. He felt reassured by her criminal integrity, to say nothing. Even to those not fully versed in lip reading, many quotes and sentences could be easily made out on the video footage that played that day.

Martin producing his warrant card and looking for Andrew Scott / Being told he was out of the office / Tracy introduced herself and was there anything she could do to help / The ACC pondered briefly, then was seen to mouth clearly - 'You may even be the preferred option!'

Tracy Scott had filled Murray in with the finer details. How he outlined his plan. The length of time he'd been waiting, for the right circumstances to arise. He would have been happy for one of Andrew Scott's men to have fulfilled the death duties. Tracy though, was still fueled with anger, hurt and resentment toward Reid. So it was personal for her and they could lay the blame at the door of DC Hayes initially, even if that only brought them extra time to deal with the accountant and the female council leader.

Again though, the question sure to be asked was - Had Murray's delayed actions cost people their lives? The maverick Inspector had no idea it was going to be Tracy Scott, herself, that would ultimately carry out the killings. Like 'Bunny' Reid, her brother would have had men on the payroll more than capable. But this was to be an exclusive private partnership between her and Martin, no other outside involvement and understandably so. He had plenty of insider knowledge - Access to case files, notes from interviews, recordings and historical information that was never made public and he wanted revenge on specific individuals. She on the other hand wanted to hurt Reid, not necessarily physically. But to destabilise his kingdom, to pull his finances and free him of every last ounce of power that he may yield. For that, she still needed to get extra close to the man himself, to seduce him and win his trust. Eroticism had a funny way of eliciting secrets. Dates, meeting times and individual names were soon forthcoming, as was her vengeance. He had an ego, and like most men, when massaged correctly the boasting began and his cloak of invincibility was soon shredded.

With hindsight there was no way that Murray could have stopped the initial onslaught - 'The Easter Weekend Celebration!' The appalling, macabre killings of Stevenson, Menzies and Johnson. In all honesty, if it hadn't been for them, he would have never been back at work as requested by James Baxter Reid. Again with the - *Circumstances and timing!*

That first trio of murders were well planned. Meticulous homework had been done and carried out. People's schedules and property layouts had been studied and taken onboard. Tracy Scott's twin persona was a definite curveball. No one saw that coming. From the girl next door, perfect mum - to chewing gum blowing Hell's Angel and devil woman! Her hair was shaved to entice Reid. Again she had genned up on the normal one-night stands that he usually went for. It was a long-haired carpet fitter that was witnessed at Stevenson's, but no one thought female. She was good. Even waving confidently at the local neighbour's. However, no long hair was visible as she rode at speed away from the Judge's exploding hillside retreat. Again with bikers, people associate the male species. Perhaps if she had only taken a different route, other than the Lanark Road, then possibly the S.H initials would never have been captured on camera and who knows where

Murray and his team would have been, in solving the case.

As if a reminder was needed, Tracy Scott's sole purpose was to bring down Reid's mini empire. It was not to witness the untimely death of 'Bunny.' Although, had that occurred, she could have lived with that also. *Circumstances and timing!* No, for her, it was to witness the mental anguish and turmoil that these events would bring to bear upon him. The pressure, the turning of the screw from his other underworld cronies who would have been impacted by his failure to deliver as promised. They, would be relentless in their follow up. As a wealthy individual herself, Tracy Scott's satisfaction and greatest delight would be gained by turning James Reid's life upside down and witnessing his journey from privilege to penury. To look on as a casual observer and watch a broken man, be returned to the gutter where he belonged.

The Assistant Chief Constable's motives, on the other hand, had possibly been even more calculating, sinister and vindictive. For it was he, that had suggested the whole scheme. To be fair, most normal minded people when presented with the idea would have told him to sling his hook. But not our Tracy. The mental imbalance must run in their family. With that said, and given the woman's recent traumatic background and experience, Paul Martin was fairly confident that resentment and anger would still be festering strongly within her. So unsurprisingly, on hearing his proposals, the young mother of two, seeking some form of sick reprisal, was more than willing to proceed.

With the scattered bones still to be formally identified, Murray now knew full well who they belonged to. It was also safe to say that the individual was in no way an innocent party in all these dreadful events. He had played his part in times past, just like all the others. None of the dead were guiltless. For Detective Inspector Steven Murray, it was important to remember that it was a dear friend many years ago, that first introduced him to the old adage of - *If you fly with the crows, you'll get shot with the crows.'*

So for the as yet unnamed individual, as well as Ellen McCann and John Samuel. They would have done well to remember that. If they wanted to be associated with a high risk or high profile situation and benefit from the healthy rewards of that association. Then they also had to accept the consequences, if things went wrong. They could not simply dissociate themselves. An equally suitable adage could now be applied to Ms Scott and Paul Martin themselves - *If you lie down with dogs, you get up with fleas.'*

It was greenbelt land - safe to say, it should never have been built upon for the foreseeable future. Twenty years they safely reckoned at the time. But things didn't quite go according to plan and Ellen McCann had let them down. She had been unable to get that particular motion passed and although she had managed to get the work delayed somewhat. Her real bosses had found that unacceptable. She had flown with the crows for many years now and had gratefully welcomed all the fine rewards and luxuries that went along with that flight plan. But during preparatory work on a field in the Balerno area a few years back, a body had been unearthed. Yes, the very location, that ironically, Ross Stevenson had purchased his premier home.

The remote, decaying corpse of 'Harry' Hayes should never have been discovered at all Or at the very least, not for another two decades. A span of time that should have seen all those involved in the disposal of his body - Either elderly, infirm or gone from this mortal earth entirely. That body find, was the beginning of the end for Ellen McCann. She no longer flew at such safe heights after that. Her reliability was gone. And just as Tracy Scott had targeted Reid's reliability, McCann now also knew her fate. No matter the deals she had pulled off for Dixon in the past and more recently for Reid. Property transactions and insider council information and secrets that had made these men hundreds of thousands of pounds previously - now stood for nothing. She knew that they would have other employees within her organisation currently learning the ropes and looking to pursue career opportunities. She was not stupid, so was also fully aware that they were biding their time. Making the most of deals that were already in the pipeline in recent years. However, it was NOT solely about the money, the finances and the profit any more. With all the investigative work that was being dredged up with Stevenson and Menzies, it was about her being a loose end. She had been living on borrowed time. If she had not been targeted by the dogs - Tracy Scott and Paul

Martin, then a local tenant from Reid's own farming community would have doubtless drawn out his shotgun and downed her as the last crow flying.

The body in Balerno five years ago had been wrapped in cellophane and sliced up the middle. Ross Stevenson's murder had been replicated deliberately to throw suspicion on to DC 'Hanna' Hayes, the deceased's daughter. Had she been patiently planning some recriminatory response during the intervening years? It certainly had appeared to be a police officer. Someone that had current access to where and how that body had been discovered and recovered. Which was also why 'Bunny' Reid had thought it was an inside job. In fairness to him, he was ultimately proved to be correct. If he had not allowed himself to be foolishly and stupidly seduced and taken in by Tracy Scott though, none of this may have happened. The name 'Bunny' knew her by, was Ashley. Nothing more, nothing less - just Ash. A... then those S.H initials again. Deliberate or not? We'll never know. Let's not forget though - It was Assistant Chief Constable Paul Martin who was the mastermind behind it. But why?

Thirty Four

'Now you might never find that perfect town. But the sun still sets on a rooftop where the city sounds like a Gershwin clarinet, and you might still be searching every face for the one you can't forget.'

- Mary Chapin Carpenter

He was always looking to progress. Even now he was only one rung away from being the sole man in charge. So he had done well for himself. He had always been driven. Never well liked though. He was, as DCI Furlong accurately described - Arrogant. Conceited. Obnoxious. Self-Centred and Bullying. He got things done, however. Although, he had no qualms about who or what he had to step on or step over to achieve HIS objective. And this particular covert mission, which was way off everyone's radar, was to be no different. Destruction of lives and property, they were of no concern to him. Never mind justice or jail terms. The man simply wanted good old fashioned vengeance - An eye for an eye. Creating a world where very soon everyone would be blind. Again the question needed asked - Why? That ended up really simple and basic - the loss of his father, Sandy.

His nickname was not derived from the colour of his hair, like Sandra Kerr's. But from the old Scot's terminology for someone named Alexander. These days they were more likely to be addressed as Alex or Zander. But when the Assistant Chief Constable's dad was born, he was christened Alexander James Martin. He grew up to become the financial whiz kid who never lived up to his promises or to Kenny Dixon's expectations. For failure to deliver, a young Alexander James - as his company name recognised him, was targeted and taken out on Dixon's orders by one - Harold George Hayes. The man who was found *Not Proven'* in a courtroom leased out for the day to Messrs Menzies and Stevenson. Again it all fell nicely to set up a grieving daughter wanting justice for her late father. Ever since his body had been stumbled upon five years ago. It was then that Martin made himself fully familiar with the case and all the background reports. From that day on, he had waited patiently for the ideal scenario to present itself. In recent weeks the pieces all seemed to fall into place. *Circumstances and timing!*

Unfortunately for Paul Martin though, he had no idea of what Susan Hayes' actual upbringing with her father was really like and that would prove to be a vital flaw in his blueprint. Once again and not for the first time, the ACC also blatantly chose to underestimate his adversary in this investigation. An individual thinker. A man who constantly stood up to Martin's egocentric bullying. A resourceful and respectful man in the shape of one Detective Inspector Steven Murray. Having regularly visited the coalface, that particular man, knew all about Hanna's father. That is what he personally loved about her backstory. Her dogged determination and drive, the fighting spirit that enabled her to break the cycle of her unhappy childhood. Murray knew from the first day that he met her several years ago, that she was naturally clever and bright. But he always figured that there was something from her past holding her back. He often wondered why she lacked the motivation to advance her career? Was it more a lack of self-worth? The Inspector knew that he had heard her say on numerous occasions, four particular words that worried him. That she always seemed to use as her less than positive mantra in recent times, like a vocal comfort blanket. A statement disguised in several formats - In her dress sense, in her manner, in the way she spoke and held herself. That seemingly innocent sentiment that she had put forth loud and clear on regular occasion was - *'she didn't deserve better.'*

Is that what she had mistakenly and innocently told herself all these years? Because more accurately Murray suspected, the truth was that she had been continually told that very same thing throughout her whole life, by her low-life, waste-of-space, chancer of a dad. Whatever had caused it, Murray, her Inspector, had always trusted her and no matter what, would fight for her. *Circumstances and timing!*

Wow, how much do those make us do? Murray questioned. Certain actions and words that are totally out of character, yet like Tracy Scott, if the motive is enough to persuade us, then a switch is flicked and we'll do whatever is required. Andrew Scott's sister had never been in trouble in her life. Even given her background, she had only ever wanted to be a loving, caring, attentive mother and up until a few weeks earlier, that is exactly what she had achieved. So there you have it. *Circumstances and timing!*

The young enthusiastic businessman, Alexander James Martin unfortunately got in tow with some bad people and was brutally murdered by Harry Hayes. Never mind any *'Not Proven'* verdict, he was most definitely your man. *Circumstances and timing!*

A man that several years later was himself considered surplus to requirements, violently slain and buried in a remote field. Probably, he was simply considered another loose end by Kenny Dixon. It made sense, it was good housekeeping - nothing more, nothing less. The discovery of his body, the *circumstances and timing,* were exactly what ACC Martin had been waiting for all these years. He had the perfect fall guy or should we say fall girl, in Susan 'Hanna' Hayes. Or so he'd thought.

Murray required solitude. He needed to return home and leave all the chaos, murmuring and gossip at the station. The Chief Constable did in both equal measures, chastise and praise the Inspector's somewhat unconventional methods before he left the building however..

"They worked this time, Steven." - Would have been the praise.

"When do you retire?" - The gentle reprimand.

Murray suspected however, that those comments were solely for public consumption and that behind closed doors a more severe and possibly official warning would follow. It was well worth it. I'd happily do it all over again, he thought. A smile simmered under the surface. Sat alone, the troubled Inspector reflected on his most recent actions. Had he tentatively stepped over the line once again? Had he crossed it previously in the past, but simply never stopped to ask the question? Was he any further forward in finding his son David's violent killer? The distorted message sent to 'Hanna' Hayes was still being worked on by forensics. Murray had thought deeply about what she had said. That her gut had felt it was in reference to his son and not the recent spate of murders. He had always valued her opinion previously, so why feel the need to question it now? Ultimately what harm would come from having it checked out properly? Hayes was only too happy to have the message examined and had left her phone in their safekeeping.

Tony Cadanza's area of expertise in the lab was IT based. Mainly the recovery and restoration of data and footage from devices deliberately damaged and broken to avoid such detection. So a mobile in working order should be child's play. Twenty minutes earlier he had sent Murray a text at home. It read: *A female - English voice - West or East Midlands*. Murray was delighted at that. He was not sure there was really much more that he could have expected from them. Although a postcode, even a house number would have been gladly welcomed and possibly which room in the property their suspect was currently sat! Cadanza however, did pass on one other piece of information that was probably even better than that. Something that Tony thought would have been helpful and useful to him, based on his present line of enquiries.

He was also privy to recent information passed on to him from Jayne Golden and her tip, tied in rather nicely with what the science guys had confirmed. Although, almost instantly he wondered - Did she have an angle? She always seemed to play the game with a hidden agenda. This time he was more wary. 'Smitten,' Sandra Kerr had said last time round. Maybe she was right, Murray conceded. Was Jayne Golden a romance waiting to be rekindled? Or was there someone even closer to home? Could there be the possibility of something brewing between the teetotal Inspector and the overly descriptive, DCI Furlong? He had fully recognised that he'd shown no hesitation in going to 'Barbra's' rescue. It wasn't the first time that day, that Murray had considered that the recent series of events had in actual fact, turned out to have rescued him!

Fully exhausted, he headed upstairs to bed. The Inspector's snoring had become much worse of late. But his recent self-imposed hiatus, had caused him to lose a substantial few pounds. Thoughtful and considerate as his colleagues were, they did not necessarily choose the most healthy options whilst maintaining their ongoing grocery deliveries. However, Murray just did not have the desire or willingness to cook or make a meal anyway. In recent years he had learned that his weight impacted and had a direct correlation with his level of snoring. So much so, even his 'black dog' would disappear at pace into another room for peace and quiet!

The man currently found himself sat bolt upright in bed. It was three thirty in the morning and with only his imaginary canine companion for company. He had just received a voicemail. Robert Coulter had left Murray a brief message with only a few garbled words. It was a day later than Murray had anticipated, which was unlike him. To be fair, no one had actually seen 'Ally' for a couple of days now, due to his demanding schedule. Which in itself was a great testament to his fine detective skills, which were obviously in high demand. It was a response to Murray's text from when the Inspector first interviewed Susan Hayes. In plain wording, the private investigator simply stated - 'I know that you will figure it out Steven, but Hanna's father... NEVER HAD A DRIVING LICENCE!'

His imagination had run wild. Conjecture, speculation and ill informed guesswork had on this occasion, left him wide of the mark and wide awake. So another four hour sleep would need to suffice. His sweat had only just subsided and his covers were stained and damp. Uppermost in his mind currently - disappointment! The near 40 year old memory that had ambushed his dreams that night was all about football. Real life annual schoolboy matches between England and Scotland in fact. Events that had taken place since 1911 and Murray's trance like state had conjured up a particular game from 69 years later.

The DI never failed to be truly amazed at how the brain worked. The abstract variation of thoughts that delicately sifted through each individual's personal algorithm, before being re-wired, transmitted and displayed in their mind. Phenomenal, Murray would always think. Although he could never quite understand it. Do any of us really?

It was Saturday 7th June 1980. At Wembley Stadium there was an England v Scotland under 16's, football match taking place. It had 69,000 people in attendance. With millions more watching on television, Steven Murray being one of them. For football aficionados, it was the game that launched future Scotland captain Paul McStay to prominence. Those watching saw a pulsating match between the two rivals' best schoolboy players. Murray a year before, very nearly was one of those players. Having played for his hometown, Paisley and District earlier in the year, he was then selected to go to the last round of trials (about 30 players) for Scotland schoolboys. DI Murray, unfortunately never made the final squad. But to this day he always wondered... If only?

Steven Murray never played in goal between the posts. He certainly never had the silky skills of an influential midfield playmaker. Nor for that matter, did he have the finishing ability required of a much needed prolific striker. No, at just over six feet tall, slim (back in the day) and with just enough aggression when pushed, he was the ideal fodder to be an old-style, no nonsense defender. A big number five. Your *'If in doubt, put it out,'* centre-half. Like one of his old managers used to say to him every week - 'They're not gonna score fae Row H, son!'

Murray's pivotal role in the team was to ensure that nothing got past him. Not really that different, from the role he currently occupied with Police Scotland.

Although he had slightly more leeway back then to lash out, kick, manhandle and rough up his opponents. However, ultimately, like now thankfully, not too many of those that he was in direct competition with, got the better of him. If they did, it would certainly not be for long.

He had woken once again feeling totally discouraged with life. A cyclone of destructive thoughts had made its way into town and had left a devastating trail of broken dreams, goals and ambitions in its wake. Mentally the overriding impression and opinion Murray had retained from the tumultuous whirlwind was, that he had failed far too often in this life. That he had fallen short over the years and that he had regularly disappointed and verbally abused his late wife. That he had frequently let down and disregarded his family and friends. Right now with everything that was going on, he had even convinced himself that he was a major disappointment to society. A dark and overwhelming depression had once again swept in to engulf him. His bipolar was waging war and its toxic side effects were taking their toll on this highly talented, but flawed individual. That combination of emotions, mixed and blended with the genuine grief of losing a child, having never really gotten to grips with the fatal hit and run of his wife and his ongoing feelings of being responsible for her death, even by default, due to his ongoing gambling addiction at the time. Had now left this man once again feeling worthless and numb. With no genuine desire to continue and possibly even more importantly to him, NO REASON to carry on.

That 1980 game had been played out in his mind endlessly before he woke. Again he couldn't quite join up the dots to discover their actual meaning. But he was convinced that there was one. So what was its significance? He was a great believer that dreams served a purpose, that you could learn from them. That you could recognise pitfalls, find analogies and adjust your stance and positioning accordingly. In his teenage years, like half the young footballers his age, every Friday night he would go to sleep playing out the whole of the next day's fixture. Who were they playing? What was the predicted weather to be like? Was it home or away? What surface would it be held on? Would it be played on their own High School pitch, which consisted of rutted, red ash? One fully guaranteed to rip your leg to smithereens if you attempted any form of slide tackle on it. Or was it to be a normal grass playing field, either with the occasional drainage problem or bone dry and worn out in key areas? Whatever surface it was to be played on, Murray then automatically imagined being picked for the team, how the game would play out and of course... scoring the winning goal! The other half of the boys his age, also dreamed of scoring over the weekend. But that was a different scenario altogether!

A little known fact these days, was that all Steven Murray ever wanted to do when he was younger was to become a professional football player. That never happened. With perfect hindsight, he had the talent, but was lazy. Over the years he now recognised that he had always had life easy. He never really was one for early mornings, long days and serious responsibility.

Physically demanding hard work was not his forte. Ironically, he had no problem working long hours, or dedicating much of his time to specific projects and was always reliable and true to his word. In the deepest recesses of his mind as he reflected back on those days, he thought much of it was a lazy gene. Possibly nowadays however, he believed it to be simply selfishness. He likes his personal routines. His own space. His weird idiosyncratic tendencies. However, on the other hand, trained medical staff will tell you that it is bipolar speaking.

That particular morning, the need to get back to reality and stop feeling sorry for himself yet again, came from an unlikely source from beyond the grave. In that classic match - Scotland won by five goals to four. But what was going on here? Murray lay back on his pillow and pondered: So what's the real score with 'Hanna' Hayes? He had played all his substitutes and needed extra-time. However, before the final whistle sounded, a red card had been produced. Sadly, the player that was to be dismissed, came as no surprise to him!

Thirty Five

'It took a while, but she looked in the mirror and she glanced at the license for my name. A smile seemed to come to her slowly, it was a sad smile just the same.'

- Harry Chapin

The gloomy hallways and corridors of the old station were uninspiring.

"Good morning, sir," DC Hayes offered up with sincerity. She was sitting behind a desk at the edge of the walkway. DI Murray joined her and sat opposite.

"Hanna!" Came his curt response.

It was followed up with a brief nod, closed lips and a concerned grimace upon his face.

'Is everything okay, sir? You look worried. A penny for them?" She smiled.

"You'll need a darn sight more than a penny, I'm afraid."

"I don't understand, boss. I thought you'd have been over the moon at the outcome."

Hayes then proceeded to rhyme off a list of things that her Inspector should have been happy and satisfied about.

"Everything has been resolved. The media loves you. You've given them enough to keep them busy for the foreseeable future. Then there is the attractive Jayne Golden back on the scene. That must be welcome news."

'Hanna,' winked at Murray whilst offering that last comment.

"Plus the added bonus that she wasn't actually involved and will most probably not be charged in connection with anything regarding the ABC Casino fiasco either!"

Murray shrugged, unmoved by any of her remarks. His head angled with deep uncertainty, like the Leaning Tower of Pisa.

"As well as the fact that you uncovered yet another corrupt colleague in the force," she added with palpable delight.

The disgraced, Ex-Assistant Chief Constable Paul Martin, in his own words would be held to account for his awful criminal actions, plus his ultimate betrayal of his fellow officers. Murray momentarily considered speaking at that point, but remained silent.

"I never trusted the man," Hayes said nervously. "There was always just something about him."

"Trust; Heinous criminal actions and being held to account for such. Now that is a very interesting concept, don't you think DC Hayes?"

'Hanna' was just about to jump straight in with both feet, when she suddenly remembered Murray's old fashioned, 'Columbo' style approach to policing. One where the Inspector is often undervalued by his colleagues and thought clueless by the criminals. Susan Hayes was not about to fall into that trap. So she thought she would play it safe with...

"Sir?" She questioned weakly. "I don't know what..."

"I had an interesting dream last night, Susan," he interrupted.

He had also opted to use her Sunday name. That gesture alone made his Detective Constable nervously sit up straight and official. She tried desperately to hold his gaze. But as always, he was animated, full of movement and had simply anticipated her plan. She began to tightly crunch up the fingers of her left hand within her right palm. Tension and stress were beginning to come to the fore in many aspects of her body language. Her right foot once again tapped continuously under the desk and her bottom lip was being continually chewed upon. Those two movements had certainly become the tell of her unease, during their meetings together.

Pausing on each word with what seemed like an eternity. She nervously queried...

"What... kind... of... dream... sir?"

"Well, from our previous conversation, I know that you have watched Joseph and his patchwork raincoat DC Hayes. Correct?"

"Possibly - His technicoloured dream coat even?" she smiled.

"That would be the one, 'Hanna.' Trust, criminal actions and being held to account..." he then once again repeated. "Let's find a spare room for a moment. I need to share, understand and hopefully clarify this strange series of events that played out during my 'match' last night."

Hayes was strangely intrigued and wanted to help. But he had done it again, because it felt as if she had been lured in. She knew Steven Murray well enough, to know when he was manipulating the situation and when she was being played. And right now was definitely one of those latter moments. Although quite what the difference was between the two remained a mystery. Unfortunately for her, she had taken a step forward and unwittingly entered into his game. A mind game in which the whistle had already sounded for kick-off.

In the new ultra modern world of open space office planning, private rooms with doors that could be locked were becoming seen as a relic of the past, a legacy of the bad, old days, something of a valued rarity.

"This will do nicely," Murray announced.

"But it's an interview room, sir?"

"And it's currently free, Constable Hayes. Do you have some concerns about using it?"

He knew, she thought. He always knows. I don't know how he knows and I can't be sure, but he knows.

"Not at all," were the words that she offered up, as he shepherded her into official Interview Room One. The exact same location that their 'unofficial' interview had taken place previously.

DC Susan Hayes was now desperately trying to put two and two together. How did he know? During her attempts, she came up with 5, 7 and 133 - She had no idea where her maverick boss was heading with this. But she feared it wasn't going to end well for her this time. Going with that 'gut feeling' that she'd seen Murray go with so successfully, so many times previously.

"You may be interested to hear, 'Hanna.'" Murray left it at that.

Her interest piqued, she just couldn't contain herself

"Hear what, sir?"

Murray sat cross-legged and in full storyteller mode. At ease and fully relaxed, he then continued.

"Whilst scouring the delightfully landscaped gardens of Gordon Menzies' estate for more intimately severed body parts, 'Hanna.' We actually came across a vehicle parked up in one of the remote outbuildings."

Hayes looked intrigued, but nonplussed.

"We ran its plates, to see who it belonged to."

"Belonged, as in past tense, sir?"

"Yes, because we believe him to be the poor individual that had been used as fertiliser, Constable."

"Oh, not so good," Hayes grimaced.

"It was under a heavy canvas sheeting. Probably only there for a day or two, given its condition. In actual fact, it was an Uber taxi and driven right up until early Friday evening. Since then it's been off the grid."

Hayes remained quiet, before offering a slightly unsettling and unwarranted chuckle.

"Could the Right Honourable Judge Menzies have been doing some moonlighting?" She expressed. "Especially, as he'd officially fully retired."

Steven Murray's normally ever-present music knowledge, linking to his current thoughts had most definitely taken a back seat these past few months. Now and again, random tunes would be sung and offered up. Nothing like his wild days, he reminded himself. But nowhere like his normal self either!

"No, I think they knew each other, 'Hanna.' I also have another most definite train of thought that I currently feel impressed to share with you."

"Go on," Hayes said calmly and professionally. Just as her Inspector was getting into full swing.

"I think you stood on the dirt at the front gates deliberately."

Oh, oh, that sounded serious and formal.

"You are not stupid 'Hanna,'" Murray continued. "In fact there is no way that you made such a rookie mistake. Like now, you normally go about your daily business in a calm and professional manner. So that was no unenforced error on your part. It was a precise movement. One thought out well ahead of time and acted on. Knowing that your boots could then account for matching the soil residue at Menzies home. Mainly because you had walked all over his grounds earlier in the day."

She looked at him sternly and went to sp…

"No, please, don't do me the disservice!" Murray frowned. "You gave us your phone, remember?"

"I only gave it to you, to help with the distorted message." There was concern and genuine alarm in her tone.

"Oh, and it did 'Hanna.' Thank you. Although its tracking, also puts you at Menzies' property several hours before the tragic explosion. We also identified a thirty second call to Uber earlier in the day."

"You what?"

"I have never called an Uber cab in my life, 'Hanna.' You'd have guessed that though, right?"

Hayes offered a tired, dismissive gesture with her hands and shrugged. Everyone in the team knew that Murray was generally hopeless with modern technology.

How it all works, links up and operates. A real certified technophobe if there ever was one.

Her Inspector's dialogue continued with, "Interestingly though, what I didn't know was what was actually involved in booking a ride."

You could instantly witness in DC Hayes' eyes, all the behind the scenes machinations going on. A frenzy of activity in her mind. Her eyes darting from floor to ceiling and East to West. Her body seemed to suddenly still. As if frozen with fear, but more likely realisation, Murray reckoned.

"You've recalled it haven't you? How, once you confirm that your pickup and destination addresses are correct, you then have to select **Taxi** at the bottom of your screen. How am I doing so far?"

"Don't do this, sir." Hayes began shaking her head.

"Then," her boss continued. "You tap, Confirm **Taxi**. And here is the magic part. Once you've been matched, you'll see your driver's picture and vehicle details and you can track their arrival on the map." He paused slightly. "Constable, how great was that? You get to confirm from a picture that he was the driver that you wanted. Fantastic! Don't you think?"

Tears began spontaneously to appear on the female officer's face.

"In actual fact Susan, that was how we were able to confirm the identity of our mystery man. Using hairs from the taxi."

His non-stop, animated gesticulation had come to the fore. He pointed at his feet. He'd simulated motor bike riding and now he had just intertwined his fingers in an almost seductive horticultural fashion. His shoulders rose and fell as the continued simplicity of his comments ebbed and flowed. 'Hanna' had been bewildered and caught totally off guard. She had thought, mistakenly it would seem, that the whole investigation was over. That a line had been drawn conclusively underneath everything. That all the team were about to move forward collectively. That various new cases were about to be assigned.

"As you know, I can ramble on endlessly DC Hayes. But as you will have also gathered by now, I believe you were at that specific location much earlier. Somewhat in advance of ringing that intercom. We've double checked the facts and using his registration number, a certain taxi driver was specifically requested. Your text stated for them to drive into the tradesman's entrance. Our dear departed, blown-to-smithereens Judge, would have never seen or heard a thing. That was a very weak link in his security system. Why even bother with fancy electronic gates at the front? When those and such as those in the know, could so easily just pop by and drive up your back path!"

'Hanna' tried her best to offer up a wholesome, sweet and honest smile. It was an expression that spoke candidly. It said to all that would listen - *And I would happily do it all again!* Murray allowed a silence to fill the air. After about thirty seconds of returning the room to his default setting, he spoke quietly and lovingly. It was a father's voice. A voice of firmness and admiration. A voice that required the truth.

"As a young girl at High School, 'Hanna.' You made it sound like it was your father that picked you up each day."

"What? No! Don't be silly, sir. You must have misunderstood me. My dad never ever learned to drive," Hayes pleaded innocently.

"Oh, I know that now, Detective Constable. So enlighten me as to who exactly did pick you up then?"

Hayes could feel his parental grip tightening. Gone were 'Hanna' and DC Hayes. Murray had just addressed her as Detective Constable... and that could not be construed as a good sign.

"They had a driver, sir. A local courier that made drops throughout the day between the three clubs. But everyday, Monday to Friday when school was in, he'd be waiting for me at the iron gates. Four o'clock sharp, regular as clockwork."

"A driver. A courier. That's helpful," Murray responded graciously. He then added those magic ingredients that had been missing - some volume, west coast slang and harshness.

"Aye, magic, young lady. You got met each day by their drug and pimpmobile!"

Susan Hayes dropped her eyes immediately to the floor.

"He was the man that delivered their goods. Human and otherwise, to each of their clubs on a daily basis. Their very own official drug runner. At some point over the years as a police officer, that obviously dawned on you. So, when did you choose to do something about it?" Murray questioned.

Her eyes darted away and again stared desperately at the ground.

"In fairness Constable, that was very nicely and neatly answered."

"Thank you, sir."

This time, her inquisitive Detective Inspector caught her eye and firmly held her gaze.

"I think I may have actually taught you lots of those little foibles and avoidance tricks of the trade," he offered with a smile. One that was equally quickly removed when he remarked sharply…

"You still never gave me a name. But of course, you already knew that."

'Hanna' Hayes reddened slightly. Caught out, as she knew that she would be. She now sat uncomfortably squirming in her seat. He was one hundred percent correct. She had witnessed Steven Murray catch many people out over the years. Today, all she had to do was tell the truth. At least that is what she'd thought. In an apologetic manner, she cleared her throat and offered up.

"His name was Joe, sir. That was all people referred to him as - Joe. Joe the driver."

"Is that so, 'Hanna?' Well that's very interesting, because the identification that has been made in relation to those finely scattered remains, doesn't tally up. The dead man found dispersed throughout the grounds of the Judge's miniature estate, was identified as one Douglas Malcolm."

"I've never heard of him," 'Hanna' stated. She then managed a confident, but forced smile to go alongside her firm reply.

Murray looked somewhat troubled and puzzled. But not for long. Because he added…

"Mmm. Really? Maybe not DC Hayes, but that's because I suspect you would have known him better in the day as…… 'Joe! Joe the Driver. The taxi driver!"

Thirty Six

'Now it's three long years since we made her pay. And the owners say that she's had her day. So heave away for the final trawl. It's an easy pull for the catch is small. Sing haul away my laddie O.'

- Archie Fisher

Steven Murray placed a long brown envelope in front of himself on the desk. It contained several sheets of A4 paper. Each folded over twice. It remained unsealed. Susan Hayes could easily make out the five words scribbled on the front of it in block capitals. They read: A REAL LIFE FAIRY TALE! In a seven minute exploration of a troubled soul, he had captured sound bites of a life. Teenage years, loneliness, stolen innocence and plans for a future that aligned both the symmetry of police work and justice! The next sound to leave his lips was deliberately musical and rather prophetic.

'Knowing me, knowing you. There is nothing we can do. Knowing me, knowing you…'

"Now, knowing that individual over the years and all the other working girls that he had access to and that he had regularly transported around like cattle, from club to club. Plus the fact that in those days, he couriered drugs all around the city, with and for various dodgy, desperate clients was not promising. These were not the actions of a man of high standing, a man of integrity and honour. So trust should surely have been an important concern for you as a parent, or so you would have thought, right? Especially if you were going to allow this sexual predator to be in a car, on his own, for thirty minutes a day with a young teenage academic. A vulnerable schoolgirl that just happened to be your own daughter. Inexplicably, you were just setting her up for trouble and his lustful advances. At least I would have thought so."

Following up on that obscure rant, Murray posed a delicate question. "Were temptation and the forbidden fruit being sent innocently on an ever impending collision course?"

'Hanna' Hayes remained stunned into silence.

"You see the thing is, I don't believe that they were 'Hanna.' Sent innocently that is. I've read up on that *fine specimen* of a man, that dared to call himself your father. I've checked things out with a few of my old contacts as well and I am sorry to say Susan that not one, not one solitary soul would speak up for him. All the feedback and comments I got back, were along the lines that he was… *'Not to be trusted; Scum of the earth; Selfish; Greedy; Sleazy and Thieving.'* I think those are enough to be going on with, don't you? The kind of man that was not only happy to leave a virtuous and modest female adolescent with a probable child molester, but a man that was also delighted to receive a substantial payment for doing so! He was very much your stereotypical villain and this story desperately needed one of those."

Hayes slowly raised her head at this. Murray however, saw a face with an expression that only just for the first time had fully recognised that fact. A blank countenance of total disbelief. No matter what had transpired in the back of that vehicle on those specific days. Never, ever once had the uniformed teenager thought that any form of paid transaction had taken place. The hurt and fragility in the face of Susan Hayes was plainly visible.

"This tale is never getting made into a Disney movie," Murray wise-cracked. "At home time, once the school bell rang and the Princess was safely ensconced inside her carriage, the driver would politely enquire as to how her day had gone. He'd then listen to her complain and moan about multiplication, geography, demanding teachers and more exam schedules. Doubtless, he soon began to console her in a variety of ways."

The tormented female Constable tightened her lips at those suggestive remarks. Relentlessly though, Murray continued and opined some more.

"Initially, the gentlemanly driver would wipe away a tear or two, with a freshly laundered handkerchief. Later, possibly he'd hold her soft nubile hand in a reassuringly tender grip. With an innocent *'there, there'* offered vocally, as he patted a clammy hand upon her knee. Possibly that level of support increased and became even more encouraging over the coming weeks, as further problematic events at school and at home unfolded. With the touch gradually rising along her leg until on the third occasion, the sympathetic pat had turned into a gentle caressing and the schoolgirl's white knee had become a much sought after, desirable thigh."

A tiny, delicate trickle of blood appeared on Hayes' bottom lip. She had unknowingly bitten through the skin whilst trying desperately to restrain herself. Her body was numb. She had never even felt any pain. At that point Murray wondered - Had the girl in his fairytale, also on many occasions entered into that particularly hypnotic, mind-numbing state?

"As with all these fantasy novels, 'Hanna,' they like to move things up a notch and take the action to another level. Did you know that the term, 'to push the envelope,' originally came from the field of aviation? It is a reference to the flyable portion of the atmosphere that envelopes the earth DC Hayes. Pilots would regularly, 'push the envelope,' when they were testing the speed or elevation limits of new aircraft."

'Hanna' had to ask. "Did you get that priceless trivia from our dear DCI, perchance?

Murray paused only briefly. Raised his hands and shrugged his shoulder…

"Guilty as charged."

"Thought as much," Hayes said. With as much relief, as satisfaction.

"So reading between the lines," Murray continued. "I would envisage that her chauffeur's initial consoling moved swiftly up the scale to comforting, then on to affectionate cuddles of warmth and understanding. Eventually, I'm guessing, along came the attempted hugs and kisses."

It was at that point that Hayes struggled to maintain eye contact. Bingo! Murray raised his voice and a serious intonation was introduced as his delivery increased in pace.

"I believe those advances would have originally been spurned by the defenceless teenager, supposedly in his care. It's only conjecture, but I would have then predicted that this carnally corrupt individual, would have in all likelihood, eventually forced himself upon her. Especially after several weeks of what we would now refer to in the trade as...... grooming."

Hayes could swear the room was violently swirling at this point. She felt giddy. Like a child being taken onto the Waltzers at the showground for the very first time. After the ride her innocence was gone. It became a memory in time, blurred and better left forgotten. The small enclosed space she had found herself in, was stilled once again.

"That day," Murray ventured. "Destinies and futures were altered forever. Career choices changed and action plans created. Silence and no acknowledgement of it ever happening seemed like the best option in a straw poll in the young juvenile's mind. Her vote had been cast, the ballot box closed and the result confirmed. There would be no mention of the subject ever again."

Hayes listened, trying desperately to remain detached from his words. Her lips puckered up, but still no opinion. At least not one that she was willing to share.

The storyteller continued. "Authorities remained in the dark. I guess it was never reported and no officials were ever, any the wiser. It was certainly never mentioned to the girl's father for fear of reprisals. Possibly toward herself, being labelled as some sort of encouraging tease - never mind what he would have done to the poor driver. Although that was without realizing that he had been well compensated on each occasion this occurred. Because in   my humble experience 'Hanna'…"

Humble my backside, 'Hanna' thought to herself, under her breath.

"… it would have been unlikely to have happened only once. This 'Princess,' this attractive, young pubescent minor, would have been subjected to a series of rapes and sexual assaults over a prolonged period of time. Possibly years I would suggest. Of that, I have no doubt."

The pair exchanged a fleeting glance at Murray's work of supposedly far-fetched fiction. Hayes swallowed hard at that. Her foot bounced on its sole and her right calf rose and fell like a nervous heartbeat. 'Hanna' struggled for oxygen and licked her lips continually. Her shoulders now began pumping furiously up and down. Her emotions were shot to pieces. She had taken a hammering. She desperately wanted to cry like crazy. Her stomach had more knots than a sailors rucksack. A multitude of emotional flashbacks that she had thought long gone and buried, were being unceremoniously trawled and dredged up to the surface once again. He knew, she thought. I knew he knew. Eventually, intensely drained, she tried to speak. It came out as a desperately light whisper.

"What happens now, sir?"

'Hanna' Hayes heard herself begin to sob gently as she asked the question.

"What do you mean?" Murray replied.

Although, not before he placed his steadying hands upon hers. He took both her trembling palms, clasped them tightly to his and rested them together upon the desk.

"Now 'Hanna,' that was just the product of my limited imagination. A strange, fabricated fairy tale. An elaborate, fictional account that I had running around in my pea-sized head for a while. How much of it could possibly be believed? Would be, believed for that matter?" he added assertively. "Plus we both know that the sweetest, most beautiful, loving and amazing, evil psychotic creature that you'll ever meet - the delectable Tracy Scott, has confessed and taken full responsibility for ALL of those deaths."

Susan Hayes stared deeply at Steven Murray. It was a look searching for some form of reassurance and hope.

"Maybe, just maybe, she is your *'One more angel in heaven,'* today?" he offered. "It's Easter time 'Hanna.' Possibly Scott, like Scullion before her, was moved and inclined to follow Christ's example and take upon herself the sins of others. In any event," he surmised, "Who truly understands how we all think 'Hanna' and how we come to rationalise major, traumatic events in our respective lives?"

At that, the fingernails of Susan Hayes dug deep into the palms of her talismanic Inspector. Once again he began to sing... *'it's tough, but we're gonna get by.'* He released her hands from the security of his safe grip and encouraged her with...

"Go get freshened up young lady. It's not everyday you get to witness an Easter miracle."

Hayes shrugged, then exclaimed… "What! Are you kidding me? Genuinely worried, she once again offered up - "I know how it looks, sir, but…"

Murray raised a hand. He had no need to hear any more.

"Do you need reminding? I was just sharing an imaginary, hypothetical yarn, 'Hanna.' A once upon a time bedtime story, that I felt inspired to relate to you. A slightly worrying and harrowing one it has to be said, but simple food for thought just the same. Something to mull over before we move on to our next case."

Hayes' mood seemed reflective. Grateful with what seemed to be a fresh start being presented to her and yet something had remained unspoken. Murray was intrigued.

"Go on," he said. "I can see that something is still troubling you."

She slid her hand slowly across her face and firmly massaged her forehead.

"Out with it," Murray encouraged.

"It's just that sometimes, sir. Often in fact, we tend to embellish fairy tales, fables and folklore. To enhance our favourite bits, romanticise them and make our lead characters more handsome, beautiful and heroic."

"Are you unhappy with my fantasy, 'Hanna?' Is that what you are trying to tell me? Would you like to enrich it further, young lady?"

"Well, no. Not so much, enrich or enhance it, sir. But maybe it lacked an unusual or surprising twist for the reader. Just a thought!"

"I'm listening, DC Hayes. Carry on."

"Don't get me wrong, sir. Hans Christian Andersen would have been exceptionally proud of your rather 'risque' narrative. But what about -

"Once upon a time…" 'Hanna' began. " … a young virgin Princess - Yes, met up at the school gates - Yes, was offered sympathy, comfort and then love - And then… NO not willingly - Abuse was forced upon her time after time, after time."

Tear ducts had begun to well up in the Constable's red rimmed eyes.

"You don't need to fin…"

"Oh, but I do, sir. Please let me finish," she began to sob. "She had no one to protect her. She wasn't stupid. She knew her father had literally sold her out. She, like everything else in his wretched life, had a price. In those dark days her schoolwork was her only ally. Her sacred refuge, shelter and safe haven. She sought comfort in her studies and managed to keep the reality of her daily situation at bay."

"Daily!" Murray blurted out angrily. Repulsed and disgusted by this alarming revelation. "Although, it is not actually a twist in the story, 'Hanna.' But it is certainly a highly unsavoury disclosure."

"No, you misunderstand, sir. In my child-unfriendly parable, Joe, Joe the friendly taxi driver never once touches or molests the Princess. Let me repeat. Never once does Joe comfort her, hug her, nor reassure her with any form of physical contact whatsoever."

"Joe was innocent of all of that, altogether?" Murray confirmed.

"In my telling and understanding of the story at least," she deftly replied.

Murray was well aware that the twist was about to come upon them. Unseen, unprepared and unrelenting. It was the ideal time to insert it into her accurate account of the retelling of the story. He then recalled how he had heard Hayes tell him in one of their early chats about how she had been scarred for life during that experience and that her life, that day, had changed forever. *Scarred for life!'* She had said.

Murray knew at the time, that response sounded unusual. They were three very deliberate words. A phrase specifically chosen to alert him to something… and he had missed it. In doing so, he had failed to notice the despairing cry for help that 'Hanna' had sent his way. Yet again he had let her down, he'd thought. At the time it was her acknowledgement of who the real culprit was. Who was actually responsible for her teenage sexual abuse and mistreatment. If he had caught it, he would have figured out sooner how it all tied in and linked up with this case.

"I can tell by your face that you get it now, sir. Do you have any songs to accompany it?" she said raising her trembling voice. "No *Adam raised a Cain, Daddy's Girl* or *Luka?"*

Resentment and bitterness were now fully detectable in her voice. Letting go of the angst could not, and would not be easy. She tried to once again regain her composure before continuing.

"You know, I'm not really sure it does enhance the story any. But at least it keeps it more grounded, closer to the truth and accurate to what really happened," Hayes added. "So Joe the driver, who was at least guilty by association and/or omission, got his comeuppance."

"Oh, he most certainly did, 'Hanna.'" Murray agreed.

The Inspector swallowed hard and raised a hand to his mouth. All the pieces now joined up in his mind and he effortlessly, then took over the story-telling once again.

"So Douglas Malcolm, aka - Joe the driver, was scattered across and throughout the grounds. The very grounds, garden and estate that belonged to the real villain of the piece."

The female Police Constable sat and listened intently.

"Our most honourable Judge - Gordon B. Menzies. A man that we have now discovered was a regular, frequent visitor to all three of your father's seedy underground clubs. He was also yet another member, certainly in recent years, of the T.I.M.E teenage trafficking club. Despite all of that though, back in the day, he was a young man with a highly visible seven inch scar on his stomach. Murray remembered seeing the pictures that Hanlon felt impressed to have the forensic team take. A man who, after court had finished, received a lift to your school and was already lying in wait for you. Or he would head straight over to whichever corrupt club your studies were taking place in and look for some extracurricular activity of his own."

Murray exhaled and paused for breath.

"I am so sorry, Susan. I let you down…"

A hand was instantly raised and Detective Constable Susan Hayes responded with…

"I have no idea what you are talking about, Inspector. I was just sharing a far fetched, hypothetical tale of my own with you!"

Easter 2016 would always be remembered fondly in the minds of those officers involved on Murray's team. Especially one suspected, Detective Constable Susan Hayes. 'Hanna' genuinely reckoned that she had experienced a 'true' Easter miracle that season. Unbelievably, she still had her job and the support of her friends and her boss it would seem. One way or another, she certainly owed 'The Big Man!' Now who knew if that was Christ or Murray? Possibly only time would tell on that score.

DC 'Kid' Curry was relieved to have his western colleague 'back in the saddle' for future adventures together.

'Doc' Patterson was delighted to witness his trusted friend, Steven Murray 'come back out to play' and leave his canine companion at home. For the first time in a long while he seemed to have a purpose in life once again.

Joseph 'Sherlock' Hanlon, like Patterson, was just grateful to have his mentor and role model back where he belonged and to see the end of late night grocery deliveries!

Still finding his feet, Sergeant Mitch Linn - 'Baldy' - Was looking forward to having a more involved role in the unit in the coming months. Him and Allan Boyd seemed to hit it off together. There seemed to be a definite chemistry developing between them.

'Skin Curdling Enema Plants!' - DCI Furlong and many of her colleagues within the legal system were mightily impressed and relieved, that Police Scotland had uncovered even more corruption within the judicial system. Including another major scalp on their own doorstep. Hard as it may be, she felt it was another decisive step forward in tackling the problems that she was specifically brought in to address. Another problem area that she was brought in to address, had chosen to post himself absent today. None of the team would know it, but in his wisdom and thoughtfulness, Inspector Murray purposefully took the day off to enable 'Sandy,' to take sole charge of the debrief. It had really been a case of revenge and retribution. It highlighted just how angst, hatred and resentment could certainly lie dormant for many years, before a certain key catalyst allowed them to resurface.

'Hanna' Hayes had her demons. Hopefully this case had helped exorcise them. The sting in the tale though, that remained between herself and Murray, was not Joe the taxi driver (Douglas Malcolm), but Gordon Bryce Menzies the up and coming... Prosecutor, Predator and Paedophile.

Epilogue

'Some bright morning when this life is over, I'll fly away to that home on God's celestial shore. Just a few more weary days and then I'll fly away to a land where joys will never end. I'll fly away in the morning when I die, hallelujah by and by, I'll fly away, I'll fly away.'

- Alison Krausse

He had told friends and ex-workmates that he was going for a well deserved break and spending a little of that pension pot that he had received in recent months. Maybe even extending his stay if required.

Steven Murray however, had tracked him down to a local hospice. Within two weeks of last visiting with him, the man was now a shadow of his former self. He was easily two or three stone lighter, with shoulders eroded and currently no actual muscle definition to his arms or legs. He sat with a traditional tartan blanket across his lap, in a well used wheelchair. Trying desperately to remain composed and focused for both their sakes, the Inspector bit on his lip as gentle tears continually ran for cover down his cheek. His chest started to vibrate gently, as his quivering voice asked softly...

"How long?"

With a faint, muffled wheeze, the mild reply offered was… "Days, not weeks."

His friend just wanted to see out his remaining time in a dignified, quiet and peaceful manner. He had wanted no fuss; no one chasing after him and certainly, no 'over the top' sympathy from ex-colleagues. Overall, he'd had a comfortable life. He'd gambled, he'd drank and he'd always been one for the ladies (sadly, even when he was still married). Even now the poor nurses had to endure his flirtatious, amorous ways.

The bold 'Ally' Coulter had made many mistakes and had amassed even more regrets, throughout his six decades here on earth. But then again, who hasn't Murray quickly asked himself internally. To his credit, his trusted colleague had tried faithfully and successfully in recent years, to make amends for many of the stupid and often unintentional times that he had overstepped the mark. Sadly, the incidents in the main, had taken place when 'Ally' had been excessively fuelled with the drink.

Today though, here sat a good man. A loving father and a loyal and valued partner-in-arms down throughout the years. His old boss, only a matter of weeks ago, could have never foreseen this current scenario. Often over the years, it was his Inspector that was the main chatterbox. This afternoon however, with much poignancy in the air, it was the turn of his recently retired Sergeant to have the final word. And although struggling for breath, he hissed and panted his way through the following.

"Inspector, you are often stubborn and headstrong. I know you seldom listen to others. You give out plenty of wonderful advice... and yet ironically, you feel under no obligation to accept it in return. Nonetheless, you have been my closest cohort and companion in recent years and I feel obliged to tell you this."

His pal gasped for breath once again, as Murray pulled up a nearby chair for himself.

"Thank you Steven, because someone will always be more handsome."

Murray appeared to jokingly question this with his facial expression, but his buddy let it go and continued on with a deep sincerity in his trembling voice.

"Someone will always be smarter. Someone will always be younger and fitter. But ultimately, Steven, they will never be you!"

DI Murray began to weep quietly. He clasped his friend's hand firmly and the two men sat together in a precious, special moment of reflective silence. A thoughtful juncture that was only broken after several minutes, when the Detective Inspector in hushed tones attempted a hidden gem belonging to Bruce Springsteen... *'Well they built the Titanic to be one of a kind, but many ships have ruled the seas. They built the Eiffel Tower to stand alone, but they could build another if they please. Taj Mahal, the pyramids of Egypt are unique I suppose. But when they built you, brother, they broke the mold."*

His friend simply looked at him tenderly and smiled.

Murray returned the gesture and segued into a slow, poignant version of... *'Ally bally, ally bally bee. Sittin' on your Mammy's knee. Greetin' for a wee bawbee, tae buy some Coulter's Candy.'*

Three days later, Robert Coulter passed away peacefully in his sleep. 'Ally' was gone. 'Taz' Taylor, his young protégé, would have been waiting at the gates, ready to welcome her old friend home with open arms.

Four weeks had gone by when an unassuming envelope was delivered by hand through the letterbox of a run down, third storey council flat in Rosyth. The young female tenant ran to her window to witness the departing exhaust fumes of a familiar Volvo. Her smooth, youthful fingers glided effortlessly underneath the seal. Once opened, the letter was short and concise.

Dear Amanda, We have great pleasure in confirming a starting date for you at our "LITTLE DEERS NURSERY" in Fife. All the relevant benefits and full details pertaining to your position are contained in full in the enclosed company booklet. Yours Sincerely, Heather Buxley (Human Resources)

It appeared that DI Murray had kept up his end of the deal also. Amanda Campbell looked around her grubby little flat, thought about her future dreams and aspirations and smiled. A smile that matched the width and depth of the Forth Road Bridge itself.

Having left behind the overcast, cloudy skyline of Fife, the Inspector had hoped for somewhat brighter weather on his short, twenty minute drive to Edinburgh Airport. It was nearly three months since her brother's funeral, but Hannah, as promised, was flying back. The introduction to his new son-in-law, Murray could have done without. However, he reminded himself of his own recent promise. One that would see him repair, rebuild and strengthen relationships. So he was right where he needed to be. The car was dutifully parked, he'd walked the short distance to the arrivals area and stood anxiously. A text message quickly alerted him to the fact that they were just picking up their bags and would both be through shortly. No turning back now the detective thought. And no 'black dog' either. That fact, had been an added bonus for the past fortnight.

Hannah Murray looked good as she stepped forward from the long line of incoming passengers. Their flight from Newark had touched down twenty minutes earlier than scheduled. She hadn't yet caught sight of her father, but he had spotted her. Although by her side he saw no one, which puzzled him. The detective in him was intrigued by this turn of events, so he instantly followed his daughter's line of sight. His gaze travelled downward along her left arm, quickly past her elbow, before reaching her bangle adorned wrist. It was there, at that point, that he was first introduced to the tiny, fragile fingers encircled tightly around a slender pinky. Swaying wildly, a strawberry blonde pony-tail made its carefree way from shoulder to shoulder. The miniature floral dress shone as bright as a Tuscan sun and her radiant grin grew and twinkled as her loving mother whispered in her ear.

"Grandpa, grandpa!" The excited tot cried out merrily, with a voice of tender, childlike innocence.

Steven Murray cried also. Although unsurprisingly, as he thought about the great circle of life, he wept magical tears of joy.

THE END

Dedicated to my wonderful family
in Pocatello, Idaho.

Shane, Jennifer, Thaddeus, Cooper and Bailey.
Not forgetting my two youngest granddaughters:
Darby and Dylann XX

.

'Walking on the road less travelled by.
Flesh and bone under an ever changing sky.
Refugee, just running from myself.
To my knees, to the one who with me dwells.
I am just a journey maker.'

- Eilidh Patterson

Printed in Great Britain
by Amazon